D1602807

The Blue Streak

ELLEN LESSER

The Blue Streak

GROVE WEIDENFELD
NEW YORK

Published by Grove Weidenfeld
A division of Grove Press, Inc.
841 Broadway
New York, New York 10003-4793

Published in Canada by General Publishing Company, Ltd.

LIBRARY OF CONGRESS CATALOGING-IN-PUBLICATION DATA

Lesser, Ellen.
The blue streak / by Ellen Lesser.—1st ed.
p.   cm.
ISBN 0-8021-1440-7
I. Title.
PS3562.E836B5   1992
813'.54—dc20   91-36437
CIP

Manufactured in the United States of America
Printed on acid-free paper
Designed by Helen Barrow
First Edition 1992

10   9   8   7   6   5   4   3   2   1

For Stanley

The author wishes to express her gratitude to: John Pickering, for his support and encouragement; Mary LaChapelle, Robin Lippincott and Debbie Sontag, for their generous readings; Ellen Levine, for her timely leap of faith; Bryan Oettel, for his confidence in Danny and me, his keen insight; and Roger Weingarten.

The Blue Streak

1

WHEN THE RINGING cut into his dream, Danny was walking down a bombed-out block in what looked like some war-torn, Middle Eastern capital. Only it wasn't Beirut, it was Brooklyn, and Danny was looking for someplace to live. He flung his arm out toward the phone, as toward a lifeline out of that recurring anxiety. February 1980, two whole months in the brownstone on Sackett Street, and still he couldn't get rid of these nightmares of hunting for an apartment, as if that search had become the convenient, all-purpose emblem for whatever he needed and still hadn't found. But he knew, even as his fingers found the cool plastic, that it wasn't a lifeline; that the phone ringing like that, in the middle of the night, could only mean trouble.

"Danny, it's Mom. Wake up. I have something to tell you."

The streetlight splashed across his face as he sat upright with the receiver.

"Listen, sweetheart, take a deep breath. Because this is really bad news."

Danny squeezed his eyes shut, and there was that picture of his father at Mount Sinai Hospital, when Danny was thirteen years old: the thin smile that didn't light Sam's eyes and all the tubes coming out of him; the ashen hand he held out to his children, that Danny's sister, Elisa, took first and wouldn't let go, so Danny had stood by the bedside, hands

3

in the pockets of the blue Bar Mitzvah suit he'd already started outgrowing and yet no man at all.

His mother had only to say it, and she did: "Your father had another heart attack." She paused for a moment, as if to let this sink in, and Danny felt that definite click inside, that sensation that could almost pass for relief, as something you've always been waiting for moves into place. The second attack, that had hung over their heads all those years, since the first had come so young, and then nothing. He took in a breath, but then she spoke again: "And he didn't pull through."

What did she mean, *he didn't pull through*? His father always pulled through; he was one of those people who were just lucky like that. Danny looked out the window to the sky that always glowed orange at night, to find out if maybe he wasn't still dreaming. In a sailboat, his father could pick his way among rocks into a treacherous harbor in the pitch dark. When gale-force winds blew their first rickety wooden Pennant aground, Sam landed on the single spit of sand beach in a boulder-strewn cove. On the day of the first heart attack, he left his office and walked to the hospital, thirty blocks up Fifth Avenue in a stiff breeze, because he was feeling pains in his chest and his arms. He had the attack right there, in the Emergency Room, minutes after he had arrived, under the supervision of the chief cardiologist. The doctor told Danny's mother that if it had happened anywhere else, Sam would have been dead in a minute, no questions asked. Enough of these near escapes pile up and it stops seeming like a coincidence.

"Sweetheart, I'm sorry." His mother's voice broke through, small with defeat but unnaturally calm.

"I don't understand. You don't— You mean he just—" The ache came hard to the back of his eyes and he closed them, but the orange kept pulsing inside the black.

She said some things in a quiet voice that didn't sound like her own. He thought she said, "Honey, I know this is hard for you." But he only heard her the way he used to hear things from in the water during a race, the shouts that were muffled into weird cries and the clearer, stronger chant of *Danny! Danny! Danny!* Only now it was coming through the phone, she was calling him.

"I'm here. I'm okay."

"You know you have to come home."

He pushed up from the bed and flipped on the night table lamp. 3:06 A.M. The numbers had the hard, irrefutable glow of digits on a stopwatch. Seeing them, Danny snapped to, as if from a dream that had lasted since boyhood. Suddenly it was like he still had a chance; like if he moved fast enough he could overtake what was happening. "I'm packing up and coming right away."

"There isn't a train till six-forty."

He pictured the junk drawer next to the fridge, where his mother kept the Long Island Rail Road schedule. "Wait a minute. You're not there all alone, are you?"

"No. Elisa and Dave are here. I called them from the hospital so they could drive me back out to the Island."

Of course, *Elisa and Dave*. His sister and her lawyer husband, who'd swept into the family like he, not Danny, was Sam's son and heir. Who'd gone to Harvard, where Danny had been dying to go but had not gotten in, in spite of all the hype from the swimming coach. "So how long have the two of *them* known for?"

"Don't be upset. She *is* the oldest." His mother, as usual, trying to make it up to him. "I had to call one of you first."

He wanted to say that she should have called him right afterward, that they could have come picked him up on their way home. But then again, he *was*, in his father's words, *way the hell out in Brooklyn*.

He heard Elisa's voice in the background: "Tell him it isn't the time for this," and the old hatred came up like that rush

5

in his ears again. But his mother must have shooed Elisa away. "Danny, sweetheart. Promise me you'll be okay. You won't do anything crazy."

Danny couldn't help snorting. *Don't do anything crazy:* it was one of those things his mother had been telling him for as long as he could remember. She'd said it whenever Danny was furious at his father, whenever he'd lost a big race or a girlfriend had shafted him. She'd said it the year before, in the middle of his senior swim season, when the orthopedist told him that if he continued to work out and compete with the tendonitis inflamed, the damage to his shoulder was going to be permanent. He knew why she said it too; from the time he was a small boy, she must have seen the look in his eyes when that feeling welled up in him, the feeling that made him smash his toys or pummel a kid at the bus stop— that wild, helpless raging, as if he could punch his way out of his body, himself. Once he was older, when he could get into a swimming pool, it was easier; he could lash out at the water, slap and kick until his cells were about to explode, and it would pass for speed if you didn't know what he was thinking. But his mother should understand that kind of self-punishing anger. Wasn't she the one who'd taken plate after plate of her good wedding china and cracked them down on the dining room table, until the blood ran in streams down her arm? And all because that one night Sam had stayed at the office a little bit later than usual.

She was calling him again. "Sweetheart, talk to me."

"I'm talking. What am I going to do? I'll be on the six-forty train. I'll be there by seven-thirty."

2

*T*HE BOROUGH OF BROOKLYN had a certain grandeur
for Danny when he was younger. It would be years before
he'd see Paris or Rome, but when he would, he'd think of
Prospect Park with its cast bronze giants on horseback; of
Grand Army Plaza: the dizzying hub of avenues, the whirl-
wind of cars pulled in from every direction, and at its center,
the arch, that had the boy hearing parade music, picturing
whole battalions, decked out not for battle but for the trium-
phal procession afterward, as if some great general had just
conquered Brooklyn. He liked to imagine his father—the
boy his father had been—charging the streets of the borough
like a fearless, benevolent stormtrooper. Samuel Winger's
boyhood in Flatbush and along Eastern Parkway took on
heroic proportions in the mind of his son. There was an aura
of danger in those back alleyways, on those fire escapes and
rattling El cars, that a suburban town like the one where
Danny grew up couldn't hope to provide. There was a
romance in having just those three nickels for the Saturday at
Coney Island: one for the rides, one for a hot dog at
Nathan's, and one for the train to go home, which usually
got spent on another screaming trip round the Cyclone,
because how was a boy of seven or eight supposed to resist
such temptations, and because if your pals were fast enough
and brave, you could run all the way up Ocean Avenue and
still make it back before suppertime.

Danny's grandmother Ida repeated the stories at every family gathering, until they were as liturgical, as embedded in Danny's personal notion of history, as the tales of the going out from Egypt or of Judah the Maccabee, who kicked the Greeks' asses right out of Jerusalem. When Sammy was seven years old, he rode the subway by himself to Manhattan (what Ida called *New York*, as if Brooklyn were still a separate city) for clarinet lessons. When he was eight, Ida started missing the nuts she kept for her Tuesday night card game, until she walked into his bedroom early one morning to find him at the open window, feeding a family of squirrels he'd trained to come in from the fire escape. When he was nine, he designed and built his own balsa wood airplane, and begged his mother to buy him an engine. That was eleven bucks down the toilet, or so Ida predicted, probably saying *ter-let* then as she said it today, in that peculiar pronunciation that also had its mysterious roots in the old Brooklyn neighborhoods. Still, she took whatever was left from her paycheck that Friday and headed to Messer's Hobby Store on Avenue J, because when had she ever denied her Sammy anything? Her brilliant Sammy, who should have been an engineer, not a lawyer, because they took the bus to Prospect Park that same Sunday and he told her where to stand at the edge of the ballfield and who would have believed it, but that *facockter* plane flew. The part of the story Ida never told, that Sam provided himself, was the fact that the airplane's first trial was also its last, since, forward-looking boy that he was, Sam had only planned for the launch, not the landing; the plane had found its resting place, as if suspended in flight, near the top of one of the oaks that bordered the ballfield.

When Danny went to see the apartment on Sackett Street, he hadn't been after adventure. He hadn't even set out to rebel, though his parents would never believe that. It was simply a minimal standard of living he'd wanted. With the monthly rent he could hope to shell out, given his dwindling savings and meager job prospects, all he could afford in

8

Manhattan was a studio the size of his mother and father's walk-in closet. Assuming he even could find one. At least unemployment made the search easier. He could be in a phone booth with *The Village Voice* on Wednesday morning when the paper first hit the newsstands, dialing the number for every hole in the wall that sounded remotely livable; he could spend afternoons chasing down shady real estate agents, or waiting on line with the other aspirants to see *nobody's* dream apartment: places with single windows looking out onto air shafts, with two-burner hotplates passing for kitchenettes; places with indelible trails of what looked like blood in the hallways, with fire escapes that brought in not squirrels but junkies and serial murderers. He didn't want to take one of those dumps. But it was three months since he and his frat brother Greg's post-graduation blowout in Europe. And while Greg was happily ensconced in business school back out in the Midwest, Danny was still camping out in his parents' house, submitting to his father's weekly cross-examinations, his stories about what *he'd* accomplished by age twenty-two. On a tip from one of the Manhattan real estate agents, he decided to take his search beneath the river, to Brooklyn.

Riding the F train from West 4th Street–Washington Square in that unfamiliar direction, he tried not to think of little Sammy's bygone campaigns, or even of Grandma Ida, tucked safely away on the far side of the borough with the other old Jews, watching with wary eyes as their neighborhoods turned around them—not changed but *turned*, the word they always used, Ida and all the rest of them: like milk turning sour. That had been Danny's only current image of Brooklyn—the old Jewish stomping grounds, and their downward slide. He didn't know what to expect when he walked up from the subway at Carroll Street, into the Italian neighborhood of Carroll Gardens.

He was the only one who got off the train, one of the few who'd been riding it. The station's tiled walls were almost as grimy as the ones in Manhattan, but his nostrils missed the usual subway stop smell, the acrid breath of urine steaming up from the concrete. When he pushed through the exit gate, he found himself climbing into a chilly salt breeze that carried the aromas of fish, bread and sausages. The exit issued onto one side of a square park, surrounded by neat, brownstone row houses. The directions to the real estate office led him away from the park, one block west to Court Street, where the food smells were coming from (the sea smell was blowing east on the wind from the harbor): the fish market, with its barrels of calamari and octopus and shiny black mussels lined up on the sidewalk; a bakery window of shellacked cookies shaped like Christmas trees and wreaths, Santas and ribboned packages; Genaro's Delicatessen, Fresh Sausage Made Daily, the sparkling expanse of plate glass curtained with great, yellow, wax-coated cheeses and desiccated salamis, dangling above a pyramid of gallons of olive oil.

Carroll Realty was next to a ravioli shop, and the woman had a place she could show him that very morning—brand-new listing, a one-bedroom floor-through, two-seventy-five. She didn't ask him for his employer or references; the only suspicious look she threw his way the whole time was when he asked what a *floor-through* was. It was an apartment that ran the length of a brownstone, front to rear, so you had windows on the street side and also in back, overlooking the garden. The brownstones along Sackett Street had wrought-iron gates fronting tiny square yards, most of them cement but a few with actual patches of grass, still green this late in the year, like oversized Astroturf welcome mats. Every third or fourth house was guarded by a plaster Jesus or Mary, and from the end of the long block rose a massive Catholic church of gray stone. The woman stopped about a dozen houses before it. Halfway up the first flight the stairwell grew dark, but not so dark he couldn't make out the niches cut into the rounded wall at each landing, the plaster Virgins and plastic flowers beneath their layer of dust: Our Lady of 383 Sackett Street.

Danny got a funny, alien feeling in the hollow of his chest, like he'd had in the dank, shadowy corners of the Italian cathedrals that Greg—a Catholic from Cleveland—had dragged him to see just a few months earlier. But when the real estate agent opened the door to the fourth-floor apartment, the light almost blinded him. At this time of the afternoon the sun poured into the big front bedroom and then back through a pair of French doors. There was a middle room Danny could turn into a den, another large space that doubled as living and dining room, a separate kitchen. Hardwood floors that just needed a little sanding and finishing. An old clawfoot bathtub. Back windows that looked out over a whole hidden world of kitchen gardens and clotheslines on pulleys and vinyl swimming pools. And since it was the top-floor apartment, he could climb the fire escape to the roof, where he could see all the other roofs, the water towers and steeples, and the taller buildings of Brooklyn's miniature downtown; where he had a view of lower Manhattan, rising like a mirage from the far shore of the river.

At two-seventy-five, the rent was fifty dollars less than what Danny had budgeted. But for the moment, his checking account had sunk pretty low, and there was the security deposit, the real estate agent's commission. If Danny could sign that day and bring in a check by the next, the apartment was his; the agent hadn't even shown it to anyone else yet. All he needed was a short-term loan to make the initial lump payment. He used the real estate office phone to ring his mother, but she wasn't home. He assured the agent he'd be back to her before five, and walked along Court Street to a phone booth before calling his father.

Sam's secretary said Mr. Winger was in a conference, but Danny told her he needed just one quick minute of his father's time. It was a few moments before Sam came on, and then he didn't say hello. He just said, "I've got to make this fast now. What is it?"

Danny had scarcely gotten through the preamble to his description before Sam cut in. "Carroll Gardens? Sackett Street? Never heard of it." He fired the phrases out at Danny and said, *Never heard of it*, as if that were the final word on the subject; as if any place he'd never heard of simply *didn't exist*.

"It's near Brooklyn Heights," Danny offered, hoping to steal some reflected glow from that most expensive of Brooklyn neighborhoods.

"Above or below Atlantic Avenue?"

He mumbled, "Below," knowing this was the wrong answer. The agent had given him a crash course on this corner of Brooklyn in Manhattan's shadow. The fashionable section was above Atlantic Avenue, up toward the bridge. The avenue itself, with its Syrian bakeries and Lebanese spice shops and couscous joints, marked the definitive border between exclusive and ethnic.

But Sam had already passed beyond that distinction. "What are you doing in Brooklyn, anyway? It's taken this family three generations to work our way *out* of Brooklyn."

Then Sam had to get back to the conference, and he'd be working late, but they could have a talk about all of this the next night, if Danny would be home for dinner. Danny never got a chance to explain the real estate agent's timetable. He hung up the phone and stared through the glass door at the rows of petrified marzipan fruits in a confectioner's window. He pushed away an image of the dusty prayer niches, and one of the old woman on the third floor in the colorless dressing gown, who'd peered out her door like a ghost when he and the agent passed. That was some line about the three generations, a classic Sam Winger if ever there was one. It had that snappy, aphoristic, incontestable Sam ring of truth. So what if it didn't really make any sense, if it had nothing to do with what Danny was actually up to?

But screw Sam. Danny didn't need a loan from his father

to get the apartment. He'd simply have to commit the cardinal sin: go home, get the faded blue passbook and clear out the savings account that Sam and Joan had opened for him on his tenth birthday—all those years of hoarded allowance, of quarters and dollars earned for raking leaves and shoveling snow, of extra tips and bonuses from his summer lifeguard jobs. *Basic principle*, Sam was fond of saying, *never live off your capital.* One more of those lines that was always popping into Danny's head in Sam's voice, just when the last thing he wanted was more advice from his father.

Danny ignored the voice this time, and the next morning got a couple of cashier's checks to close out the bank account. He also looked in the *Times* at the want ads and found the notice of a lifeguard opening at the Brooklyn YMCA, just two subway stops from Carroll Street in the Manhattan direction. The personnel manager agreed to interview him that afternoon, and gave him the job on the spot. New York State high school freestyle champion, four years Ivy League varsity, lifeguard and swimming instructor experience up the wazoo: the guy said he couldn't have tailor-made a better candidate. Danny had been a little nervous about what he was doing, but now he felt sure. All the pieces were fitting together, like a winning relay race, like a little kid's crawl stroke when the coordination finally came—with the lack of resistance, the ease, that for Danny had always spelled destiny.

So he was steeled to face his father at dinner that night, to present him with the one thing Sam hated most from his children: what he called, in his nasal Brooklyn-French accent, a *"fate" accompli*. The lease was signed, the moneys were paid, and Danny had agreed to start at the Y the following Monday. But when Danny finished his presentation—complete with quotes from the real estate agent about how Carroll Gardens was the next wave in desirable Brooklyn neighborhoods—Sam stood up from the dining room table, set his chair back in its place, and pronounced with perfect calm, "You aren't going to do this."

"But it's already done." Danny shot a look of appeal to his mother, but Joan was sitting impassive, staring down at her plate, not letting on what she thought about the whole business one way or the other. "And anyway, you can't tell me what to do. It's my money."

"And I'm your father. Or maybe that only means something to you when I'm footing the bills."

Danny could see Sam was setting a trap for him. "I didn't say that."

"Oh, but that's exactly what you said. I'm just a bank account. Otherwise, what I say doesn't count around here for anything."

Danny didn't know how to answer him. He had to admit that Sam had a point; Danny *had* felt a giddy sense of freedom, signing the withdrawal slip and taking the checks, figuring his decision was truly his own, since he was holding the purse strings. The same kind of freedom he'd felt when he took off for Europe—except for the hundred dollars his mother slipped him at the airport, to "buy himself something nice," all on the money he'd saved from his lifeguard salaries. The freedom he'd dreamed of so many times as a boy, imagining his father was dead so he could do whatever he wanted.

Now Sam was pacing the length of the dining room table, the vein that ran down the left side of his forehead into his brow standing out, livid green under his winter-pale skin. "I practically kill myself working to give you everything you want, and this is the thanks I get in return?"

Again, Danny turned to his mother. Wasn't that Sam's stock response whenever he wasn't getting his way? It wasn't Danny's fault, it started with Sam himself: this idea that paying for things should give you control over people. In his head, he heard the answer his mother always gave Sam when he pulled that shit on her: *Don't pretend you did it for me. I never asked you to work nights and weekends. I never said I needed a fancy house, or a boat. I just wanted a husband, a father who was there for his children—a family.*

"I tried to talk to you about it yesterday on the phone, but you were too busy."

"That's right. I was busy. Some people around here have to work for a living."

"That's exactly what I'm trying to do. I got a job, didn't I?"

"You call that a job? That's a job for some deadbeat jock with nothing else on the ball. No son of mine is moving to Brooklyn and throwing away an Ivy League education to watch people paddle up and down the pool at some broken-down Y."

"Then I guess I'm not your son, 'cause I'm doing it. You never were much of a father, anyway."

Now Joan jerked her head up, like she had been slapped. "The two of you can disagree. But that's enough of this nonsense."

Sam turned on her with such venom, she could have been the one taking a lifeguard job. "What nonsense? If I've never been much of a father, and he says he isn't my son, then some things are going to start to change around here."

Joan was standing now. "For example?"

"For example, my will. I wouldn't want any of my money cramping his style in the future."

"Don't be ridiculous."

Sam snapped at her, "Just stay out of this," in that tone that made it sound like she wasn't his equal, his wife, but some secretary out of the typing pool. Danny was about to tell him to leave her alone, but Sam whirled back on him. "You go up to your room. The discussion is over."

Danny wasn't finished with dinner, but he stood up, shaking his head. There was no sense in even stooping to argue. The family had been placing bets on it practically since Danny could walk: could they get through a meal without the boy being sent away from the table? Sam had even tried the stunt the night of Danny's graduation and everybody had laughed—finally even Sam himself—because Danny was twenty-one years old and they were out at a restaurant.

If Sam thought the threat about changing his will was going to scare Danny off, he had something coming. Wasn't it the kind of ultimatum Sam was always tossing out and retracting, as if time and love were ever-elastic? *You'll never drive this car another mile. You'll never swim one more lap. You'll never step foot on this sailboat again*—when the very next Saturday he was hauling Danny up out of bed, snapping up the window shades so the kid got a load of the wind in the treetops.

Of course his father wasn't going to disinherit him. Danny had put the idea immediately out of his head. But now there was no way to be sure how Sam had been feeling or what he'd forgiven. The night of the fight was the last time Danny laid eyes on his father.

3

THE CHIMES IN THE CHURCH TOWER rang the half hour, startling Danny out of his reverie. He went to the closet and found his one suit, a dark blue, like a grown-up version of the Bar Mitzvah suit. Sam had made him buy it before graduation, even though Danny told him he'd be wearing cutoffs and his swim team T-shirt under his gown. Naturally Danny would be needing a suit, Sam had said, for job interviews—though the only interview Danny had gone to in the intervening months was the one at the Y. Though his father had never bothered to ask, Danny didn't mind lifeguarding again so much, really. Once he shut off the bad memories, it left him a lot of time to think. It had to be better than waiting on tables. And what was so terrible about working a job that just paid the rent, that wasn't calculated to *get you* anywhere?

Sam's life had always marched forward according to an inexorable and precocious timetable. At thirteen the youngest Eagle Scout in Brooklyn history. A freshman at Brooklyn College at the age of fifteen. At twenty-one a law school graduate. By thirty a founding partner in a Park Avenue firm. At thirty-six admitted to the Mount Sinai Intensive Cardiac Unit. And now, a couple of months shy of his forty-sixth birthday . . . All that constant driving, all that success, and look where it had gotten him. Kind of like Danny's pushing and pushing in the years that he swam.

17

What did he have to show for it except a scrapbook, a medal case and a busted shoulder? Where was the automatic virtue in always moving as fast as you could? Was it such a sin to just stand still for a moment?

Sam thought so. Just a few weeks before, Joan had phoned Danny from Elisa's apartment—a call casually but transparently engineered so that the two kids would talk, since they so rarely did when left to their own devices. Elisa said she'd heard he was working at a pool, and asked if he was going to start swimming again. He was about to ask what the hell he'd do that for, when he heard Sam call out in the background, "He's not swimming. He's just treading water."

Danny pushed that thought away and focused again on his clothing. All his decent shirts and socks and his quasi-presentable jeans were in a pile on the closet floor. All through college, when Danny went home, it was not with a suitcase but with a laundry bag, everything dirty, which he'd present to his mother upon his arrival like it was a gift, like what she really wanted out of life was to be doing his wash again. But this time he couldn't do that. This time he was returning not as a child but as the man of the family—whether his brother-in-law was trying to beat him to it or not. To make the six-forty train, he should be at the subway by six. There was still plenty of time for a visit to the all-night laundromat.

He crept down the stairs with the laundry bag over his shoulder like a housebreaker making off with his loot: the last thing he wanted at this hour was a run-in with his landlord, who lived in the ground-floor apartment. The front door to the brownstone closed with an audible clack, even though Danny eased it shut with his free hand, and the iron gate squeaked as usual, but then he was out on the street, his breath a ghostly white cloud in his wake. It was colder than he had expected, colder and quieter. Between the streetlight and Manhattan's perpetual glow to the west, the deserted block was bathed in an unreal half light, like one of those mysteriously illumined night photographs. A few houses down he started, thinking there was someone standing in front of a brownstone, but it was only one of the plaster religious statues—Jesus or Mary, he couldn't tell which: the figure was shrouded in plastic for winter protection, filmed with a layer of frost. He looked back toward the church and saw the whole row of them at attention, like anonymous sentinels.

The laundromat was at the corner of Sackett and Smith streets. Danny was always surprised when he came home late from the subway to see its oasis of light amid the dark storefronts (in this neighborhood, the shopkeepers didn't need to burn bulbs to discourage breaking and entering); who from these blocks of solid Italian family wives would be out doing her laundry at three or four in the morning? Save for the lone attendant, the place was empty now, probably had been for hours, but it still had the heat and laundromat smell—that mixture of bleach, bodies, steam air—that reminded Danny of swimming pools.

For years he had lived for that smell, until his last couple of seasons in college, when the tendonitis in his shoulder had gotten so bad that what he smelled and tasted more than anything was his pain, the sour saliva that filled his mouth after the shots of cortisone; the adrenaline before a race that was no longer pure psych and desire but once again had a juice of fear in it; and afterward, staying down in the water so he wouldn't have to look at the faces yet, the chlorine and salt down the back of his throat: *Tough luck about Winger, he can barely break fifty now.* The last time he swam in the Easterns, his junior year, he hadn't wanted to get out of the water at all because Sam was there—the one meet Danny expressly told him not to come watch but he did, insisted upon it, as if it were more important to see his son lose than to have witnessed all the victories Sam never made it for, from Danny's first blue ribbon for the town pool to his trophy in the State High School Championships: a string of wins that was dubbed "the blue streak" in the local sports pages.

When Danny finally climbed out, he didn't want to look up at the spot where he knew Sam and Joan would be standing, waiting to get his attention—Sam with a stopwatch hung around his neck, frozen with the precise duration of each lap of Danny's shame, down to hundredths of seconds. They could go home early now, since Danny hadn't qualified for the finals, and of course they would try to convince him to leave with them, to stop and get a good steak somewhere, instead of waiting all day to ride back in the dark on that bus. He went to the locker room and stood in the shower for a long time, letting the heat work into his shoulder. He dressed slowly enough he might have been freshly injured, when it was just the usual pain, the pain he felt now whenever he pushed himself.

They were in the lobby when he came out with his coat and his gym bag. His mother rushed right up and put her arms around his neck. "How bad is it?"

"Not too bad."

Sam didn't say anything until they were all in the car. Then he twisted around toward the backseat to face Danny. "You're going to have to figure out what you want to do with your life." As if Danny had been planning to make a profession of swimming, and that had only just fallen through. As if Sam had been biting his tongue all those years, waiting for just this opportunity.

Now Danny loaded the wet clothes into the giant drum dryer. He didn't feel anything in his shoulder, not even a twinge, but he could remember the pain—the way it had taken the one thing he had ever done really well, the thing that was his, and turned it against him. It was as if the trajectory of his career had been a message coded into his body: first the potential to go as fast as he did, then the limit, the pain, that said he couldn't go any faster.

Danny watched the clothes tumble and rise, tumble and

rise in the dryer, until the heat and motion unanchored him. In his dream, he stood in the enormous, echoing vault of a swimming pool, not the one from the Easterns but the pool up in Albany, where he'd taken first in the States in the hundred-yard freestyle. He and the other swimmers were up on the blocks, the bleachers were full but there was no cheering; the crowd was frozen into that silence just before the *Swimmers, take your marks, get set* and the starting gun. He was ready to go—standing there on the block in that silence was like containing pure motion, like someone in the bleachers holding back a great shout. But the race wasn't going to start until Danny's father had gotten there, as though by prior arrangement, like everyone knew ahead of time Danny was going to win and this was just an exhibition replay set up for Sam Winger's benefit. Maybe something had come up at the office, or Sam was in a traffic jam somewhere. What else could be keeping him? But the other swimmers and the coaches and spectators did not seem to mind, like it was only natural for them to be waiting.

Danny shook his arms out and sucked in a deep breath, ballooning out his rib cage the way he liked to do to psych out his competitors. Then he felt the hand on his shoulder. But when he opened his eyes, it wasn't his father; it was a young woman's face, bending over him.

"Excuse me. Your clothes are dry. I figured I ought to wake you."

Danny was confused for a moment. Then he said, "My father died," partly to remind himself why he was here, partly as some sort of explanation for *her*.

"Oh. I'm sorry." Her hair was tucked up into a cobalt beret, but he could tell by the way the hat hung that there was a lot of it.

"I've got to go home," he said.

The smile she flashed him was sad but hopeful as she walked across to the line of washers. "Where's home?"

He gave a self-deprecating shrug of the shoulders. "Long

Island." *But my family's from Brooklyn, originally,* he wanted to say. *My father grew up here.* She was feeding sheets and towels into a machine, and he moved to his dryer. Usually he just shoved the hot clothes back into his bag, but now he carried them to the table and started folding them, smoothing down the front of his shirts and buttoning them up to the collar. "You live in this neighborhood?"

"A few blocks over." She tilted her head north, in the direction of Atlantic Avenue, toward the streets where the Italians gave way to a mixture of Hispanics and Palestinians. When her machine was loaded and she'd put in her quarters, she folded her bag up under her arm. "Well, good luck."

He tried to smile for her sake. "Yeah. Thanks." As she walked out the door, her long tweed overcoat swung with her step. *Good luck.* As if his trip home were some kind of race he was entering.

4

THE SUN WAS ALREADY UP when the train shot out of the tunnel on the Long Island side. The light slashed in through the window, snapping Danny out of his game of pretending to be a commuter, some budding junior exec or law firm associate, traveling to the office early to get a jump on the day. He'd figured he probably looked the part, minus the gym bag he carried instead of a briefcase. He was wearing the suit—he'd decided he couldn't pack it without wrinkling it all to hell—and the camel's hair overcoat that was a hand-me-down from Sam, a none-too-subtle hint that Danny stop dragging around in his old letter jacket. The only problem was that there was no crowd of *other* commuters in which he could lose himself, jostling and fighting for seats on the train. This train was practically empty, heading from the city out to the burbs, when any self-respecting member of the work force was going in the other direction.

There wasn't much warmth in the triangle of sun but Danny leaned into it anyway. He'd been out of the cold for almost an hour, between the subway and Penn Station and now the train itself, but still he couldn't stop shivering. At quarter past five, he'd been all packed and ready to go, and couldn't sit around the apartment just waiting. He'd struck out on foot, heading north, figuring he'd pick up the subway in downtown Brooklyn. The chill had come right up through the thin wool suit pants (light wool for the most versatile, year-round wear, Sam had told him) but he'd kept walking up Court Street, where already the air was yeasty with rolls and Italian loaves baking, into the neighborhood where the woman from the laundromat lived, past Atlantic Avenue, with its smells of roasting pistachios and baklava, its cumin and cardamom, into the Heights, and then west to the Promenade. He rested his bag on one of the benches and stood breathing hard. His lungs burned from walking as quickly as he had in that cold, and his mouth was full of metallic saliva.

When he got his wind back, he gazed across the river, following the spans of the Brooklyn Bridge over to lower Manhattan. Later, the sun would come up behind where he stood, from out of the ocean on Brooklyn's far side, beyond the boardwalk and beach that rimmed Coney Island. But already the sky above Manhattan was brightening to a medium turquoise that looked almost unnatural, like some theatrical backdrop behind the stage set of skyscrapers. Before he'd moved to Sackett Street, he'd never even known the Promenade existed, this broad lip of walkway suspended over the artery that linked Queens and Brooklyn, just inland of the piers along Brooklyn's shore. He'd figured that once a truce was officially called with his father, he'd take him and Joan to one of the fancy Heights cafés for Sunday brunch, and then for a walk out here. Even Sam would have to admit that the view was phenomenal: the Brooklyn Bridge arcing up and away from you like some great stone-and-steel rainbow; the way Manhattan looked from the other side of the river, all the buildings rising cleanly, impossibly, from that finger of island; the Hudson and the East rivers flowing together; the ships; the Statue of Liberty.

When Danny was a kid, he'd sometimes dreamed that he was learning to fly. Since he'd moved into Sackett Street, he'd had a few of those dreams again, and this was the kind of clarity that the city had in them. In the dreams, he'd be in

24

the air above the East River, or right over Manhattan, skimming the tops of skyscrapers like a low-dipping plane. The flying part wasn't easy—he always woke tired, remembering the sensation of working to stay up in the air. What was effortless was the dreaming creation of the city from that perspective: every block, every building, in three dimensions, in such precise, realistic detail; the line of bridges traversing the river, connecting Manhattan and Brooklyn like links in a chain; the lights strung along their spans like shimmering necklaces.

The bridge lights still glinted, but the turquoise of the sky was shading toward a paler blue, and though Danny tried to shake it off with the cold, he had the palpable sense of a presence, a spirit hovering, working to stay aloft as he did in the dreams, not over the Promenade itself or the river but over Manhattan, that in his mind was Sam's adult turf as surely as Brooklyn had been little Sammy's. The sun would be up before long; as he turned to go back to the subway stop, he thought of the sunrise he'd once seen from a plane, flying above a dense cloud cover, the light bursting forth into that vast and flawless blue upper atmosphere, so like a child's vision of heaven, and he wondered how it would be if there really were spirits: the labored hovering over what had been their life, or that moment of perfect release, that ascension.

The train rattled through the neighborhoods of Queens row houses, then slid across the marshy inlet edging Little Neck Bay, the fields of tall weeds and grasses straw gold in the slanting winter sunlight. When Danny was a boy, the view out the train through that stretch had always seemed like a flash of wilderness, and he would imagine running away and hiding there, crossing the tracts of reedy marsh grass on foot. Today, speeding by, the marsh looked scrawny, encroached upon; actually, Northern Boulevard was just on the other side of the tracks. The houses of Little Neck sprung up and streaked past his window; in another couple of minutes he'd be at his station. How many

25

hundreds of times had he taken this trip?: all through junior high and high school, whenever he went to the city with friends; coming home on college vacations; and then almost every night this fall, before he'd moved out to Sackett Street. He picked up his gym bag and walked ahead to the doors. As the train started to slow, he looked up and caught his reflection in the sooted door panel. The overcoat and the suit surprised him; for a moment he almost reminded himself of his father. He stared, and his image flickered as the sun darted in and out from behind the buildings and onto the glass, like a candle flame, a spirit, flickering.

Climbing the steps from the platform, Danny drew the camel's hair collar up and around his neck. The town bus was waiting, as he'd known it would be, and now it all went like clockwork. As soon as the driver was sure he had everyone from the train, the bus pulled away. It heaved and lurched up Middle Neck Road, past the glittery shoe stores and clothing boutiques and overpriced delicatessens. Past the crass edifice of the temple the Wingers belonged to, that looked more like a giant warehouse than a place of worship. Past the bagel store and the pizza place, where Danny used to play hookey from Hebrew School. Past the old Village Green, and the corner where his elementary school had once stood, the red brick building since razed to put up senior housing. The bus made its wide, slow-motion turn onto Steamboat Road and yawned through the short, sleepy strip of the black section. It picked up speed by the indoor tennis courts and the park, where Danny had always gone as a kid to shoot baskets, until his muscles grew so loose and stringy from swimming he could no longer trust them on land. And then it tugged up the last hill to Danny's stop.

When Danny took the steps down to the exit door, he could feel the night in his legs. He only crossed the street when the bus and its wake of exhaust were memory. But as slowly as he walked, it was barely a minute before the white house with blue shutters slid into view. Danny had imagined that the house would have visibly changed somehow, but it looked the same as it always had: the immaculate half acre of lawn, laid down strip by strip like carpeting lifted ever so gingerly out of the back of the truck from Green Acres Sod Farm all those years ago, when Danny could barely hold his piece of grass and soil without the edges crumbling; the lawn Danny had mowed and fertilized and strafed with weed killer to his father's exacting specifications long after all his friends' parents had hired gardeners; the shrubbery, pruned and sculpted by Sam himself with his arsenal of clippers and electric hedge trimmers that he wielded like some kind of mad surgeon or chain-saw murderer, or like that old fart of a barber in town, who didn't stop until you had a crew cut, whatever you'd asked for—Sam out there at the end of his hundred-foot extension cord, with Joan screaming over the buzz, "That's enough! There won't be anything left," and Sam just smiling, pruning away, as if it were the world's most relaxing activity. The electric garage door was closed, but Danny could picture the sky blue Mercedes diesel sedan that Sam had insisted was strictly a survival and economy measure when he bought it after the second energy crisis, and that Grandma Ida refused to step foot in, scowling whenever the subject came up: "*Meshuggener*, don't you know they're all Nazis?"

Danny walked up the front steps and stood at the door for a moment, suddenly convinced that last night had all been a dream, that his father would be inside, in his bathrobe at the kitchen table, eating Special K with skim milk and reading the business page. He was so sure that he pushed the door open, stepped inside and called out, "I'm home." He had barely set his bag down when a dark shape rushed at him along the hallway that led from the kitchen. It wasn't his mother, it was his aunt Barbara, Joan's brother Buddy's wife, in a black dress with a short, fitted jacket that looked more suited for a cocktail party than a bereavement. Elisa and Dave were one thing, at least they belonged, but Danny hadn't figured anyone else would be at the house yet. Barbara stopped a couple of feet from him, her hands flying about the lapels of his overcoat, brushing at them like they were covered with lint. "Here. Let me hang this up for you."

"I've got it." He slipped the coat off before she could grab it. "Where's Mom?"

"She's inside, making a couple of phone calls. Come on. I'll fix you some breakfast."

Barbara was just shy of anorexically thin, but her husband and Danny's two cousins on that side were chunky; though she barely nourished herself, feeding other people seemed to be her main role in life. "I'm not hungry," he said, and stepped around her to make for the kitchen.

His mother sat at the table, the receiver pressed hard to her ear, her looseleaf address book and a legal pad laid out in front of her, nodding her head but not saying anything. She had a coffee cup by her side; up on the counter sat the plug-in, thirty-cup pot she used for duplicate bridge games and Thanksgiving dinners. She turned around to him, face drawn and gaze steady. She was wearing jeans and a sweat-shirt; she had no makeup on and her hair wasn't curled, so it hung down like a girl's by her shoulders. ". . . I know you do. Listen, Danny just walked in the door. I'm going to hang up now."

She nodded once more, then placed the receiver back in its cradle without her eyes leaving him. She stood and walked toward him, her arms open. "Baby, I'm sorry." And then it was the musty hairspray smell of her hair, how tightly she squeezed him. He waited for her chest and shoulders to start shaking along with his. His mother, who Sam was always calling the faucet. Who'd wept at the opening credits to *The Sound of Music* and *Gone With the Wind*, and cried so hard during the final chapters of *Bambi* that Danny and Elisa had had to get Sam to finish reading it. But she didn't cry now. Instead, she released her grip, stepped back and looked at him with that same glazed calm. "Did you get any sleep?"

He wiped at his face with his coat sleeve and shook his head. "I went to the laundromat. Where's Elisa?"

"She took Dave to the station. He was going to square everything away at his office and pick up the rest of their things. She must have just missed you."

Barbara stepped in from where she'd been hovering by the door to the kitchen. "Buddy and I got up and drove over as soon as Mom called us. Buddy went to see to the girls, and his office. He'll be back as soon as he can."

Danny nodded and looked around the kitchen. He had that feeling of presence again, but stronger now, more intimate, as if Sam were just in the living room, or upstairs. On the refrigerator, among the tennis schedules and Beth-Israel Sisterhood bulletins, were the usual pictures, that Joan hadn't thought or had time to take down. The sumo wrestler with the quadruple belly, that she'd clipped from some magazine and posted as a reminder for Sam, who the last couple of years had started to get thick around the middle. A suntanned, shirtless Sam waving from the cockpit of their new sailboat. Sam and Joan in the basket of a hot air balloon over the Serengeti in Africa, Sam and Joan along the Great Wall, Sam, on the back patio, holding a microphone, totally bombed, making the toast that turned into a speech at Elisa's wedding reception. There was Danny himself, at age seventeen, lifting up out of the water on the last lap of a hundred butterfly, his mouth drawn into an O, like those pictures of wind gods sucking in air, under his Mark Spitz–lookalike moustache. And next to that, in the corner, the photo of Danny and Sam that past spring at Danny's graduation.

What Danny remembered about that day was being pissed at his father: for refusing to take the girl Danny was seeing at the time out to dinner; for bending Greg's ear with the advantages of a law over a business degree; for sitting there with that tight-lipped, disappointed look on his face when all the students who'd won prizes and special citations were called to the podium. The strange thing was that the picture showed something entirely different. Danny's robe hung open to reveal the middle letters of the words, *Varsity Swimming*, Sam was wearing a madras sport shirt open at the neck, their arms were draped around each other's shoulders, and they were both laughing, like somebody had just cracked a joke. Danny had never thought he looked anything like his father. Sam had sandy blond hair and blue eyes and Danny was dark like his mother, with hair that was almost black in dim light despite all the years of swimming pool chlorine, and olive skin that had always had Grandma Ida scrubbing at his neck and ears, figuring they must be dirty. And yet, in the photograph, there was a general air of resemblance about their two faces, the pair of open mouths and the heads thrown back.

He turned away from the picture, back to his mother. "So, last night. You know . . ."

She completed his question, in a tone so even it floored him: "How did it happen?"

He nodded, but then Barbara was on him, taking his arm. "Why don't you sit down and let me make you a bagel. I don't think Mom is really—"

He shook her off. "He's my father. I want to know what the hell happened. Or maybe everyone else around here should know it but me."

"Shhh. It's all right." His mother had taken hold of his hands, as if she were afraid he was going to strike Barbara, and in that moment he almost could have. "Let's go into the den and sit down. We might as well get through this now before people start coming."

"What people?"

"Your aunt Esther's flight gets in from Utica at eight-thirty. She's going to rent a car at the airport and go pick up Ida. My parents are flying up from Florida. Tonight, after dinner, your father's partners are going to come. Henrietta and Aaron could be here any minute. And everyone else. The immediate world is on its way over here."

He didn't know why it should surprise him, why he'd imagined this event as his own, as something for the immediate family. When had they ever had Sam to themselves? Why should it be any different now? His mother must have been on the phone since the sun came up. There were all of his parents' friends, garnered over twenty years of suburban dinner parties and tennis leagues, bridge rotations and yacht club regattas; there were Sam's longtime clients, most of whom had also turned into friends, since at some point Sam had saved each of their skins on the kind of scale that engenders eternal gratitude. There would be a phone call, and then half a dozen other calls would branch out from that one, like some urgent chain letter moving out over the wires until the news spread. It exhausted Danny to think of how wide the waves that circled out from his father's life traveled, how many people were touched by them.

In the den, he perched himself at the edge of the couch. Sitting back on it would be too comfortable, too deep a falling into the wide, downy cushions that used to draw him into naps at the end of the day, home from practice, dozing but also aware of the sounds of Joan in the kitchen, the smell of baking potatoes, of meat broiling. His mother sat on the upholstered rocker, facing him. She set her feet in their boating moccasins square on the floor in front of her and placed her arms on the chair arms, stiffly, as if she didn't inhabit her gestures but only performed them from memory. "It started a week ago. A week ago Saturday. Dad had a fall on the tennis court."

"What do you mean, *had a fall?*"

"It was his Saturday morning tennis game. You know, with Herb Steinberg, Mel Ascher . . ."

Danny got a picture of those men his father's age in their designer tennis whites, bellies softening with booze and rich food but arm and leg muscles taut, mediocre tennis players but fierce competitors, like Sam himself, who'd won his office tournament two years running against men Joan said

31

were not only younger and stronger but much better players. It was a wonder to watch, she'd told Danny. Sam's serve was slow and he didn't have much of a backhand, but sooner or later his opponents would start making mistakes, screwing up on their timing. His game was no match for theirs, but mentally, psychologically, he overpowered them.

"They'd just finished their warm-up, and Dad had first serve. He put a nitro under his tongue."

As he listened, Danny visualized the white pills in the little brown vial that Sam carried everywhere in his breast pocket and whose appearance, in the middle of a walk or a game or an argument, had always scared Danny, always made him look for signs of the pain on his father's face, his father who'd just stand there, mouth open, looking blank for a moment, who'd say, if they were alone, "Don't tell your mother, okay, tiger?"

"Not because anything was wrong. He said that's what he always did. That's what Dr. Bleetstein told him: to anticipate strain, and not just react to it. So he took the nitro, and set himself up for the serve. But he never hit the ball. He blacked out. He got a bump right here"—she touched the side of her forehead, right where Sam's protruding vein would have been—"and he was all black-and-blue where his glasses smashed."

"He fell on his face?"

She nodded. "Herb says he was only out for a couple of seconds, but someone called an ambulance and they made him go. When I got to the hospital, he seemed fine, just a little bruised up. He said he must have been overtired. We'd stayed out late at the Goldbergs', and he'd had a few drinks. They have a nine o'clock court, so he didn't take time for breakfast. He just grabbed a cup of coffee on the way out the door. Anyway, he insisted that's all it was—his head had gone light. He swore it wasn't his heart. And all the tests backed him up. The EKG was fine, everything was fine. They sent him home with a portable forty-eight-hour monitor."

32

"So that was a week ago Saturday?" He tried to think of what he'd been doing that morning, but couldn't remember. What he meant to ask was why he hadn't been told. His father passes out on the tennis court, falls literally flat on his face, gets rushed to the hospital—and Danny isn't even let in on it? It wasn't like he'd moved to Outer Mongolia. He was on the near side of Brooklyn, a couple of subways and a half-hour train ride away. Sure, he and Sam had fought about the apartment, the lifeguard job, but what hadn't they fought about? They could have made up. Danny could have come out to the house. He could have told Sam he hadn't meant what he'd said that night.

"Everybody seemed to think it was nothing," Joan said, as if by way of excuse. "He saw Bleetstein that Monday, and he said your father's heart was better than it had been since he'd known him. That's what Dad said too. He said he'd lived with this thing long enough he could tell. Bleetstein said they should do another angiogram, just to make sure. He'd been trying to get your father to have one for the past few years anyway. But he said it was no emergency. Dad said he'd take a week off at the beginning of March, so that's when they scheduled it."

She stared off into the air above the table then, as if she were puzzling out something, as if there were something in what she'd just said that she did not understand. The whole time she'd been speaking, she'd sounded bewildered, like she was reciting the events but couldn't really make sense of them.

He made sure to speak the words gently now: "So what happened last night?"

"Hang on. There's another whole part to the story first."

Just then, the electric garage door buzzed into life on the other side of the wall, the familiar drone that had woken Danny from his naps on the couch, night fallen outside the den windows, Sam striding in with his briefcase and a draft of cold air. Danny looked toward the door his father would

33

come through from the garage as if it might be him this time, with that same feeling he'd gotten earlier at the front door, that this was all a dream, or a hoax. Sam would march in, Joan would start crying, and then they'd all have a big laugh over how crazy it was, their actually believing him dead.

The door opened, there was a shuffle of steps and a papery crinkling of packages, and in walked Elisa. Danny's mother may have been numbed past tears, but his sister had definitely been crying. Her eyelids were puffed up and purple, and her cheeks were dotted with those pink blotches she'd gotten as a kid when Danny, finally big enough, would take it into his head to pummel her. Her perfect, fixed nose was all red and swollen from blowing it. Whenever he first saw her, that tiny, straight nose surprised him, even though it had been eight years now (she'd had a choice: the nose job or a big sweet-sixteen party); the mental image he seemed to revert to when they were apart was of what she'd looked like beforehand, with the Winger beak, in spite of the fact that Elisa, with her mother's collusion, had done her best to destroy all photographic evidence of that earlier, undoctored self, his real sister. The joke of it was that she'd never told Dave, and sworn the whole family to secrecy. Like the guy wouldn't open his eyes and figure it out for himself one day. Like she was genuinely afraid that if Dave had known, he wouldn't have fallen in love with her.

Danny stood, but he didn't move toward her; he stared at her face and tried to think what to say. You didn't say you were *sorry* when you too were inside the circle of loss. His mother had said it but she hadn't meant it that way. She'd said she was sorry because she figured she'd fallen down on the job of keeping her husband, their father, alive; because she figured she was somehow responsible.

Before he could think of anything, the phone rang, and almost at the same time the doorbell sounded. Barbara rushed in from the kitchen to grab the packages from Elisa, who went to answer the phone. Joan looked across the room toward the front hallway. "Danny, honey, would you mind getting that? It's probably Henrietta and Aaron. You could hang up their coats, okay?"

"Sure." Danny hopped up; he was supposed to be useful. But he didn't want Sam's cousins to come, didn't want the *immediate world* coming or calling up on the telephone. He wanted to sit quietly in the den with his mother, to find out the part of the story after Sam's fall. He opened the door but it wasn't Henrietta and Aaron after all. It was a giant column of fruit wrapped in cellophane, a man half hidden behind it.

"Mr. Winger?"

The disguise of the suit again. "No. Mr. Winger's—I mean, yes, I guess so. I am."

The guy wasn't interested in the nuances of Danny's identity. He handed over the fruit basket. "Card's taped to the ribbon inside."

"Okay. Thanks." Danny shifted under the weight of the basket. He carried it into the kitchen like a dubious trophy and set it down on the counter. Elisa was off the phone and Joan was back in the kitchen too. For a moment they all stared at the gift, the pears and apples and grapefruit so outsized and waxy, so perfectly formed, they could have been artificial. Then Barbara swooped down on it, tore the top of the cellophane and pulled out the little white envelope with the card.

" 'With our deepest sympathy,' " she read. " 'The Weinsteins and the Millers.' "

Joan nodded, still staring at the pieces of fruit, like they were some alien and possibly dangerous substance brought into her kitchen.

But Barbara wasn't paying any attention. She wheeled around to the holder by the telephone for a pen, and wrote "fruit basket" under "deepest sympathy." "We need to keep track of everything as it comes in. I'm going to just put this in here"—she dropped the card into the box where Joan kept mail that hadn't been sorted yet—"and that's where all the cards go. And write on it what the gift was. Okay, kids?"

Danny tried to catch Elisa's eye, to smirk about Barbara's officiousness, about being called *kids*. But Elisa was looking too serious. His gaze fell back on the tower of fruit. "How much of this stuff you think we're going to get?" He imagined a funeral chapel filled not with flowers but baskets of apples and oranges, and Barbara directing, telling the attendants where to place each arrangement.

Barbara hoisted the basket and teetered with it toward the garage, calling back over her shoulder, "You'd be surprised. It's wintertime, so you have it easy. You can just keep everything outside where it's cool. When my friend Audrey's Burt died, she had to rent an extra refrigerator to keep all the cold cuts from spoiling."

From the living room, the antique wall clock started to chime. The clock had been one of Sam's mechanical obsessions; he was always winding and tuning it, taking it apart and reassembling it, comparing its readings to Greenwich mean time. As Danny counted the notes, it struck him for the first time that all those years of listening to his father's clock were the reason the chimes of the Sackett Street Church of Our Saviour got on his nerves so much.

Eight A.M.: it must have marked some threshold of decency for the *immediate world* his mother had spoken of, because now the phone—both phones—did in fact start ringing in earnest. Joan manned the kitchen extension, and maintained that grave, not wholly comprehending expression as she mostly said *Yes, I understand, I know you are, yes. The arrangements will be listed in the* Times *tomorrow. With the obituary. Heart attack. Yes.* In the den, Elisa somehow managed, in spite of the tears that rolled down her face like some aquatic system independent of her immediate functioning, to click into that telephone manner she used at her law office, that she'd even pulled on Danny the couple of times he'd needed to call her there. *Thank you so much, Mrs. Goldfarb. I really appreciate your saying so. I'll pass the message along to my mother as soon as she's free.* Danny trudged back toward the kitchen, disgusted. Elisa had as foul a mouth and pissy a temperament as anyone, but she had this ability to turn on a killing politeness, to metamorphose into Miss Manners in the blink of an eye, and so with baby-sitters, neighbors, grandparents, aunts and uncles, even with Sam and Joan, Danny had always been the one who was blamed for everything. *How thoughtful of you, Mrs. Bleetstein. It means a lot to all of us that you feel that way.* Up from what saccharine inner reservoir was she dredging this bullshit? And why did the news of a death send all these suburban yentas scurrying to their push-buttons, as if you had nothing better to do at a time like this than to be speaking with *them*?

He sat back down at the kitchen table and laid his head across folded arms. As soon as he shut his eyes, he had a vision of his father's face the night of their fight, how red it had gotten. And how Danny's own cheeks had burned the next morning, listening to Sam talk to his mother downstairs, waiting until Sam left for work before he ventured out of his bedroom. After that, it had taken a few days to organize his move, but Danny hadn't stayed over at the house again. He'd slept on the floor at Sackett Street until his new bed was delivered, and only went back to the Island during the day. When Joan confronted him, he denied that he was avoiding his father. "I've been in your hair for three months. I just want to get the new place set up, that's all." When she asked him to come home for dinner on one of the nights of Hanukkah, he said it wasn't a very good time. She sent him a miniature menorah and a box of Hanukkah candles along with a check, and he lied and said yes when she asked him if he was lighting them.

Not that he would have necessarily seen his father even if he had gone home. How many nights had the candles sat in their holders in the big brass menorah with Elisa and Danny

37

hovering over them, practicing the blessing under their breaths, waiting for Sam to materialize? Half the time he didn't show up before bedtime, and Joan would go ahead and light the candles herself, only quickly, without the usual flourish of the shammes and just reciting the blessing, not chanting it. And then the kids would be sent straight up to bed so Danny missed his favorite part, watching the colored wax drip slowly down over the brass until the flames swelled, then sputtered and snuffed themselves out with a hiss. He would just see the candles, whole and upright with their even lights, and then, in the morning, the empty brass holders.

Danny felt a hand on his arm and looked up to see Barbara. "Wouldn't you like a nice bagel and cream cheese? I have a piece of lox I brought along from home. Eating something will make you feel better."

He was about to snap back at her but he checked himself. He was hungry, and besides, if he ate it would make *her* feel better. "Sure. What the hell. Give me the works. Maybe there's some tomato and Bermuda onion."

"Hey, why don't you get off your ass and make it yourself?" Elisa had come in from the den; she was in between phone calls. "You should know how by now. Unless you've got someone fixing your meals for you out there in Brooklyn."

"Give me a break. Barbara offered, okay? Get off your high feminist horse for once."

"Kids." With her hand over the telephone mouthpiece, Joan was wearily shaking her head. "Not now, okay?"

He glared at Elisa, then moved around to the counter next to the sink, where Barbara was cutting the bagel. As hungry as he was, the food she took out all looked glossy, unreal, like the fruit in the basket. When Barbara finished slicing, spreading and assembling, he motioned for her to leave the plate on the counter. He picked up the bagel and closed his mouth around a huge bite, as if getting it down quickly

38

would help make up for eating it in the first place. But he almost choked on it, because just as he was starting to swallow, a horn blasted in front of the house. No doubt another fruit basket, with a delivery guy that had no respect for the grieving.

He went into the den, still chewing, to look out the front windows. It wasn't a delivery van but a mustard brown Chevy. Struggling out of the car were Henrietta and Aaron, his grandmother's cousin and her husband, and so some obscure but tenacious relation to his father, to him. Aaron must have accidentally hit the horn while sliding out of the driver's seat, and Henrietta was busy berating him. Danny couldn't make out the words, just the general tone of her carping, and the way that as her mouth moved, her other features shifted and distorted like in some grotesque facial tic. She was a short, stubby woman, whose body, as Danny had decided at some Thanksgiving dinner or Passover seder years back, was distinguished by an almost complete absence of waist: viewed from the side, there was virtually no distance between the bottom edge of her pyramid breasts in the front and the point at which her ass started to stick out in back of her. Aaron might have been of reasonable height, except that he was so stooped over, not so much from age as from forty-odd years with a wife like that. His forehead and balding crown jutted out, shiny and vulnerable, as if he were forever waiting for the next blow. On his own, he was a sweet man. At family gatherings, when Henrietta was giving someone else an earful in a different room, he could sometimes be caught smiling, or playing with babies. But with Henrietta beside him, he wore a perpetual grimace, and popped a piece out of his roll of Tums whenever you thought he was actually opening his mouth to say something.

Henrietta took a series of little steps up the front path, carrying a couple of aluminum roasting pans wrapped in silver foil, walking like the pans were a strain but probably never giving a thought to trusting her husband to help her. No doubt it was some brown, stringy pot roast, or one of the two-ton noodle kugels Joan was always accepting graciously and then dumping into the garbage can as soon as she could, hoping to set back the local, gourmet raccoons. Henrietta was moving slowly enough—and Aaron would never go so far as to walk in front of her—that Danny had time to decide he wasn't up for this, run back to the kitchen to grab the plate with his bagel, and hightail it upstairs before Henrietta stepped up and leaned on the doorbell.

5

DANNY'S BEDROOM was back to looking almost the same as it had when he was a boy, after several years of a different incarnation. On Saturdays in junior high he and his friends rode the train to the city and discovered Greenwich Village, which had inspired the original redecoration. It was 1969, but they weren't looking for drugs or free love, these jocks from the suburbs, though that's what Sam and Joan were afraid of when they found out it was the Village, and not the Empire State Building or Statue of Liberty or museums that were filling those Saturday outings. Danny and his buddies liked to look at the hippies in Washington Square, watching them like you might the natives of some exotic, incomprehensible culture; the lives of those creatures with the long, greasy hair and peasant clothes and beads, just boys and girls, really, not so much older than they, liberated from parents, from schools and temples, from teams, were just as hard to imagine. But watching the hippies was only a part of it. They loved the bright, narrow shops with walls covered floor to ceiling with buttons: CANDY IS DANDY BUT SEX WON'T ROT YOUR TEETH. SAVE WATER—SHOWER WITH A FRIEND. LUCY IN THE SKY WITH DIAMONDS. And even better than the button stores were the black-light, psychedelic poster shops, where the shapes and colors pulsated and moved around on you even if you'd never so much as been near any acid, the Jefferson Airplane was deafening, and where, one Saturday when Danny must have picked up some kind of contact high in the park, he could have sworn he had a vision of God after staring up for too long at the Day-Glo corona of Hendrix's afro.

Sam and Joan put their foot down at the black light, but still, one Saturday night, Danny took down the map of New Amsterdam in the seventeenth century, the etching of New York harbor, the quartet of sailboat lithographs with the green felt mats Joan had cut out herself, and the watercolor of a tugboat on Long Island Sound Danny had painted in the fourth grade, and stacked the lot in the back of his closet. Day-Glo didn't quite cut it if you couldn't have a black light, like his friends Mitchell and Steve had bought out of the savings from their allowances, so Danny settled for Brigitte Bardot, standing chest-deep in the sea on the French Riviera, breasts afloat and nipples like lilly pads right at the surface; Richard Nixon in his victory pose, with the caption, *Would you buy a used car from this man?*; and a blown-up picture of a pig mounting another pig: *Makin' Bacon*.

When Sam and Joan came back from their bridge game, Danny was already asleep, in the midst of one of those unsettling dreams where the girls he'd seen in Washington Square, with their unshaven legs and their unfettered breasts through the gauzy white of loose peasant blouses, got mixed up with the girls he knew from school and Temple Beth-Israel Sunday School and the Arthur Murray Dance Studio, where everybody sent their kids so they could fox-trot and cha-cha-cha at Bar Mitzvahs—girls like Naomi Weissman, who shivered when he touched her breasts through the three layers of sweater and blouse and bra, who let out a little, awed *Oh!* when his hand had once strayed too far up the leg of her center-creased blue jeans, but who was determined not to let down her defenses; Naomi suddenly there in the park in one of the see-through shirts with those sweet, pointy tits of hers, smiling at Danny, beckoning him over to the patch of grass where she was shaking to the beat of a group of conga drummers, spreading her arms out wide so he could see *them* bobbing and dancing, just out of reach.

Even in the dark, when his mother stepped in to check on him, she must have noticed something wrong with the walls, because just at the moment when it was happening in his pajamas, the light shot on, and he was awakened by her cry. *Sam. You have to come in here and see this.* And then more softly, heartbroken: *All those beautiful pictures . . .*

Danny sat up in bed, shielding his eyes from the sudden, merciless light, making sure the blanket was covering his pajama pants. Sam came in and stood in the doorway, his gaze resting for a moment on Brigitte Bardot. He gave the other posters only the most cursory inspection, then turned to his son. "What did you do with the other pictures?"

Danny motioned his head toward the closet. "In there."

"Did you line them up so they won't get broken or scratched?"

Danny nodded.

"With the glass facing glass? Not front to back?"

He thought for a second, then shook his head no.

"Okay. You'll set them up right in the morning. Now how did you hang these posters up?"

"Tape."

"Did you take my good masking tape from down on the workbench?"

Danny shook his head again, hoping this was the right answer, that Sam didn't want him poking around in his things. "I just used some Scotch."

Sam shook his own head now, almost sadly, the way he always did when confronted with incompetence or stupidity. "That'll take the paint right off. If you're going to do something, don't go off and do it half cocked. Tomorrow you can retape them, if it isn't too late already."

"I can repaint the walls if they need it," Danny offered. For a couple of years he'd been wanting to paint his room blue so it would look like a swimming pool.

43

"We'll see about that." Sam stifled a yawn. "Okay, let's all get some sleep."

"But, Samuel, those pictures." Joan had been staring at the walls the whole time, like at the photographs of those ravaged Vietnamese villages in the papers and magazines. "You're prepared to live with this?"

"I don't have to live with anything. It's his room. He'll get tired of it soon enough." Sam turned and crossed the hallway to his own bedroom.

Joan gazed at the posters for another minute, almost like she might start to cry, and then walked up to the bed and kissed Danny's forehead.

When she was gone, and their door was closed, Danny slipped out from under the covers and turned the overhead light back on. He went to the poster of Brigitte and pulled back one taped corner, and sonofabitch if his father hadn't been right as usual. Stuck to the little roll of Scotch tape was a square chip of white paint; the wall bore the mark of the matching square of bare plaster.

Through junior high and high school, the gallery of images changed, with the changing fortunes of rock bands and Hollywood idols, political candidates and brands of beer, with Joe Namath quarterbacking for the New York Jets and Mark Spitz sweeping the '72 Summer Olympics. From time to time, Danny would peer into his closet at the neat row of wooden-framed pictures, glass against glass, and feel a pang for the classic, seafaring decor of his childhood; for the boy who loved nothing more than the Saturdays and Sundays he spent with his family on their small wooden sailboat on Long Island Sound, chubby in his orange life vest, his father letting him hold the tiller but keeping his own hand on it too, so Danny would feel the pull of the wind and water and his father's pull also, like it was one more of the elements he had to contend with.

He didn't really mind when he came home for Thanksgiving break freshman year to find his poster collection rolled up in the closet, the walls repainted pale blue, and the old pictures and prints reinstated, all of them but Danny's tugboat, which really did look like a little kid's picture by then, however precocious it might have seemed when he'd painted it. And that was more or less the state his walls were in now, except for the diploma his mother had insisted on having matted and framed, his college medal case, and the bookshelf he had mounted over his desk to hold the stacks of old *Swimming Worlds* he had plotted and dreamed over.

From downstairs, he could hear Henrietta, then Barbara; hear the phone ring. Outside, he heard a van pulling up to the house, and at the window watched a man walk up the front path carrying an enormous plastic platter of cold cuts. On the other side of the room, he lay down on his old, single high-riser bed, with the second bed tucked underneath it, that had pulled out and popped up with a metal screech on the nights when his cousins Nathan and Cindy slept over. He closed his eyes, but there was no way he could sleep. He flashed on an image of Nathan from when they were still boys, before all the craziness started in Nathan and Cindy's family, before the craziness of the sixties and early seventies carried Nathan away. It was the first time they took Nathan out on the sailboat, and he couldn't swim. Danny was already winning races for the team at the local swimming pool; he lent Nathan his orange life vest, which he hadn't worn in a couple of years. Nathan was three years older than Danny, much too big for the overstuffed, baby preserver. Still, he strapped it on tight and sat there in the cockpit looking like he was going to be seasick.

The face of his Danny saw now was the one Nathan wore when the wind came up, and Sam brought all the sails in close-hauled so the boat heeled way over. It was such a look of naked, unknowing fear that Danny had never forgotten it; it would be the face of Nathan's he would remember years later when the news would come early on a Saturday morning when Danny was a sophomore in high school: Nathan had taken flight out the window of his high-rise dorm at the Massachusetts Institute of Technology. He had dropped a couple of tabs of acid, the campus police could ascertain that much, but still it amazed Danny to think that his cousin had not been afraid, out there alone on the window ledge, the lights of the campus ranged below him like stars, like jewels glinting through a black water, this boy who couldn't swim, ready to dive for that ocean.

The knock sounded softly, and then the door pushed timidly open, the way it used to when Sam had sent Danny up to his room from the table, and Joan would come up sometime later and sit at the edge of his bed, brush the hair from his forehead, speak to him quietly about swimming or school—anything but what had happened downstairs with his father. Now she came in and took her usual place and Danny sat up against the blue corduroy bolster, the needle-point pillow of a ship's compass.

"I'm sorry, turkey"—her tenderest nickname for Danny, ever since the day of his bris, when he was just eight days old, and was carried in to the *oohs* and *aahs* and *I'm telling you*s of the relatives, squirming and naked on Grandma Ida's silver platter like a Thanksgiving bird.

"Stop apologizing. It isn't your fault."

"I mean for all the phone calls. The interruptions."

"That isn't your fault, either. None of it is your fault."

She raised the manicured arcs of her eyebrows, as if to say she didn't swallow that for a minute. Everything was her fault, according to her own obscure system of logic and blame—always had been. There was no use in arguing that with her.

"So. You got up to where he had the appointment for the angiogram next month, but everything was okay."

She stared down at her hands.

"You did come up here to finish telling me, didn't you?"

She shrugged her assent, but before she spoke she gazed off again, toward the sailboat lithographs, the spot where

46

Richard Nixon had hung. "Everything seemed to be fine, but he had this headache, after his fall. Bleetstein referred him to a neurologist—Dr. Spector, who's supposed to be the big man at North Shore Hospital. Spector saw him Wednesday and said nothing was wrong. He said your father had fallen and banged his head, he'd probably gotten a bit of a whiplash, he should just take it easy for a few days and take some Tylenol when he needed it for the pain. Because it was here"—she pulled her hair up from the back with one hand, and with the other touched two fingers to the spot where the tip of her neck met the base of her skull—"so the whiplash made sense."

He nodded, like he was right with her, but it still seemed to him that she was delivering a long preamble, only loosely connected to the story of the previous night. What did all this headache and whiplash business have to do with a heart attack?

"He went to work Thursday and Friday. We played in our regular Friday night bridge game. But he wasn't himself. Like in the first hand he bid four no-trump and won the bid, and then he went down two tricks, for absolutely no reason. No one could believe it. Not so much that he lost, because he looked tired, but that he never yelled at me."

Danny couldn't help smirking. His parents were notorious for bickering at the card table. There was rarely a night that they'd come home from duplicate bridge when Joan wouldn't swear that it was the last time she'd play with him. Sam didn't like losing, but if that's what the cards had dictated, he would put up with it, and was capable of admiring the way someone else played out a good hand, though he'd usually explain at the end how they could have taken an extra trick or two. But if the cards went his way and he lost, or didn't win as big as he figured he should have, he was insufferable. Danny had heard it himself when the rotation brought the game to the Wingers' house. Whether it was her fault or not, Sam found a way to blame Joan, and didn't hesitate to berate or instruct her in front of their friends, with the game still in progress. *That can't possibly be all you have. What did you raise the bid to three clubs for?* And then, before the same hand was out: *Think before you put down a card. Did you see what Judy played last time? Haven't you understood the first thing I've been telling you?*

When Danny was little and they'd been playing at somebody else's house he'd wake to the sound of the garage door slamming, and when his mother came in to kiss him good night, her cheek would be hot and slick. But as the years went on, she got to be a fairly sharp player, and also more stoical; only if Sam behaved especially viciously would she cry, and if there was even the faintest possibility that she'd lost them a trick, she was the first to admit it. Maybe that was the reason they'd been such a good match: his propensity for dishing out blame stood in direct proportion to her capacity for assuming it.

Joan had her hand back at the base of her skull, running her fingers up and down as if there were some kind of answer there. "He said the pain was shooting up from that spot, and when we were driving home from the bridge, he said he heard a whooshing sound in his ears. So first thing Saturday morning we had the hospital get hold of Spector. He said he didn't know anything about whooshing sounds—that that had nothing to do with what he'd been looking at. He said if Dad had a whooshing sound in his ears, he should go see an ear, nose and throat man."

"So did he?" Danny was sitting up at the edge of the bed now, alongside his mother. He'd forgotten the heart attack for the moment; he suddenly felt like he was on the track of something, that what his mother was telling him was fraught with some obscure but crucial significance.

"The guy Spector recommended couldn't see him until the following week. So the nurse suggested the Manhattan Ear, Nose and Throat Hospital. You know, on Sixty-fourth Street. On weekends it's run like a clinic. She said Dad could just walk in there and see someone. But by the time we were done with all of the phone calls, he said he was tired. He just wanted to stay home and relax. I told him he could relax in the car—I was driving him to Sixty-fourth Street.

"Of course once he agreed to go, he insisted on driving himself. Then we hit an accident on the parkway—the road was backed up from the Throgs Neck all the way to La Guardia. Before we even got into the city, he was carrying on like a lunatic. *I told you I wanted to stay home. What do I need this aggravation for?* He got out at the hospital and I circled till I found a parking space. By the time I got in there, he was tearing the place apart. There were about twelve people waiting, and only one doctor on duty. He said he wasn't sitting there, he was hungry, he wanted to go have some lunch. We went and had a burger, and then we drove back home."

"So he never saw anyone?"

She shook her head no. "I canceled our dinner date for that night. We just stayed home the rest of Saturday and all day Sunday. Sunday we read the paper and watched a tennis match on TV. After the match he wanted to work on a shelf he's been building to fit behind the head on the boat. I did a few things around the house, and then I broiled some lamb chops for dinner. *The African Queen* was on Channel Nine, so we got into bed early. He didn't want to admit he wasn't feeling well—you know how he is. But he kept taking Tylenol and rubbing the back of his neck."

He hated to ask but he had to. "Then what happened yesterday?"

She stood up and went to the window, and he looked out too, from the bed, at the icy blue sky, the bare branches of the big, front-yard maple. "In the morning, when we woke up, he looked terrible—green. He said he felt okay, it was only the headache still. But he must have been a little worried himself, because he let me talk him into sending Jeffrey to his ten o'clock court date downtown, to present some papers on Roland."

49

"Who's Jeffrey?"

"Oh, Jeffrey Skinner. He's the junior partner in the corporate department. Nice young guy. Bright. Your dad gives him a terrible time but he seems to enjoy it. He told me he'd learned more in a month with your father than in three years of law school and six years of practice combined."

"That's great," Danny said, scarcely managing to conceal his sarcasm. At the moment he wasn't too keen on hearing about some apprentice workaholic's love affair with his father. "So he didn't go to the ten o'clock court date."

She nodded and went on with the story as if she hadn't detected his tone. "That way he could stay out of the traffic. I tried to talk him into staying home altogether, but he wouldn't hear of it. He said he had a big day. So he left around ten. I went to the garage door and watched him drive out. There was nothing I could do to stop him, but I had this bad feeling." She came and sat down on the bed again.

"I kept calling his office that afternoon. I just wanted to speak to him, to see how he sounded. But he was in back-to-back meetings all day. Then I got a call from Florence to say the Roland meeting was running late, he wouldn't be home for dinner, that they'd call out for some sandwiches. I actually thought about getting in the car and driving into the city so I would be there when he got done. But I knew he'd only get angry. Like you can't ever make the suggestion that something might be too much for him.

"So I waited. And the next thing I know it's ten-fifteen and the phone rings. It's Jeffrey. They stayed after the meeting to finish up a few papers and then your father started clutching the back of his head. Jeffrey asked him if he was all right and he said fine, it was only this headache, he had to do something to get rid of this headache. So Jeffrey went to find him some aspirin, and on his way back he heard Dad call out something but then stop, in the middle of a word. He said he couldn't make out what it was. By the time he got to the chair, your dad was throwing up. Jeffrey went to lift up his head, and then he realized that he was unconscious."

Danny tried to picture his father in a pinstriped business suit there in the chair like that, but he could not. And what had Sam been trying to say? Could it have been someone's name? Was it possible that Danny had crossed his mind in those final moments? He felt his mother's hands taking his, and he squeezed them, probably too hard for the hand with the wedding band, the diamond engagement ring.

"We don't have to finish this right now. There's plenty of time for you to hear the rest later."

"No. Go on." He took back his hands and swiped at his eyes and nose. "I want to hear it all before everyone comes."

"Well, there's not much more to tell, really. The ambulance was on its way when Jeffrey called, and I guess it got there a few minutes later. I put some things in a bag for your father—his toilet kit, some pajamas, a robe, a clean change of clothes—and I got into the car and drove in. The funny thing was, I was perfectly calm. It was like I'd been rehearsing that moment in my head for so many years that I knew exactly what to do. It was like something I'd already done before. When I got to the hospital, Jeffrey was there in the waiting room. The doctor came out and said it didn't look good, but they were still trying. The ambulance crew had gotten him on the respirator right away and they had his heart beating. But none of his other vital signs were doing anything. They couldn't get anything to come up. Then in about half an hour the doctor came out again and said he was sorry, they couldn't do anything more, they had lost him."

"But why? If they had his heart beating . . ."

"But it was only beating artificially, on the machine. It wouldn't go on its own. And there was no brain activity. The doctor said the damage must have been extensive enough that it was too late by the time the ambulance got there."

Danny stood up and walked to the other side of the room, where he leaned against the edge of his dresser. Something wasn't right about what she was saying. There had to be something more to it. He thought again of the whooshing sound in Sam's ears, like hearing the ocean through a seashell, except from inside, and of that last word or half word: what his father might have known in that moment.

"So that was it. Except I went in to see him."

He looked at her, surprised, though of course that's what she would have done.

"To see him. To say good-bye. And I did. The doctor brought me in and then he left me alone with him. And I kissed him, I smoothed back his hair. But you know, it was funny. I did it, but I knew that it wasn't him. I knew it the minute I stepped foot in that room. It was his body, but it wasn't him. Whatever it was that made him Sam was already gone. Whatever used to look out at me from behind those blue eyes of his."

Danny got an image of the soul departing with the breath from between his father's lips like a twist of smoke, a vapor. And where did the soul go, when it left the impersonal body? Did it expire in that same moment, a fragile, last exhalation? "So what happens now?"

"There's going to be an autopsy this morning, and then he'll be brought to the funeral chapel. Crestwood—you know, the big place, out on Northern Boulevard. If everything goes according to schedule, we'll hold the funeral tomorrow."

"And that's it." He said this with an air of mock finality that was actually a pleading for more, though he wasn't sure what else he wanted her to say or to do. What she did was stand up and go to him, take him into her arms, with that same mechanical, weightless embrace of a sleepwalker. He leaned into it anyway, and rested his cheek on her hair. He might have stayed like that a long time, but they both jumped at the sound of a car door.

Danny didn't look, but his mother did. "Oh, Jesus. It's Ida."

6

*S*AM'S FATHER, Danny's Grandpa Moe, had also died in the hospital, but only because at the last minute Sam and Joan had insisted he go; for weeks Grandma Ida had fought to keep Moe at home, in his own bed, where she could take care of him. Joan always said that Ida had killed Moe by keeping him home, with those blood clots traveling up his legs and his heart so weak. She also sometimes said it had been her own fault, since she was the only one with the detachment to see what Ida was doing. Because by the time Joan called the ambulance, with Sam holding Ida down, she was kicking and screaming so—*They get him in that hospital, they'll finish him. Let it be on your head. God forbid, your own father. A couple of murderers here in my house*—Moe was really well beyond saving. That's what the look on the doctor's face told Joan, when he pulled her and Sam across the hospital corridor into a supply room, digging hard into each of their arms: *This is Nineteen Sixty-eight. How could a pair of educated people like you let a thing like this happen?*

Danny didn't remember exactly how long Moe had lasted—whether it was just a few days or a couple of weeks—but what he couldn't forget was the image of Ida, once Moe was dead, refusing to be separated from her husband's body. Ida was religious, but she wasn't an Orthodox Jew; she only invoked the strict observances when it was dramatic enough, or inconvenient enough for others, to suit her contrary purposes. So that night she announced that Jews did not for an instant leave the side of their dead until the body was safely en route to the funeral home, of which there was a good one right in her neighborhood. Sam for once in his life was past words, but Joan tried to talk sense to her. *Mom, we're all exhausted. We can go home, get some sleep. If you want we'll come back first thing in the morning.* But for all Ida knew, by first thing in the morning, Moe's body would turn up missing. She wasn't budging an inch from that room. She'd call the police if anyone tried to remove her.

Once more there was a look from the doctor, not angry this time but mystified, as if these were people from out of the Dark Ages. Still, he gave his go-ahead for their vigil. Joan had told Danny, years later, that after one or two in the morning she hadn't been able to keep her eyes open, but every time she jerked awake from those fitful patches of sleep she saw the same thing: Ida looking down at Moe—at the outline of Moe underneath the white sheet—absolutely dry-eyed, with the same scowl she'd turned on him all the years he'd been living, as if it were his fault she had to sit up all night.

Danny watched from his window as Ida made her way up the front path, on the arm of Sam's sister, Aunt Esther. Ida was tall for a woman of her generation, just shy of five eight, with size eleven triple A feet—an extraordinary endowment that she was pleased to advertise, and that had found its way through the genes to Elisa along with the nose, only the feet were past fixing. As a young woman, Ida had been known as something of a beauty in the Jewish society along Eastern Parkway—Danny had seen the hand-tinted portrait of the girl with the gray-blue eyes and long legs in the flouncy, skirted swimming suit on the boardwalk at Coney Island—and she'd maintained through the years a regal, even imperious, carriage. But now she walked with a doddering step that Danny had never seen before, and a stooping, defeated curve of her spine, as if the weight of the news were physically bearing down on her.

And yet, broken as she might appear, Danny knew from experience: you should never underestimate Ida's ability for making trouble or causing harm. She had a genius for boring into people in their most vulnerable states, at the most unthinkable moments—a genius for finding and laying blame. It was from her Sam had gotten it.

She had done it that day years ago in Mount Sinai Hospital after Sam's first attack, when Joan had taken the children to visit him: a visit only wangled—since they were still below the minimum age—by special permission from the chief cardiologist. Elisa monopolized the hand of Sam's that wasn't all taped up with tubes, but Danny finally came closer, and pressed in to the bedside. He'd tucked the blue, first-place ribbon from his meet with the junior high swim team into the pocket of his Bar Mitzvah suit, and now brought it out to show Sam, who looked past the ribbon to the boy's face, as if that were the real prize, his eyes shining with an acceptance Danny had never seen there before: the gaze of someone who hasn't lost what he loves, but had that first close brush with losing it. And Danny was part of this, no matter how much his father picked at or punished him— he knew in that moment he was. Only then Sam started to cough like he'd swallowed down the wrong pipe; his face went red; the mountainous blips on the TV screen above his bed changed shape and got taller, rose up more quickly and then—more quickly still—disappeared. It was then Ida started.

She'd been staying out at the house to help take care of the kids while Joan ran back and forth to the city to be at the hospital, and so she'd come along for this visit too. She'd sat in a chair in a corner away from the bed, outside the spotlight just about as long as the woman was capable. But now she was up, flying across the room, pulling Danny and Elisa

55

away from their father. "Who ever heard of letting children into a hospital room? With a man lying sick in bed like that." She whirled around to face Joan. "You should never have brought them here."

"Mother." Sam had his breath back, just barely, and was leaning up in the bed, as far as the tubes would allow him. "Calm down. You'll have the nurses barging in here in a minute."

"Calm down? You're telling me I should calm down? You're the one who's in bed half dead from a heart attack. And you know who to thank for it?" Ida spun back on Joan, the tendons in her neck taut as bowstrings. "It's her you can thank," really shouting now, "with her *kvetching* and belly-aching and nothing's ever good enough"—Danny's mother, standing there in the navy knit dress she'd been wearing for several seasons now, her cloth coat hung over a chair, her hair that had been set in pink plastic curlers at home, never once (except the day of the Bar Mitzvah) done at a beauty shop; Danny's mother, who only fought and nagged at Sam to *slow down.*

Joan fell back in a chair, like someone had struck her. Danny and Elisa drew back to the wall by the door. Sam fought to get free of the tubes as the blips on the screen scattered crazily.

"He was a lawyer before you ever laid eyes on him. The smartest boy in all Brooklyn. You're lucky he even looked at you. And this is what he gets in return?"

She was still going when the nurse charged in and grabbed her arms from behind. "You're going to have to come with me, ma'am. Mr. Winger can't have this kind of disturbance."

"Nobody comes and pulls me out of here," Ida snapped, even as the nurse was pulling her across the room. The door closed over the words, "I'm his mother."

In a minute, another nurse rushed in and went straight for Sam. She checked and resecured all his tubes, and pulled out a mask attached to an apparatus that had been waiting all the while by the bedside. In almost the same motion, she had the mask on Sam's face. "Just a few minutes of this, Mr. Winger. Until we've got everything slowed down." Then she turned to Joan, who had gotten up from her chair. "I'm afraid you and the children will have to leave also."

Most of Sam's face was hidden under the mask, but Danny could still see his eyes, an expression he might have misread as helplessness or fear, until, just as Danny was backing up to the door, his father winked at him.

From below, the doorbell sounded, and Danny pulled himself away from the window. He got to the top of the stairs in time to see Ida collapsing into Joan's arms, sending up a wail that almost didn't sound human. When she lifted her head from Joan's shoulder and started to speak, it took Danny a minute to make out her words: "What I lost. Oh, my God, what I lost. My beautiful son." She covered her mouth with her hand but kept repeating, "My brilliant, beautiful Sammy."

Aunt Esther stood behind her mother with her hat in her hand. The set of her lips looked as much bitter as grieved. *Brilliant, beautiful Sam:* Esther must have been hearing that since the day they brought her baby brother home from the hospital. Probably no one had ever called Esther beautiful; she was squat and badly myopic and froggy-looking like Grandpa Moe. And while she didn't get shorted on brains, she never had much of a chance to make use of them. According to Joan's version, Esther had wanted to be a doctor, and got accepted into a special honors program at Brooklyn College for premed science and math. But the cost of going to Brooklyn College meant living at home with Ida and Moe, so instead she married George Rosensweig right out of high school and moved upstate so they didn't have to listen to Ida complain. Crazy George, who'd always made Danny laugh, with his fat cigars and dirty jokes and plaid trousers, with the fresh way he'd talk to Ida, even in front of the cousins, telling her she could kiss his bare *tuchas*, saying if she really wanted to see a *schmuck*, he'd be glad to oblige; pulling her out of a chair to dance when no music was playing, pretending he didn't realize his hand was hiking up her skirt, grabbing at her behind. "Filthy! Stupid!" Ida would shout at him, slapping him off with her hands or a magazine if one was handy, while Esther, Sam and Joan covered their mouths and ran into the kitchen. "This is the kind of *dreck* I've got for a son-in-law?"

Esther went to college at night at a branch of the State University once Nathan and Cindy were out of diapers, and then got her State Teacher's Certification, which was a good thing, because Uncle George never held on to a job for more than a year or two, and there were long periods when he didn't seem to be working at all. Every time they got together he'd go into a whole song and dance about the latest business scheme he was launching, pushing a cigar on Sam in exchange for his "expert legal advice," and Sam played along with him, all the while casting skeptical looks at his sister, who shrugged her shoulders and shook her head, miming *meshuggener* when George wasn't looking. George started taking off when Nathan was in junior high, but for a few years there he kept coming back, and staying a month or two or three before taking off again. Esther didn't believe him when he told her he was leaving for good. But sure enough, she got the letter from his attorney, saying he was filing for divorce on the grounds of "mental cruelty."

Danny hadn't set out to eavesdrop the night Esther drove down from Utica with the letter. He was on his way back to bed from the bathroom when he heard her sobbing and Sam and Joan talking in comforting but grave tones. He crept down a few steps to listen. From what he could piece together, George had been holed up in the basement for weeks at a stretch, barely putting anything on but the same dirty underwear, either refusing to speak or ranting and raving about the women he said were going to move in with him.

When Joan asked Esther why she hadn't told them, why she herself hadn't sued for divorce and gotten him out of the house, for the sake of the kids at least, all she could talk about was her mother: what her mother would say, how her mother would use it to make her even more miserable.

Now Esther stepped forward to pry off Ida's coat from behind, and Ida only gave her a scowl, as if Esther were trying to cut her performance short. Still, Esther took her mother's arm and led her into the den toward the couch, saying she would make them a nice cup of tea, that they would just sit quietly for a little bit. But Ida pulled her arm away and grabbed Henrietta. "He was the only thing in my life. The rest—forget about it. Nothing but *tsuris*. He was the only thing I had to hold up my head about."

Esther got a look on her face like her mother had slapped her, turned and fled upstairs to the guest room. Joan ran up after her. Aaron muttered something about using the toilet, and Henrietta clicked her tongue: "It's no wonder the man's got a hemorrhoid the size of a golfball." Barbara sat Ida down and assumed responsibility for making the tea, and Henrietta decided to help in the kitchen, just in case Ida should start in on *her:* what did she understand about what Ida was going through, since she was childless, since she'd married a man who couldn't even give *that* to her? With Elisa still answering phones, Danny found himself standing there alone with his grandmother just as her eyes seemed to clear and she noticed him as though for the first time. She patted the place by her side on the couch. "Come sit by Grandma now." A glimmer of light came up in her eyes. "I'll tell you a few things I bet you never heard about that father of yours."

Yes, I know: He made a plane and flew it in Prospect Park. He was first clarinet in the Erasmus High marching band, and the way he used to look in those parades through Grand Army Plaza, with that sharp hat and the golden braid on his uniform that you stayed up half the night before ironing . . . But she never got around to the stories. By the time he reached the couch she was weeping again, twisting her fingers up in her handkerchief. He sat down next to her but then froze. He had a horror of touching her, had since he was a boy, when there was nothing that made him squirm like Grandma Ida, leaning into his face to clean it with a handkerchief she'd put to her lips and moistened with her own saliva.

"Seventy-seven years old and I should live to see this?" She gave a dry, honking blow of her nose. "Am I such a terrible person, he had to do *this* to me?"

At first Danny assumed she meant Sam—that she was seeing his death the way she'd seen Esther's failed marriage, as something the child had done to their mother. But then he saw the way she was looking up at the ceiling.

"Didn't I go to shul all these years? And all those pledges for Russian Jewry. They didn't make me president of the Flatbush Hadassah four times for nothing."

She didn't mean Sam, she meant *He*, and Danny couldn't have held her even if he had wanted to: she was up from the couch, pacing with her new stoop, rubbing together the arthritic claws of her hands like she did when she got her skin rashes.

"He should have taken me instead. What do I have to live for? My Sam—he had everything in front of him. What kind of God is that? A *meshuggeh* God! What good is He?"

Danny pushed himself to stand up. Ida was practically shouting now, her hands were all red, the vein in her forehead, like Sam's, was standing out, bluish purple. But before he could move to stop her, Henrietta ran in from the kitchen. "Cousin Ida, you've got to take it easy now. You're going to make yourself sick."

"He was so smart. So successful." Ida lowered her voice and let Henrietta lead her back to the couch. "The people in my apartment house, all the fancy attorneys, they ask me, 'Are you Sam Winger's mother?' And you should see the look on their faces. 'Sam Winger,' they say. 'Isn't he the big man on Park Avenue?' "

"I know, I know. Sit a little while, would you?" Henrietta eased her down. "Barbara's bringing some tea. You can't get yourself all excited like this. You've had a terrible shock. You keep this up, we'll be calling an ambulance."

"So call the ambulance. What do I care? I'm no good for anything." When Barbara brought the tea, Ida didn't look at her, or utter a word of thanks, but she took a sip, then made a face as if it were bitter. "I should drop dead, it would be a blessing. Why didn't He leave my Sam, and take me? What good is a mother when something like this can happen? All my life I believed." She looked up from the teacup to Danny, a wild glint in her eyes. "Let Him strike me down if He's up there, but I don't believe no more."

She went back to sipping her tea, with her pinky and fourth finger raised, as if her new godless state required a defiant dignity. Now Danny understood why Ida hadn't blamed Joan, the way she'd blamed her for the first heart attack, the way she'd blamed Esther when Nathan jumped out the window. This was too big to have been brought about by any mere mortal; this was a tragedy of cosmic proportions. Ida's belief had withstood the Holocaust, the torment of Soviet Jewry, the Arab armies lined up and waiting to drive the Israelis into the sea. But this individual death—the death of her handsome, accomplished son in the prime of his life—was more than the edifice of her faith could support.

"Hey, Danny, would you pick that up?" It was Elisa from the kitchen; the phone was ringing on the end table next to him.

He grabbed it. "Hello?"

"Yes. Is Mrs. Winger there?" A man's voice, that sounded edgy under the businesslike tone.

Danny got command of himself: he could do this as well as Elisa. "This is Mrs. Winger's son, Danny. Can I help you?"

"Daniel." The man cleared his throat. "This is Arthur Abrams from Crestwood Funeral Chapel. Let me offer you my most sincere condolences."

Abrams' sincerity had a slippery feel to it, like a track worn too smooth with use. "Thank you. Can I help you with anything?"

"I wish that you could. It seems we've run into a bit of a snag here."

Danny swiveled on the couch so his back was to Ida and spoke more softly. "A snag?"

"Yes, it seems so. It concerns the location of your father's body."

"The *location*?" He glanced back at his grandmother bending over her teacup. "Hold on, okay?"

He hit the hold button, dropped the receiver and called back over his shoulder to Ida, "I'll be right back." He took the steps two at a time; at the upstairs landing he could hear the low murmur of conversation—Esther and Joan—from behind the closed door of the guest room. He swung into his parents' bedroom and went for the phone. "Mr. Abrams." He was surprised at how hard he was breathing, just from the stairs. "Now, what exactly is happening?"

Abrams cleared his throat again. "Well, as you may know, your father's body was to be shipped from the hospital first thing this morning to the New York City Medical Examiner's Office, where the autopsy was to be performed. I know it's difficult to put you through these details on a day like today. Are you following so far?"

What did the guy think he was, an idiot? "Yeah, I'm following."

There was a pause, during which it sounded like Abrams took a swallow of something. "When I called the Medical Examiner's Office to find out what time they'd be ready to release the body, they had no record of having received it. So I called the hospital, to see if *they* had a record of shipping the body to the M.E. The first person I spoke to said she was sure the body *had been* sent, that it wasn't there anymore. But now they tell me they can't find any paperwork. They say the body could be in transit, but I've been calling both places for over an hour now, and they're only fifteen blocks apart. For the moment, until they locate the paperwork, neither one will claim any responsibility."

Paperwork? The body? This was Sam Winger the guy was talking about. "So you mean they've lost my father? Nobody knows where he *is*?"

"Well, no, not exactly that. The body is either in one place or the other. It's just a matter of clearing up the mix-up on paperwork."

"Or maybe the driver got the address wrong. Maybe he's cruising around somewhere up in the Bronx. Maybe he had an accident."

"Listen, son—Danny. I know how this must upset you, but it will all be straightened out. You're dealing with the New York M.E. and a large city hospital. It's a major bureaucracy. Sometimes things move more slowly than you or I would prefer, and that's why I'm calling. I just wanted to tell your mother that I won't know for a couple of hours yet if I'll have the body in time to get ready for tomorrow morning."

"And if you don't?"

"We'll have to hold the funeral Thursday morning instead."

"So they're looking right now? You told them this was an emergency?"

7

*W*HEN DANNY HUNG UP THE PHONE, he sat down on the bed, there where he'd stood, on his father's side. Joan must have taken Sam's valuables from the hospital and set them down on the night table when she got home, in the same spot where Sam himself would have set them if he'd made it home that night: the old Timex he'd refused to trade in, no matter how many gold watches Joan had offered to buy him for birthdays or anniversaries; the fat leather wallet, molded to the curve of that infamous Winger *tuchas*, that started to spread on Elisa whenever she gained a few pounds and that Danny had noticed catching up with him too, now that he wasn't swimming; a jumble of keys and loose change, as if Sam would be back to claim them, sweep them off the tabletop into his cupped palm and then jingle them down to the pit of his pants pocket.

Danny opened his father's night table drawer (his mother had a matching table on the other side, and they never slept in reverse, so Danny could creep into the room in the dark when he was a boy and the big new house had still frightened him, and know which side to go to, to shake his mother awake): a toenail clipper, a few plastic shirt stays, a shoehorn, a brown vial empty except for the white, powdered residue of Sam's nitroglycerine. Danny thought of the red and white foil packs he used to find at the back of the drawer, unwrap and puzzle over, until one day he decided to try blowing one up; it worked pretty well, so he went downstairs and asked Joan why his father kept balloons in the night table.

He slid the drawer quietly shut and stood up again. That guy Abrams had a hell of a nerve, the way he kept repeating *the body*. Whatever his mother had said about seeing Sam last night—about it not being Sam anymore—still, after all, it wasn't just some anonymous *corpse*. If nothing else, it was the body Sam had lived in for going on forty-six years. *The house of the body*, Danny thought, and then: *the temple of the body*. Now the temple of his father's body was probably being driven around midtown in some van, with a guy up front smoking cigarettes and playing the radio; or, even worse, lying forgotten, untended, in some room in that hospital, where nobody even knew who he was.

For some reason the thought of that made Danny picture his father on his back on the living room rug, where he sometimes lay down for a nap after dinner. Sam always snored whenever he slept, even if he'd just dropped off a few seconds before; as if from being wide awake he sank instantly into some deep, senseless cavern. When Danny was a boy, Sam would sometimes pat a spot by his side on the rug and cajole Danny into lying down next to him, taking his hand, even though the boy would be jumping with energy. Danny would watch his father's eyes roll back and his eyelids droop, and he'd close his own, pretend he was trying to sleep. But then a couple of snarls would rip from Sam's throat, his jaw would drop open, and Danny would make his escape. The surprising thing was that while his father's whole face had gone slack, his grip on Danny's hand tightened, so Danny had to pry his fingers loose, one by one. After he had, his father's hand didn't close back up into a fist; it just lay there at his side, palm up, open.

Now Danny adjusted the vision, and saw his father laid out in his new, silent sleep, face slack with his soul's departure—what his mother had seen last night. Then he remembered the other part, the thing he'd heard twice—from his mother, from Abrams—but hadn't really digested: an autopsy was being performed. It wouldn't be the body inviolate, dignified, *lying in state*. The house, the temple of his father's body would have been broken into. Who knew what it looked like? Danny's mind was scrambling to remake the picture in the wake of this new confusion when the floor creaked behind him. He jumped aside from the bed, as if he had no right to be there.

"Oh. Sorry, sweetheart." His mother sounded as startled as he was, but quietly. "I didn't know you were in here."

"Yeah." He looked around for some likely excuse, but there was only the one. "I was just on the phone."

"Who was it?"

"Abrams from Crestwood." He knew—even as he was saying this, without having thought it out in advance—that he was only going to tell her part of the truth. "He said things are moving slowly at the Medical Examiner's Office. Some kind of backlog or something. So we might have to put the funeral off until Thursday. He'll call back in a few hours when he knows for sure."

She shook her head. "Of course your father would normally be the one to deal with something like this. To light a fire under them." Her gaze went blank for a moment before she snapped herself back. "But okay, I guess we'll just have to wait. I only hope to God they can still get everything done in time for tomorrow. I don't know how much more of this I can stand."

He said, "I know," though he wasn't sure exactly what *this* was; why it would stop once they'd had the funeral. "Listen, Mom?" He shouldn't be asking this now, but he couldn't help himself. "How come you requested the autopsy?"

"Well, I didn't exactly *request* it." She turned to the mirror over her dresser a moment, and rearranged a few strands of her hair. "An autopsy's required by law if a person dies in the emergency room—if they're not a regularly admitted hospital patient. You can get out of it on religious grounds, but the doctor said it was better to let them go ahead with it. For you kids. And for your kids."

"Why for us?"

"Just in case they find something you ought to know about, for your own health."

"Like what are they going to find? We know he had a valve defect, which *I've* probably inherited. We know he had high blood pressure. We know there was probably all kinds of shit in his arteries." Danny's mind jumped back to the regimen his mother had launched after Sam's early heart attack, for Sam but also for the children too, though between him and his sister, Danny had borne the brunt of it: thirteen years old, a budding competitor, but he could only eat eggs once a week, red meat twice, he had to switch from butter to margarine, to drink that watery skim milk. And when he got mad and started to shout, his mother wouldn't listen to what he was saying but only tell him he had to calm down: a temper like that was just what had landed Sam in the hospital.

"I know it sounds silly and probably nothing will come of it. But the doctor said now and then they turn up something they weren't expecting—something that can make a difference for someone else in the family."

Danny must not have looked very convinced. He was thinking that if the exercise was in effect largely for his sake, he would have told them to skip it; thinking that it was because of the autopsy his father's body was missing now.

"Don't worry about it, turkey." Joan rubbed a hand up and down Danny's arm. "I think it's what your father would have decided—that we should know everything there is to know."

Her thoughts seemed to drift off until a look of panic passed over her face. "Listen, don't say anything about this in front of your grandmother, okay? If you go by the book, Jews aren't supposed to have autopsies. As it is, there are going to be enough headaches about how things are done."

She started toward the door but turned back. "Maybe you should take that suit off now and hang it up nicely, so it will be fresh for tomorrow."

Tomorrow, or Thursday, or maybe next week—if they don't find "the body." As her footsteps sounded back down the stairs, he thought about his mother's reasoning—that going for the autopsy was what Sam would have done. He could picture her deciding, carrying on the debate in her head with Sam playing devil's advocate, her ear tilted as if she were actually hearing a voice. How many times in his life had Danny heard those imaginary arguments in his own head? And how many times had he flown in the face of his father's position?—going off to drink a couple of beers with some of the guys after practice; sneaking his mother's car on Saturday nights when his parents were out, and he still only had his learner's permit, not his regular license; signing up for easy courses, the ones with nicknames—"Rocks for Jocks," "Nuts for Sluts"—instead of buckling down in upper-level history, poli sci; clearing out his bank account and signing over the check to Carroll Realty. The irony was that now he could really use Sam's advice. What would Sam do, in Danny's place, about their losing his body? How *would* he light a fire under them?

Once he stopped to think, it wasn't any great mystery. For starters, Sam would never leave it to Abrams. He'd be on the phone himself, with the Medical Examiner and the hospital both. And they wouldn't be polite, informational phone calls. Sam would raise hell, and make it clear that he'd keep raising hell until the body was found. He'd threaten six kinds of lawsuits. He'd find some hotshot client or partner or friend with connections in the right high places. And he'd let the whole business go only so far on the phone; if he couldn't get there himself, he'd send someone else to raise hell in person.

There was only one problem: Danny wasn't exactly cut out for the role like his father was. When he acted mad, he wasn't very effective. He could see it in people's eyes, whenever he tried to *pull a Sam*. He could almost hear them thinking: *this is just some young hothead*. They figured it was safer to let him blow off steam, but they didn't listen. He remembered his father sitting at the big oak desk in his law office, chewing somebody out on the phone, sounding wildly indignant but utterly articulate too, then pausing a moment to smile at Danny and wink, and only then did the boy realize the tirade was all theatrical, the anger carefully meted out for effect. Danny had his father's temper—people were always saying that—but he didn't have his father's control; he was like scattered, weak fire, and his father was a submachine gun.

Much as Danny didn't like to admit it, there *was* someone right for the job close at hand. Someone who was a lawyer and knew how to talk like one; who was always threatening to sue anybody who so much as stepped on his little toe. Someone who'd be able to get to people with the right connections. And he wasn't *there*, at the house; he could make as many calls as he needed to. That was the other thing about Danny doing it: how could he be on the phone making irate demands without Joan or Elisa or Esther hearing him? Without Ida sniffing out the fact that something was wrong? And there was no reason for any of them to get wind of this. In a matter of hours, the whole sorry business would be cleared up. Sam—Sam's body—would be in the competent care of Crestwood Funeral Chapel.

It took a couple of minutes for his brother-in-law to come to the phone. Danny accepted his condolences, but cut short his apology for not getting back to the house yet. "Look, I don't have much time. I've got to get off the phone. It's a good thing you're not back. There's something you have to help me with."

Dave made him go through everything a second time, slowly, as he wrote it all down. He had Danny find the little phone directory from Sam's law firm, and took down a few names and extensions. He agreed that no one else needed to know, including Elisa; that when he called back, he'd pretend to be someone else asking for Danny. Then there was silence over the line, and Danny was on the verge of thanking him, until he heard footsteps coming up the stairs. "I've got to hang up now."

When Elisa stepped into the bedroom, Danny was already standing, and she was the one who looked guilty. "Oh."

"I know," he said. "You didn't think anybody was in here."

"Mom said I should stop taking calls and go lie down awhile." She looked sheepishly past him, and he understood she'd been planning on lying down on their bed.

"What's wrong with your own room?" Like Danny's, Elisa's room was intact, a living shrine to her childhood—what Joan referred to as the Pink Palace, complete with flowered wallpaper, canopy bed, the sappy needlepoint pictures that in junior high Elisa took up the hobby of making, since she didn't go out with boys: sitting with a bag of colored wool at her feet, stitching bouquets of flowers or bonnet-clad maidens—not calmly, in a sort of trance, like their grandmother Bea, but furiously, muttering under her breath, always jabbing herself in the finger, pushing the needle through those tiny, square holes as if she were stabbing somebody. "The thing is, it would be better to keep this room free. For the phone. In case you do fall asleep."

She nodded, but still she just stood there and looked at him. It was the same way she used to stand there when they were kids and he wanted to get rid of her, as if she knew something was up, as if she were purposely hanging around to foil some delicate scheme of his. "Listen, I want to show you something I found last night."

"How about showing me later, okay?"

"Come on. It'll just take a minute. This is the perfect time, anyway. Mom's busy dealing with Ida downstairs, and I don't want her to see. I don't think she could handle it."

Without waiting for an answer, she walked over to Sam's mahogany highboy and slipped open the middle, thin drawer, where Sam kept his tie clips and cuff links, his handkerchiefs, and odd papers and souvenirs. It figured Elisa, the nosy one, would be rummaging. From the back corner she pulled out a small cardboard box, slid the few buttons and silver dollars on top to the side, and then produced a black-and-white photograph. She scarcely looked at it before she handed it over, but still her eyes teared up, as if she already had the thing memorized.

Sam was in profile, in an army uniform, his pale hair shaved close to his head, looking as fit and thin as Danny would in the middle of swim season. He stood at attention only he didn't look stiff, he looked exhilarated, as if the army were just a more advanced version of Eagle Scouts, and for Sam it probably was—in those months right after Korea, in Officers' Training with his new wife on the base, and then on his way to the Pentagon to serve as a lawyer. He was beaming up at an older man the way a son might look at a father he loved. The man had enough bars on his chest to be a major or general; he wasn't smiling, but appraising Sam with obvious pride. On the back was penned: "Fort Benning, GA. March, 1955" in blue ink, in a neater version of his father's familiar handwriting. Danny was about to start figuring, but Elisa had beaten him to it.

"It was just a few months after their wedding. Mom was already pregnant with me." She took the picture back from him and looked at the front again with a satisfied air, as if Sam beamed the way he did at least in part because *she* was on the way. Then her gaze traveled back from the young Sam to Danny. "He was the same age you are now. Twenty-two. Isn't that incredible?"

Danny studied the strong, naked curve at the back of

Sam's skull, his squared shoulder, that radiant face. Did Elisa realize she was insulting him? Because what was incredible about their identical ages wasn't the element of coincidence; it was the comparison, and how short Danny fell. It was how he'd spend the rest of his life scrambling to catch up with a father who'd already stopped running.

8

SOMEHOW DANNY IMAGINED Dave would be calling
back in a matter of minutes, to say everything was fine,
they'd found Sam, or at least to report on all the calls he
was making, the connections he was bringing to bear. The
fact that he didn't gave the rest of the morning a different,
warped feel, as if the hours were passing both more slowly
and more quickly than usual. Probably the distortion of
time was also a function of Danny's not having slept. He
was beginning to feel the way he used to at school when
he'd pulled an all-nighter, only this time it wasn't on
speed—those ragged white crosses he'd only use at exam
time *spring* term, when swimming season was over, or the
good stuff one of the frat brothers figured out how to
manufacture in chem lab the fall of their senior year, and
that Danny started taking (and not just for studying) because what did the perfect machine of his body matter
anymore, until the night he was staying up for the second
time in a row on a weekday, just by himself in his room,
and he did another line around three, because that middle
stretch of the morning was dragging.

The business with his heart didn't happen right off. It was
a few minutes after he'd snorted the line and was walking
around his room thinking what to do next, when it started.
He was buzzed enough to hear it before he felt it, thumping
right out of his chest. Then the crazy fluttering traveled up

toward his windpipe like fear, so though he could still breathe he was scared he wouldn't be able to.

His friend Greg's room was just down the hall. Greg's first response to Danny's pounding was a muffled "Fuck you" that must have been coming from under the covers.

Danny banged on the door again. "Open up, man. I mean it. I think I'm having a heart attack."

In half a minute, Greg's face appeared in the doorway, squinting against the hall light. "You doing that meth again?"

Danny nodded.

"You asshole."

Greg pulled him into the room and turned on the light. He pushed Danny down into a chair and told him to shut up and sit still. Then he rolled a fat joint and made Danny smoke practically all of it (Greg took just a couple of hits for himself). And it worked: after a few minutes Danny could feel everything slowing down, his heartbeat getting regular.

"Greg White's first aid station. Twenty-four hours. At your service."

"You saved my life," Danny said.

"Right." Greg tapped out the end of the joint.

"No, I mean it. It was the weirdest sensation. Like all of a sudden my heart started racing, with these shallow beats. I didn't know what the hell was happening."

"You didn't know what the hell was happening?" Greg stood up, more wired than Danny now. "I'll tell you what was happening. Your shoulder hurts and you know you're going to have a shit season, so you start snorting crystal meth and staying up all night to *totally* trash yourself. Don't you ever think about your old man and *his* ticker? Unless you're going for some kind of record. Like maybe you could kill yourself before graduation."

Danny shook his head and put a hand to his chest; he imagined the steady parade of blips on an EKG printout, and the tiny, extra ascension the cardiologist had shown him on Sam's, the special fingerprint of his father's flawed heartbeat. Greg was right: he should get rid of the rest of the meth. He'd give it to Peterson, at the other end of the hall. He was the only guy in the house who wasn't some kind of jock; he was planning on being a writer. When Danny hit the bathroom in the early morning before heading out to the pool, he'd sometimes run into Peterson filling the plug-in hotpot he used for his instant coffee, saying he'd been up all night, that he had just a couple of pages to go before he finished a short story. Peterson may as well have been a jock—he wrote like he was running a marathon; he could probably churn out a novel by the end of the term if he used the meth instead of that instant Maxwell House. But Danny didn't say any of this to Greg. It all went through his head in one wave, with the shape a thought had on pot but the speed of the crystal methedrine. When he started to talk, he was already on the next swell.

"Do you know how I started swimming? I don't think I ever told you this. I didn't want to do it. My mother *made* me." Greg had gotten a couple of beers from a cooler, and Danny took a long pull on his. "It was the summer after second grade. They'd just finished building Parkwood—you know, the big public pool—and we joined. They had this whole swimming program: all levels of Red Cross instruction, and a team that had workouts twice a day in the lap section. There was also a playground, off in the woods at the back, and a snack bar. And there were a shitload of kids. So my mother had this idea that if she signed me up for a Red Cross class and got me onto the swim team, I could spend the whole day there, Monday through Friday, and always have something to do. Like my father kept reminding me, he was shelling out enough to join the damn pool. We might as well get our money's worth."

Greg was starting to look tired, and Danny was about to

say screw it, I'll let you go back to bed, but Greg took another sip of his beer. "So were you a natural? An instant superstar?"

Danny snorted. "Are you kidding? I was this little wimp. You should have seen me. I'd get there in the morning for practice and the water would be ice cold. If I hadn't known my mother would run into the coaches, I'd have hid out in the playground. I guess I was eight, but the lowest age group was eight and under, so I was swimming with all the other little jerks whose parents were pushing them into it. Like these six-year-old girls and shit. But still, I could barely keep up. At the end of the workout they practically had to haul me out of the pool. I was so bad they stuck me in backstroke, which *nobody* wanted to swim. So there I was, zigzagging along the lane, getting my arms caught up on the rope, smashing my head into the side at the end of each lap. Sucking up all this water."

Greg smiled. "Cool kid. So what did you do it for?"

"I'm telling you, they made me—my parents. First it's, you'll sign up and give it a couple of weeks and see how you like it. Then two weeks have gone by and my father gives me this line about quitting. *When you're part of a team, you don't quit; you don't let everyone down.* As if anyone would have missed me."

"So when did it change? When did you start to get in-to it?"

Danny shrugged. Of course, when he thought logically about those first years, he knew that it had been gradual. Struggling up and down the lane practice after practice, summer after summer, with Pete or Tommy, the coaches, bending down to him when he got to the wall, shouting to make sure he could hear through the water: *Move it! Pick it up! Pull!* On the Saturday mornings of meets, hanging shivering off the starting block, half in and half out of the water (it had been summer, but he always remembered those mornings, and the water, as cold), never thinking of winning, hoping only not to come in dead last this time; not to lose too many seconds on the rope or hitting the wall, because then Pete would yell at him—that old sour dread at the block, not wanting the race to begin and yet wanting it, holding his breath for the gun, so he could whomp down on the stinging flat of his back and thrash out his two laps and then it would be over with. Because in those days, when he tried to go fast, swimming did feel like thrashing, as if the water were some heavy, entangling element, or the weight he had to fight against was all in his body, his Winger behind—what Pete and Tommy called his *fat ass* when the mothers weren't listening.

He knew it was only little by little that he learned how to backstroke straight down the lane; that he started to feel lighter, almost at home, in the water; that the fear rose up only right before his own race, so he could really watch the other kids' races, and cheer for them, and the fear itself began to seem less like fear, more like a surge of adrenaline. He knew it didn't happen magically, overnight, like someone casting a spell on him. And yet that's how it had felt, the summer he turned twelve, the Saturday morning the second freestyler for the eleven-twelve age group had twisted his ankle.

Danny had swum thousands of laps of crawl in practice, but he'd never thought much about it, except as relief from the thrashing and blindness of backstroke. When Johnny Fassler limped up to the team in his street clothes and told Pete he couldn't race that day, the coach scanned the eleven-and-twelves. His gaze didn't settle on Danny because he thought he could *do* something. It was because Danny had only his one race to swim, and most of the other kids had two, even three; because Pete was used to giving Danny the shit work. "Hey, Winger, you better get ready to move that fat ass of yours. You're taking Fassler's fifty free."

Danny just nodded, and snapped his towel at the air when Pete wasn't looking. His fifty backstroke didn't go any better or worse than usual, but something felt different afterward, knowing he was going to swim again, and all the frustration and adrenaline and regret that was still coursing through him could be put to some use. He didn't think so much about the other swimmers when he got up on the block (standing there in the sun, instead of hanging below in the water); he just thought about purging himself, working off all that sour energy. At *Swimmers, take your marks, get set*, he bent over and gripped the lip of the block, but the boy next to him went off—a false start—and Danny stood up again.

From the block, he felt like he was towering over his lane; like the twenty-five yards to the wall wasn't as far as usual: a long stretch of a racing dive and then just a few breaths, as if there would be a wind at his back, or a current to carry him. He looked past the wall, out past the rows of chaise lounges to the edge of the concrete, into the woods, and thought about the woods and the lake at his grandparents' summer place, the big boulder at the edge of the little cove with their dock, where he'd go first thing in the morning—to fish with his cardboard and string, or just look out at the mist rising. For a moment he wasn't on the block, about to swim a strange race; he was just a boy on a summer morning, filling his lungs. Then the kid who'd made the false start was back in his place, and Danny bent again to the words that seemed to have lost their terror, that sounded like they were coming from far away.

The dreamy way he was feeling did not make him slow. He was off at the gun, and he started stroking the instant he hit the water. He went six or eight strokes before he took his first breath, and his arms felt easy and sharp, like they could slice through the water. He didn't hit the flip turn perfectly, but well enough to get a good push off the wall. That's when he spied the boy to his left, the false starter, pushing off an arm's length behind him, and the one on the right, kicking up a white cloud in his face underwater, but not out of reach. Danny never caught him, but he got a sense of what it would be like to want to, to try. The false starter never caught Danny. When he slapped at the wall and jerked his head up, he knew he'd never really finished a race before; he'd only just gotten through them.

Off in the distance, beyond the sound of rushing water that stayed in his ears, the heaving gusts of his breath, the team was clapping and cheering. It didn't dawn on Danny that it was for him. Not until Pete and Tommy ran up alongside his block and hoisted him out of the water. Tommy said, "Where the hell did you get that stroke?" with a tone of bafflement, almost as if Danny had done something wrong, had taken something that didn't belong to him.

He was still gasping for air. He just said, "What stroke?" but he knew exactly what Tommy had meant. When *had* his arms learned to move like that? When had the water started loving his body? Pete slapped him hard on the ass, and then clamped a hand on the back of his neck. He had come in second, behind a big-shouldered boy from Syosset who was almost thirteen. Not only had he topped Johnny Fassler's best time, he'd finished ahead of Parkwood's fastest twelve-year-old freestyler.

His teammates surrounded him, smiling, snapping at his legs with towels, slapping his back, as if suddenly he were a different person; and he knew that he was. The stroke he had used wasn't his, but from then on it would be.

When Danny told his mother at the end of that summer that he wanted to join the Nassau County AAU team—to work out three afternoons a week and Saturday mornings, all fall and winter, to get some *real coaching*—she must not have known what to think. Getting some exercise and staying out of trouble during the summers at Parkwood was one thing; she'd never intended to turn her son into some kind of fanatic. It was Sam who convinced her to let him, convinced her they could manage their end of the carpool (though of course *he* never once drove). Even then Danny knew by the way his father looked at him—tentative, measuring—that it wasn't the swimming he cared about; it was what he suspected might be the sign of some *drive* in the boy—a drive like the one Danny's sister had shown for her schoolwork, a drive like Sam's own. All those years Danny swam and swam harder, Sam must have hoped it was that kind of pure motivation, that could be transferred to another arena when it was time. He never would have guessed that Danny was driven by superstition—only working to keep up with his luck, to make sure no one ever saw through him, to earn the gift he'd received on that summer morning.

It was like a story Peterson from down the hall had once told him, shortly after they'd pledged for the frat. Danny wanted to know what had given Peterson the idea of becoming a writer.

"It was plagiarism."

"Sure." Danny laughed. "Plagiarism and bullshit."

But Peterson looked dead serious. He explained that in the fourth grade his class had put out a newspaper. Everyone was supposed to contribute a story or drawing or puzzle. Peterson copied a poem from an old *Highlights for Children* he dug up in his brother's room and turned it in with his name on it. "It was just this dumb thing—about the universe and planets and stars. Some little kid contemplating the immensity, that sort of shit. But it was pretty good, for fourth grade. It had this nice meter, and it rhymed and everything."

Peterson's teacher went nuts for it, the girls started mooning over him, and his parents got all worked up; they bought him this fancy, two-volume set, *The Wonder Book of Young People's Poetry*. By that point, he figured he had two choices: either admit to everyone he had copied the poem, or start learning how to write another one like it—and fast.

Danny asked Peterson if he still ever felt like a fake, and then Peterson did laugh. "After all the hundreds of pages I've written? Come on. That was one lousy poem. It was grade school, for Christ's sake. It was half my lifetime ago." But for Danny, it didn't work that way. Even when he was winning

80

and winning big—when he was voted captain of the high school swim team, when he took first in the States, when he was getting letters from college coaches all over the country—part of him knew he was still that fat-assed kid from those first summers at Parkwood who couldn't do anything right, the same way his sister, even after her plastic surgery, must deep down still have been the girl with the big, hooking nose who only got asked out by the worst dorks in high school.

Maybe that was why he'd reacted the way he had when the tendonitis hit. He put up with the pain for as long as he needed to, to save face. He let his mother and Coach Lowery drag him around to a dozen orthopedists and sports doctors and acupuncturists. He pretended to believe them when they said he just had to be patient, the shoulder would come back. But he knew it wouldn't; he knew how he felt in the water. It was easy to hate himself, the way he had done as a boy, as if he'd never *stopped* hating. As if hating yourself was something like swimming, that you never forgot: even after so many years, you could slide back in, as if it were your rightful element.

It was the kind of self-loathing he tasted again, in a sudden, bitter surge, at the thought that his father could be so fed up he'd even consider disowning him. At the thought that even if by some miracle Sam's body turned up in time, things still would not be set right. That there was nothing Danny could do, now or ever, to set things right with his father.

9

*B*Y *THE TIME SAM'S CLOCK* was chiming two P.M. and Dave hadn't called, Danny didn't think he could stand it much longer. The more the minutes alternately slid and crept forward—the more his grandmother rubbed her hands and practiced her blasphemies, and his sister's eyelids swelled from their rims like a matched set of blisters; the more Aunt Esther paced the rooms of the house, squaring a pile of cocktail napkins, straightening a picture frame, and Barbara kept trying to feed people—the more Danny practically dove for the telephone when it rang. Already his mother was saying she should have heard from Abrams by now, that they needed to get the obituary to the *Times* before the afternoon deadline. If the funeral was going to be the next day, they needed to confirm with the rabbi and the cemetery management; they needed to drive out to the chapel to settle on all the arrangements. Danny could see her eyes darting crazily with all the details, and that panic taking hold of her like before a big party or holiday dinner when she was running behind. He wanted to tell her she shouldn't worry, they'd have plenty of time; the funeral was going to be Thursday for sure—at the earliest.

"If we haven't heard from Abrams in half an hour, I'll call him back myself," he said. Abrams, or Dave. What could be keeping the asshole? He'd sounded so confident, in control. *Don't sweat it, kid. Just sit back. Big brother-in-law Dave will take care of it.* Danny locked himself in his parents' room and dialed Dave's direct line, but the number was busy. He pulled the scrap of paper back out of his pocket to get the main switchboard number, but before he picked up the receiver again, the ring sounded. He forgot that it could be somebody else, any one of hundreds of people. He picked up the phone and spoke as if in mid-conversation. "Thank God."

The response he got snapped him right out of it; it was a woman's voice that said, "Danny?" And it wasn't the Long Island accent he'd been hearing all morning, but the upstate twang that had deepened and grown more clipped in the years after Nathan died—his favorite cousin. "Shit, Cindy. It's you."

"Yeah, it's me. I guess things have really fallen apart back there. That's how you answer the phone now? What ever happened to *Winger residence, Daniel speaking . . .* ?"

That was the line Sam had taught him as soon as he was old enough to pick up the phone, and tried to make him recite right through high school. He pictured the half pout, half smirk on Cindy's lips, like Nathan's only not so obnoxious. "Yeah, well, I thought it was going to be Dave. I've been waiting for him to call for ten years here. Where are you?"

"Home."

When she said it, he pictured the little yellow house with the peeling paint on the outskirts of Utica, the ravine out back that the grown-ups never crossed, and beyond it the creek they used to follow without Elisa or Nathan, up past their ankles in spring, pretending to be explorers or escaping criminals. But of course she didn't mean *that* home—Aunt Esther had sold it years ago, after George left. She meant the apartment in Portland that Danny had never seen, where she'd been living since she quit college and moved out there, cutting Danny off along with the rest of the family.

"I changed my mind."

83

"About what?"

"About coming. I wasn't going to—that's what I told my mother. That it was too long a trip. That I wasn't up for a funeral. But hell, I keep thinking about him. You know: *Uncle Sam*. About stuff from when we were kids and all."

Danny didn't say anything.

"Do you realize it's been five years since I've been back? And she said she'd pay for my ticket."

"Your mother?"

"Yeah. Speaking of which: how's she holding up?"

"I don't know. It's hard to tell around here. Everybody's so busy trying not to set Ida off."

"Right. Jesus: Ida. That must be something. Well, anyway, I booked a seat on the red eye tonight. I'll be there first thing tomorrow morning, your time. Unless the flight is really late I should make it in time for the funeral."

"The funeral's not going to be until Thursday."

"What do you mean? I thought . . ."

"Believe me, you don't want to know. I'll come pick you up at the airport."

"Okay. If you can. Otherwise I'll just take a cab. As I recall, things get a little crazy coming up to a funeral."

"So I'm realizing."

"Listen, speaking of crazy, my father hasn't called there or anything, has he?"

"Uncle George? No. I mean, not that I know of."

"That's good, I guess. But don't be surprised if he does. If he tries to pull something."

"How would he even know? I'm sure my mother didn't think to call him, and your mother wouldn't . . ."

"I don't know, but the man has his spies. He's always finding stuff out about me and calling me up, pretending like he wants to play father. Plus, he's always had a thing about going to funerals. He used to do it even when he still lived with us—look through the obituaries for anyone he knew even the littlest bit, and then go. That's the one thing he and

84

Ida could get together on. You know, how she never looks at the news—just skips ahead to the obits to see which one of her so-called friends has died."

Danny gave a snort of laughter, but his heart wasn't in it. He wished she wasn't sounding so flip right now. He would have liked to tell her about moving to Sackett Street, and the fight with Sam. To have her reassure him that it was ridiculous, imagining for a moment that Sam would go ahead with his threat.

The thought of the disinheritance made his mind jump back to Dave. "Listen, Cindy, I better not tie up the line. What airline? When does your flight get in?"

For Nathan's funeral, Danny's family had driven upstate, with Ida in the backseat between the two children. Nathan's body, or what was left of it, had been shipped back to Utica from Massachusetts; as they drove, Danny kept picturing a black zippered body bag like the ones he'd seen on the TV war news. Sam and Joan barely spoke for the whole five-hour trip. Nobody answered Ida when she piped up with, "The kid was so smart—a regular genius, for all the good it did him," or, "If he'd had a real father . . ." Danny tried to shut her out and think about Nathan, to make sense of the fact that he'd never see him again: the long, skinny body under the blankets on the bed next to him, the enormous, stinking feet that always stuck out the bottom, the mop of brown hair he never shampooed enough, because nothing of the body had ever really mattered to Nathan; to make sense of the fact that his dying was not like the deliberate act the word "suicide" typically conjured, but an accident, a mistake. Sure, he had plenty of reason to be confused and depressed: just look at his personality, not to mention his family. But why couldn't he work it out on some impossible computer program or physics equation, like he always had? What was a nerd like Nathan doing messing around with LSD, anyway? But it was too frustrating to try to hold the two thoughts together—Danny would never see Nathan

85

again, and it was all a mistake. A mistake was something you were supposed to be able to fix or make up for.

Danny and Cindy never really got to talk that weekend in Utica. Aunt Esther wouldn't let Cindy out of her sight, as though, now that she had lost one, she had to hold on for dear life to the other. At the service, Cindy wore a black velour dress and black boots. Danny found himself staring at her, at how suddenly grown-up she looked, how remote. Uncle George didn't come to the house but he showed up at the small funeral chapel, reeking of cigars and rubbing at the beard he'd grown since leaving Aunt Esther, going from person to person soberly offering his hand as if there was no blood on it.

Esther pretended she didn't see him, that he didn't exist—a strategy she'd designed in advance, dead-sure that George would make an appearance. Ida brandished her handkerchief and started to shout: "It's you who killed him. You ruined his life. What other reason would he have to get mixed up with drugs in the first place? A smart kid like that. To jump out a window?" Everyone stood frozen a moment, as if for once Ida was only voicing what the rest of them thought. Then Sam took her by the arm and led her out of the waiting room. George approached Cindy next. She shook him off when he tried to put a hand on her shoulder. "Look at your wonderful family now," she said.

The rabbi who conducted the service was new in town, and young, and hadn't known Nathan. The things he said might have held true for any eighteen-year-old that had died, of any natural cause. He didn't mention that Nathan had been a science and computer prodigy but a loser when it came to people; he didn't speculate about whether Nathan had ever been laid, or if he'd felt himself in the presence of anything like God when he dove from the window ledge. He didn't say that it had all been a mistake, and explain how mistakes were also a part of God's plan. He was a Conserva-

86

tive rabbi, so he read a lot of stuff in Hebrew that didn't mean anything.

Danny's mind wandered away from the service, to remember the model of the human anatomy his family had gotten Nathan one Hanukkah, and how carefully Nathan had put it together, not letting any of the other cousins help or even touch the thing afterward: the symmetry of the white plastic skeleton and then the strange, molded shapes of the organs, in shades of red and liver and gray, that to Danny had looked uncannily real, like bits of things you would see at a butcher shop. The only one Nathan had let so much as breathe on the model was Sam. But there was nothing surprising in that; Sam was the only one Nathan had never directed his sneer at. Whenever the families got together, Nathan and Sam would disappear for a couple of hours to play chess or tinker with one of Nathan's engineering or chemistry projects. There were plenty of times, growing up, when Danny had suspected his father would jump at the chance to trade sons, like Cindy always said she wished that she could change brothers.

The consolation he found at those times was the fact that Nathan never would have been much for sailing, especially the way Sam did it; that when they dragged him to Parkwood, he'd only sit at the edge of the kiddie section and stick in his feet; that he'd surely have drowned if he'd ever taken the plunge into Long Island Sound the way Danny had.

It was one of those blustery Saturdays, the autumn after Danny's Bar Mitzvah, just before they took the sailboat out of the water for winter; Danny was wearing heavy jeans, a ski jacket, even a hat and gloves. There were a lot of boats out, getting in their last runs, and the sea was choppy, but Danny wanted to take the tiller. Sam wasn't holding it with him like he had when Danny was younger; he was trimming the sails, taking in and letting out, adjusting and readjusting. But at the same time he was on Danny with a running critique. *You're heading too much into the wind. Fall off, you're luffing. Watch the telltales. Now don't overcompensate.*

This was no different than Sam's usual conduct on the boat, or anywhere else for that matter. As he was forever making clear, he was captain, and Joan was first mate. Elisa came next in the chain of command, by virtue of seniority; Danny was only the measly second crew member. But wasn't a captain supposed to look after the morale of his crew, to every now and then give praise for a job well done? Wasn't he supposed to *build* esteem instead of eternally chipping away at it? Suddenly it was as if thirteen years of that chipping rushed like blood into Danny's ears. "If you don't leave me alone and let me do this, I'm dropping the tiller."

"Don't get smart with me, young man. Pay attention. Come up now. I said come up!"

But Danny had let go and the boat was turning. If Joan hadn't been there to grab the tiller and bring them back up into the wind, the boom would have swung across and cracked Sam in the back of the head. Danny scuttled out of his mother's way; she was too busy regaining control of the boat to yell at him. But Sam was coming at him across the cockpit, hand raised. Danny's face was cold enough so he tasted the blow more than felt it: the salty gush of blood inside his lip. He swallowed it, wiped his mouth with the back of his glove. He had had enough of the captain hitting him, too. "You touch me again and I'm going overboard."

His father wasn't listening; he was bearing down on him. "What are you trying to do? Get us all killed?"

"That's it! I'm going."

"Daniel Winger, sit down this instant." It was his mother. But Danny was already stepping over the teak grabrail they rubbed down and oiled every spring at the boatyard, stepping out onto the narrow strip of side deck. The last words he heard were his father's: *The kid is a lunatic.* Then he dove, a little like off a starting block only not so flat, more in an arc, aiming deeper. For the moment he was in the air—hearing the whoosh of his flight and of the boat that was speeding away from him—he had a sensation of weightlessness, of the purest, most total revenge. All that changed when he hit the water.

He hadn't thought about the way the freezing Sound would slam him like a punch to the chest, the way his jacket and pants and sneakers would start dragging him down. He hadn't thought about the waves slapping into his mouth, or the danger of other boats coming. Most of all he hadn't imagined how hard it would be to rescue him. How they'd have to tack back and forth around him three or four times—he lost count: on the first pass, tossing the life ring that fell short, so he had to thrash his leaden arms to get up to it; then Joan shouting to him to stay where he was, to keep calm, while Sam at the tiller tried to edge in tighter but not too tight, and Elisa hauled out the ladder they used for swimming in summer. Finally, when he thought they were going to whiz by him again, his father pulling hard up into the wind so the boat stopped dead, the sails flapping and beating like flags in a hurricane.

The boat was so close—the ladder hanging over the side, their three anxious faces—but his arms and legs were so heavy and cold, it seemed to take a few minutes to reach it. His father got his hands under Danny's jacket sleeves, into his armpits, and helped haul him up. "I'll sail the boat," he told Joan. "Take him down below and get those clothes off him."

In the cabin under the bunks were towels, clean socks and sweatsuits, an extra jacket of Sam's. Once Danny was dressed again and huddled inside a sleeping bag, Joan lit the alcohol stove and put on a kettle for instant hot chocolate. Sam steered them right back to their mooring, without a question or complaint. No one said a word about what Danny had done, as if it had all been an accident, and the only thing that mattered was that he was safely on board, that he didn't come down with pneumonia. Later, Elisa would tell him that he was a jerk, and then adopt a new taunt for him when he was mad—the faint cry, as if through a storm, of *Man overboard!* His mother would whisper into his hair, "Don't you ever give us a scare like that again," when she tucked him in that night. But for the moment—for the first time that he could remember after something went wrong—they weren't arguing or laying blame. On the launch that picked them up and motored them ashore to the dock, Sam sat down next to Danny. He wrapped his arm tight around him, rubbing his hand up and down Danny's arm and saying only, "You warm enough, tiger?"

10

WHEN THE PHONE RANG AGAIN, Danny grabbed it, just to break off the sound, but he was still motoring ashore on that launch, huddling against the warm bulk of his father.

"Dan. I'm glad it's you."

"Dave." His brother-in-law was the only person who called him Dan, and he hated it.

"It isn't easy breaking into the line there."

"You've been trying?"

"For about an hour now. Off and on."

"Oh." He stood up to snap himself to. "So what the hell is happening?"

"Let me first tell you what I've been going through. You find a reasonable human being at one of those places and they're going to check it all out and get back to you. Then when you don't hear anything you call them back and they're gone for the day, or the next one insists there's no one by that name working there. So you have to start over. The whole thing is unbelievably Byzantine. I must have been on the phone with a dozen different people at the M.E.'s Office, and forget the hospital."

Dave rattled all this off quickly, in a voice that rose in pitch as he went. Danny had two, equally unpleasant thoughts: that Dave hadn't made any progress at all, and that this whole song and dance was a buildup to announcing that Sam had been found, with Dave casting himself in the role of hero: David versus the Goliath of New York City bureaucracy. "So what are they saying? Have they found my father or haven't they?"

"Well, not exactly. The hospital found the papers that certify they sent the body to the M.E.'s Office." Dave had made enough of these phone calls, he was talking about *the body* now too. "They say that happened early this morning, so the ambulance driver's off duty now, but they're supposedly working on tracking him down. Meanwhile, the M.E.'s Office is still claiming they never received it."

"Received *him*."

"What?"

"Never mind. Just keep going."

"There's not much more to say for the moment. I've got everyone from the janitor up through the Assistant M.E. checking into it. But apparently when there's a screwup like this over there, it sometimes takes a while."

"Like how long of a while?"

"There's no saying. I mean, do you realize what the Medical Examiner's Office is? It's the coroner's office—the city morgue. Like if some junkie gets knifed on a streetcorner in Harlem, that's where he goes. If they dredge some corpse out of the river—"

"Okay. I get the idea. So what are you going to do?"

"I'm going to get out of here and come back to the house now."

Danny felt a panic seizing him, but he held himself to a whisper. "You can't come back. How are you going to keep talking to all of these people?"

"I'm not. That's what I'm calling to tell you. This was all a great idea, if it worked reasonably quickly. But I think the game's up now. I've given the M.E.'s Office the number at the house, so they can call if something turns up. You're going to have to tell them."

Danny didn't say anything. Of course he'd known all

along that it might come to this, but still, the idea of actually saying it, of seeing the looks on their faces . . .

"I mean, tell your mother and Elisa."

"I know what you mean."

"If you want, you could wait till I get there. We could tell them together."

Danny hesitated a moment, but then shook his head. "I better do it myself. Mom's pretty antsy. I don't think I can hold her off for much longer. She's about ready to call that jerk from the funeral chapel herself."

"Abrams isn't a jerk. He's been very helpful."

"Right. Too bad he couldn't do anything."

"Everyone's doing their best."

Just like Dave: Mr. Harvard Superior himself suddenly going soft on the world, just to be contrary, or maybe to cover his own ass. "Sure. But you know what Sam would say."

"No."

Danny grinned to himself. Dave wasn't so buddy-buddy with his father after all; anyone who was would have known the answer: *Their best isn't good enough.*

Joan and Elisa were downstairs in the kitchen, huddled with Henrietta in front of the sink. Henrietta was whispering with a vehement, livid expression, hissing out her words for the emphasis she usually got from raising her voice, sending a spray of saliva toward his mother's and sister's faces. "It has to be in a shroud," she was telling them. "A shroud. Do you understand what I'm saying? That's how Jewish people get buried. Even Reform. She's crazy on this one, Joanie. I'm warning you."

She, of course, had to be Ida. Danny cleared his throat, and Henrietta snapped her short neck around to glare at him.

"Sorry to break in here. But, Mom, I have to talk to you and Elisa a minute." He glanced at Henrietta. "Upstairs."

93

"Can't it just wait till we finish . . . ?" His mother raised her eyebrows in Henrietta's direction.

Henrietta had her hands on her hips and was scowling. Or maybe she wasn't, and that was simply her face. It was like all the older women in that branch of the family, from Ida on down: along with the wrinkles and folds, permanently nasty expressions had been sculpted on their faces, as if their inner sourness, not time, were molding the flesh. Henrietta did not want to be interrupted, especially now, when she had the makings of a good crisis brewing. She was as bad as Ida in her own way, though she always managed to put herself forward as innocent. Ida would fill her cousin with her grumblings, and then Henrietta would broadcast them, as if she herself had no stake in it ("You know how I am, Joanie, I hate an argument"); as if she was only passing the word along in case anybody was interested.

But the debate about Jewish burial customs would just have to keep. Until there was a body there wouldn't be a burial, in a shroud or anything else. He met Henrietta's look straight on. "No, it can't wait."

"It's tough on Henrietta," Joan said quietly as they climbed the stairs.

"Right now it's tougher on us," Danny answered, though he knew she didn't mean the death, but life in general.

He didn't want to deliver the news in his parents' room, so he steered Joan and Elisa into his own. He sat them both on his bed, against the blue bolster Joan had added to make it more like a couch for the daytime. He leaned against the edge of his dresser, sliding back the wooden model of a Chinese junk he and Sam had built on weekend afternoons when Sam was home from the hospital after the first attack, but still had to be taking it easy—the intricate rigging of tiny ropes and miniature canvas sails, whose tension they'd spent hours adjusting, sagging now, as if the wind had gone out of them. Danny cleared his throat and swallowed, but he still wasn't ready to speak. Elisa broadened her gaze with a weary

94

skepticism that could bloom any minute into impatience. He turned to his mother but she just looked back at him dully, exhausted beyond surprise. He could see it in her eyes, what she must have been thinking: *What could the kid have to say that was worth so much fuss and secrecy?*

"Okay already. You dragged us up here. Now get on with it," Elisa said finally. "We don't have all day."

"Actually, we probably do have all day," he said.

She stood up from the bed. "Listen, I don't know about Mom, but I'm not in the mood for one of your games right now."

"This isn't a game. And it's not about me. It's about Dad." He swallowed again, harder this time. "Dad's body."

"His *body?*"

At any other time, he would have almost been glad his news was as bad as it was, just to show her—like all the times when he was a kid and wished he'd break an arm or a leg or even actually die, and it would be worth it, whatever the pain, just to get one look at Elisa's face, at all of their faces. "You know how he was supposed to go from the hospital to the Medical Examiner's Office, for the autopsy?"

The color was draining from his sister's cheeks, and his mother looked at him like she was waking up.

"See, well, you know . . ." *No, I don't know:* that's what Sam would tell him when Danny was saying "you know" a lot, dogging him until he could barely get out a word without stammering.

Let the boy speak, Joan would say. *You're only making it worse.*

No, I won't let him speak. We aren't raising an imbecile.

"It's like, he never got there. Or he's there, and they're saying he isn't."

He stopped, poised for the inevitable volley of questions, but it didn't come. The two of them just stared at him, their brows screwed up like they weren't following. He wasn't doing this right; he was supposed to sound confident, reassuring. "I mean, he's there. He's definitely there. It's just a screwup in paperwork."

"Paperwork?" His mother repeated the word like she used to with technical swimming terms he would throw at her.

"Look, I'm doing this wrong. Let me start again, okay? Let me just go step by step."

"That sounds like a good idea," Joan said.

He shook out his arms and wiped his palms down his jeans. Once you told it straight out, there wasn't that much to the story. There was the original call from Abrams, and his own call to Dave. There were the calls Dave had made, and where he had left things. He spoke with his eyes down, and only looked up at them when he'd gone through the basic scenario, and was about to launch into the pep talk he'd rehearsed in his head: This was just a temporary delay. It would probably be all cleared up within a couple more hours, and if not, then by first thing in the morning.

But he stopped at the sight of them. His mother had her face in her hands, and Elisa looked not stricken but angry. She started pacing the room, just like Ida or Sam, the way she always did when she was working herself up into a frenzy. "So you've known about this since what time?"

He counted back in his head and then generously rounded off. "Since noon or so."

"Noon?" She practically shrieked it, as if the fact of how long he'd known was somehow more terrible than the news itself. "I don't believe you would do this."

"Do what? What did *I* do?"

She wheeled around toward him, her face in that ferocious expression that used to make her nose look like the beak of some bird of prey. "Forget about me. Forget the fact that I've been waiting for Dave to get back here for hours now. Did you ever think about Mom? Don't you think she had a right to be part of this? To maybe help make a few decisions here? But no. Here's your chance for a secret mission, right? To be the big man."

Danny stared at her with his mouth open. He'd figured they'd say he should have told them, and not taken the burden all on himself. But it had never dawned on him that he'd be attacked like this. Of course he'd only been trying to do the right thing, to protect them.

"I did it for you. Can't you see that?" He turned to his mother, whose face was still hidden, moving side to side in her hands. "I did it for you, Mom."

But his mother didn't seem to be listening. Beneath her hands she was squeezing her eyes shut, and repeating something under her breath. After a moment the words came clear: "It's my fault, all my fault."

Danny got down on his knees in front of her and took hold of her wrists. "It's not your fault. It's *mine*. I was stupid. I should have told you when Abrams first called."

She lifted her head and looked at him like they were talking about two different things. "It's my fault he's missing." She pressed her hands to her forehead, as if she felt a sharp pain. "I should have done what Ida did the night Moe died. I should have stayed with him. I should have never come home last night." Her voice dropped to a whisper: "I should never have let him go yesterday."

Danny twisted around to Elisa, hoping she had some answer, but she had clamped her hand over her mouth, as if what Joan was saying were true. He turned back to his mother. "What were you supposed to do? Tie him down and hold him by force?"

She took a fistful of her hair in each hand. "Something. *Something.*"

Danny felt a pressure building inside his head. He gripped his mother by the shoulders and shook her. "Why does it always have to be somebody's fault? Sometimes things just happen. Can't something *just happen?*"

Before Danny could stop himself, a pair of hands was closing around *his* shoulders, pulling him back from behind. He whirled around to see Uncle Buddy, Joan's brother.

97

Buddy was an inch or two shorter than Danny, but much broader, and strong; Danny could still feel the burn of his fingers where they'd dug into him. But it was Buddy who flinched, and put an arm up to shield his face. It was only then Danny realized his own fists were clenched; that Uncle Buddy thought Danny was going to hit him, thought he'd been hurting his mother. "Hey." He jumped back and flashed his spread palms. "I'm not socking anyone. We're just having a little discussion here."

"Some discussion." Buddy turned to Joan. "I just walked in the door downstairs and heard shouting . . ."

"We're okay." With Joan's face uncovered, you could see she'd been crying. "Really. Everyone's fine."

But she didn't look fine at all. Danny wanted to go and put his arm around her, but he was afraid. Suddenly she looked so small to him, and so fragile.

Buddy moved in where Danny would have gone, and drew Joan up into the shelter of his big, fleshy arm. She tilted her head to rest it against him.

"Come on, kid," Buddy said. "I'm going to pour you a drink."

"Buddy, we've got a problem," she said, but she let him steer her toward the door.

"It's okay. Come take a load off your feet. Everything's going to get taken care of."

From the door he turned around to Elisa and Danny. "Why don't you kids calm it down in here? We've got enough excitement already." Then back to Joan: "Mother and Dad are downstairs. I just picked them up at the airport."

Joan inhaled a long breath with her eyes closed. When she opened them, she turned back to Danny. "We'll talk about this a little later, okay? I better go see Grandma and Grandpa."

Danny nodded, and tried to hold her gaze; with his eyes to say he was sorry, to say *don't you be mad at me too*. But Buddy was already swinging her around. Danny watched their two backs fade into the dusky light of the hall, and imagined he could almost see what connected them: the child's games, the pet dogs, the secrets whispered in houses long ago sold. He'd never thought of his mother and Buddy as especially close, but how naturally they moved together now, gliding toward the stairs like the flesh of a single body, brother and sister.

11

THE SAME WAY Danny pictured his sister, in her absence, with her original nose, he tended to think of his grandmother Bea as she had been when he was a kid, before what Joan always referred to, in hushed, almost reverential tones, as *Grandma's accident.* This was a phrase that had always struck Danny as off somehow, because the accident wasn't *hers;* it was just a fluke of fate that had nothing to do with her. The year Danny was fourteen, the year after Sam's heart attack, the Teitlebaums were standing on the tarmac at the Mexico City airport, about to step onto the boarding ramp, when a student pilot crashed his small plane, and the propeller flew into the right side of Grandma Bea's forehead.

Joan was at her mother's bedside three months later when Bea awoke from the coma, and Danny had heard a hundred times the story of what Joan had seen. The first thing Bea did was put two fingers together and bring them up to her lips, like she was holding a cigarette—she'd smoked two packs of Lucky Strikes a day since before Joan was born. But then a look of confusion came over her face. She took the fingers away from her mouth and studied them, as if they were someone else's, the gesture entirely alien. (She never smoked another cigarette in her life.) Then she noticed her daughter, and tears welled up in her eyes. She opened her mouth to speak, but no word came out for a long moment. When it did, her voice sounded hoarse and cracked, but that was to be expected. What sent Joan running for the nurse, not in joy that her mother had come to, but in panic, was what Grandma Bea said. After Joan's months of waiting—of sitting night and day at the bedside, of struggling in her high school Spanish to get some sense out of the doctors and orderlies, of heartburn and diarrhea from the food in the hospital cafeteria—her mother hadn't spoken Joan's name, or said, *Knock on wood, I'm alive*, or, *Oy gottenyu!* Her mother had looked at her and said: "Strawberry."

In the months that followed, all the doctors and therapists credited Bea with a recovery nothing short of miraculous. Before the year was out, she would be looking, with the help of a wig and plenty of makeup, almost like her old self— except for the depression on the right side of her forehead, where the metal plate had been installed, and that cockeyed expression of trepidation and surprise on her face: she knew exactly what she *wanted* to say, but was always waiting to see what her mouth would come out with.

But Bea had a terrible Hungarian will. Legend had it she'd even won out over Ida, when Ida hadn't wanted Sam and Joan to get engaged the summer before he went into the service. Bea invited all the neighbors from around the lake where the two kids had met (the Teitlebaums owning their house, the Wingers just renting), put out platters of chopped liver and miniature stuffed cabbages, poured everybody a glass of New York State champagne, and then announced the engagement. For years, there was a heated debate as to whether Sam had ever actually popped the question. Joan always insisted he had, in so many words, the evening before, as she and Sam were baby-sitting for Nathan. The way she told it, they were leaning over Nathan's crib when Sam said, "Wouldn't you like to have a couple of these someday?" She looked into his baby blues and said yes, she would, and he kissed her.

That was enough of a proposal for Joan, or at least it was by the time Bea—who always waited up for her daughter after a date to see if there was any good news—had gotten through with her. But Sam swore up and down he had never proposed (how could he have, with his mother bending his ear night and day about staying single?); that it was all Grandma Bea's machinations. He'd wink at Elisa and Danny, ever a willing audience for this oldest of their parents' disputes. It excited the children to think of that time before they were born as the subject of competing mythologies; to imagine their parents' union—their own existences—hinging on such a delicate and mysterious balance of forces. "Your Grandma Bea was one tough customer," Sam would say, pulling a reluctant Joan to his side. "And you know how hard it is to argue with such terrific chopped liver."

Up to a point, Bea applied her fierce will to the task of regaining control of her speech. After years of work and the services of half a dozen speech therapists, she could exchange the usual niceties. She could take a cab and shop for dresses or needlepoint patterns and wool. She could meet Danny's friends and they'd never guess that something was wrong with her. But she seemed to have given up on any more elaborate communication, on ever really becoming herself again, the vivacious, busybody self that Danny remembered. Maybe that was impossible, or maybe it was just too much effort, when everybody who mattered already knew her anyway, and remembered as Danny did; when Grandpa Irv was so willing, even anxious, to speak for her. It was only every so often that Bea had something that needed to be said—that no one, not even Irv, could guess at, or give her the words for. Then the old fight would come back to her face. She'd wave her hands or bang on the table; she'd squeeze her eyes shut and shake her head if anyone interrupted her. Then, slowly, with visible effort, as if it were a matter of controlling wayward muscles, she'd speak, and usually deliver the kind of gem the family would be repeating for weeks, the way you repeat the remarkable sentences a precocious child utters.

Today, when Danny followed the sound of the commotion downstairs, he knew Bea must have come out with one of her beauties, because Buddy and Barbara, Joan and Elisa, Grandpa Irv, even Bea herself, were all laughing and at the same time wiping their eyes. "It's too late for that, Mom," Joan was saying, taking her mother into her arms.

Danny whispered to Uncle Buddy, "What did she say?"

Buddy gave him an appraising look, then leaned in so he could whisper back: "She said your mother could move back in with her and Irving now."

Joan and Buddy led Grandma Bea to the couch, where Ida was clucking her tongue and muttering, "What's she making such a fuss about? He wasn't her son. Sure, a mother-in-law can feel bad. But a mother . . ." Grandpa Irv lowered himself into an armchair, refusing all offers of something to drink, holding his hat—the same plaid wool duster he'd worn for years—in his lap, as if he were waiting for an appointment.

Irv's golf game had always kept him in shape, but now he looked frail and thin in the overstuffed chair, his bald skull brown and papery. Danny wasn't used to thinking about his grandfather's age. When he looked at him, he still saw the Grandpa Irv of the lake house, waking up at six so he could run out to the course and get in a fast eighteen before the sun rose too high; perking coffee and making the Levy's Real Jewish Rye toast that Danny always smelled in his bed, that drew him out from under his covers into the kitchen with the high-back, knotty-pine benches, where Irv would toast the boy a couple of pieces and butter them, so Danny wouldn't get hungry when he went down to the lake, though sometimes he waited till Grandpa Irv stepped out onto the dew-soaked porch with his golf bag and then just crawled back into bed, and dozed and dreamed until Grandma Bea was up fixing everyone's regular breakfast. The Grandpa Irv with the wooden speedboat he'd bought in the forties—varnished and waxed until it gleamed in the sun—standing in the back with his seventy-five-horsepower Evinrude outboard, that he'd gun so they'd skid bouncing across the lake until the grandchildren screamed, and then he'd slow down until they begged him to race again. Grandpa Irv in his lime green or canary yellow slacks and matching striped polo shirts, his white patent leather loafers and belts, so when he'd show up for a family dinner Joan would tease him that this wasn't a country club, and Bea would shake her head, like there was nothing she could do with him; who'd say, "What's wrong with a little color?" and figure he should know, all those years in the Garment District selling men's haberdashery— "What's wrong with a little color?" too when he drove up to the house in his first fire engine red Cadillac with the white vinyl roof, the car that Nathan dubbed, with his usual sneer, the Pimpmobile, but that the other cousins begged and clambered to ride in, and Irv, with a mischievous gleam in his eye, said all right, but they had to each pay him a nickel.

Funny how you could go for years without noticing the way someone was changing, and then see it all in one moment, like this one, when Danny looked at his grandfather and thought of his wizened Italian landlord from Sackett Street; thought *old man:* that tired, bewildered look on Irv's face, his mouth hanging open, his eyes staring straight ahead as the women fluttered around him.

Dave came back not long afterward, his tie loosened and his collar spread open, looking like he needed to put his feet up and suck down a beer. Danny wanted to warn him but Elisa got to him first, and hauled him up the stairs by the arm before Dave had even gotten his coat off. Dave deserved the shit about keeping the screwup a secret even less than Danny did, but no doubt Elisa was letting him have it. Still, Danny had to hand it to Dave: the guy must have had a way with her; it wasn't long before he appeared at the top of the stairs to call Danny, and ask him to bring his mother up too. Dave and Elisa were in Joan and Sam's bedroom. Dave had just hung up with Abrams, who was putting in a last call to the Medical Examiner's Office before he packed it in for the day. Abrams had reassured Dave everything would be cleared up by morning, and ready to move for a Thursday funeral.

Joan just nodded and paced a couple of times in front of her bed. "We have to come up with a story." She took a few more steps and then turned to face them. "For Ida. For my parents. They're all expecting the funeral to be tomorrow, and we can't tell them the truth. My parents are upset enough as it is, and Ida would tear me to pieces. I can just hear her now. There has to be some other reason for waiting till Thursday. You know Jewish custom dictates having the burial as soon as possible after the death. When Sidney Scharf's widow delayed his funeral a couple of days, Ida was still *tummuling* about it months afterward."

She was right. They needed a lie, and a good one. "Can't we just say they were backed up at Crestwood?" Danny was thinking aloud.

"It's got to be better than that," Joan said. "We would have known about Crestwood's schedule this morning. And you know how Ida is. She's the resident expert on funeral chapels."

"How about something with Rabbi Rosenbaum?" Elisa had jumped up and was pacing now too. "Like he was already booked—he couldn't do it tomorrow."

Joan pursed her lips, calculating, but then shook her head. "That wouldn't be enough for your grandmother. She'd say Dad was too important for that—that the rabbi should have dropped everything. She'd probably read him the riot act as soon as she saw him."

"So how's this?" Elisa wasn't one for letting an idea of hers go. "We tell her Rosenbaum's out of town. We say he couldn't get back until tomorrow night. Then we tell

Rosenbaum what's going on, so he can play along if she says something."

It took a little convincing, but Joan agreed in the end, *thou shalt not lie* notwithstanding. It was a reasonable plan, though Danny wasn't so pleased his sister was the one to come up with it. Especially since, as she went to get the phone book for Joan, she couldn't refrain from shooting him one of her little looks—the kind that no one else ever noticed; the kind that used to send Danny tearing across the room at her. How many times had he been spanked with his father's wooden fraternity paddle, until the carved "Phi," "Beta" and "Upsilon" were practically branded into his bare hide, and not so much as a finger was laid on the angel Elisa? "She was just sitting there," Sam would insist when Danny tried to explain that mocking light in her eyes, the maddening way she curled one side of her mouth down.

While his mother held on for the rabbi, Danny drifted into his parents' walk-in closet, pretending to just glance idly about but searching the shelves on his father's side, alongside stacks of tennis shirts and behind rows of shoes, for the fraternity paddle. It used to hang from a hook on the wall by a leather thong, ostensibly for display but more likely, Danny had always suspected, so it would be ready at hand, and visible as a deterrent. After Sam's first heart attack, the week before his release from the hospital, Joan was clearing the house of his vices: a humidor full of cigars, the bottles of scotch and gin, the none-too-secret stores of salted peanuts and pistachios. Danny suggested the paddle should also be classified as a health hazard—"Have you ever seen how red his face turns when he's spanking me?"—and his mother agreed; she said Danny was getting too old for the spankings anyway.

She somehow imagined that it would be no big deal—that Sam would be too preoccupied to notice the paddle was missing. But he noticed the very first day he was home: Danny won the banana split he had wagered his mother.

Everyone, including Elisa, kept their pact and played dumb. They told Sam they had no idea what could have become of it. They made a great show of ransacking closets, and assured him the paddle was bound to turn up—maybe the cleaning woman had stashed it away somewhere. Sam never swallowed the act for a minute. He interrogated Danny and Elisa with his most searing gaze—the human lie detector, they called it. He tried to tickle the truth out of Joan once he was getting his strength back. But the conspiracy held.

Faced with the graver trials of his son's adolescence, Sam resorted to a belt, and even the flat of his hand, but those methods never took hold; they lacked the symbolic potency, the precise combination of force and control, intimacy and reserve, that had made the paddle so uniquely effective. Danny was a senior in high school when Sam unearthed it in the far corner of the uppermost garage shelf, during a hunt for a carton of old sailboat fittings. He tried to pretend he was only kidding when he found Danny and Joan in the kitchen and brandished the paddle, saying, "Okay, over my knee. Which one's first?" the way he used to when he had call to spank both his children.

Sam never hung the paddle back up. He and Joan had redecorated their bedroom by then and he claimed it no longer fit, but Danny was sure that wasn't really the reason. He figured that for Sam the symbolism of the paddle had shifted: no longer the father's justified anger and punishment, like the just wrath of the old Hebrew God, but the instrument of his own humiliation at the hands of his family. When he was at his weakest, they'd gone behind his back; they'd ganged up on him. Outwardly, he'd been a decent enough sport about it, but the paddle—ever afterward the butt of an open family joke—stayed hidden away in the closet. Still, Danny could picture him taking it down now and then, running his fingers along the glossy surface, silky from coat upon coat of shellac, testing the weight on his palm, thinking back on the spankings not in anger but with a kind of tenderness, as if recalling some fond occasion from his son's boyhood, a moment when they'd been especially close.

That wasn't why *Danny* wanted the paddle. Suddenly it occurred to him that the whole fiasco with the lost body was not just bad luck; that it was, in some obscure way, his father's own doing. If there were spirits, wouldn't it be just like Sam's to start right in meddling and screwing things up? Sam, who could never just do things like everyone else; Sam, as usual, making life difficult. That paddle had been right on one of these closet shelves, so where in the hell was it now? Danny wanted to slap the gleaming wood on his own palm as a reminder of the one time his father had not called the shots, the time Danny had gotten the best of him.

12

"*IT'S TOO MUCH FOOD.* This is what your friends are sending you? All this *chazerai*? Who could eat all this?" Ida shook her head as she surveyed the dining room table, stretched with extra leaves to its full expanse so you could barely squeeze around either end of it, covered in Joan's good white embroidered tablecloth since none of the everyday cloths were long enough, but without the usual accompaniments of china, silver and crystal; instead, the table was set with plastic glasses and cutlery and paper plates, arrayed with a smorgasbord of plastic and aluminum serving containers.

It was barely five-thirty, early for dinner in a household whose mealtime had always been scheduled around waiting for Sam: Danny and Elisa half asleep in their seats, and Joan saying, "Five more minutes, okay, kids? Everything goes into the oven in five more minutes if your father hasn't walked through that door." Tonight Joan had said they were expecting visitors later; it would be easier if they got dinner out of the way. Danny knew that was only part of the reason. The other was Irv and Bea, whose dinner hour had been ritual long before Irv's retirement and the winters spent eating Early Bird Specials in Florida restaurants. The Teitlebaums had always eaten at five, even quarter to if Bea could manage it; Joan and Buddy were the only kids on their block who had to come inside and wash up at four-thirty. If

Irv didn't get his meal on time, he was capable of throwing a tantrum. On Thanksgiving, when Joan liked to serve the turkey at six, Irv always carried on about how he could smell it, the bird was perfectly done, why was she leaving it in there to get all dried out? It was all she could do to keep him from hauling the roasting pan out of the oven. But tonight, Irv had no cause to complain and it was just as well; the production of the meal gave everyone something to do, something neutral to focus on.

Usually, before the relatives gathered around the big table, Sam and Joan went through several delicate rounds of diplomacy over the seating, factoring in who couldn't stand who on general principle, who'd insulted who at the dinner before, who you could risk putting Ida with, who you had to protect from her—shuffling and reshuffling the guests until they arrived at the least potentially explosive arrangement, so Elisa could set out the gold-edged place cards written with her meticulous calligrapher's script. Tonight there had been no formal assignments, just Joan, her eyes darting from face to face, chair to chair, then telling everyone where to sit with the pretense of being offhanded. Uncle Buddy was sent to Sam's usual place at the head of the table. Next to him on one side sat Aunt Barbara, and next to her, Esther; opposite them, Bea and Irv. In the center of the table, across from each other, Henrietta and Aaron faced off. Ida was next to Henrietta, and Danny next to his grandmother. Across from Ida and Danny were Dave and Elisa. Joan would have her usual seat, at the end near the kitchen, so she could be jumping up and down and running to get people what they were missing, and they could all be screaming, "Joanie, sit. We've got everything. Eat your own dinner, it's getting ice cold."

For the moment, though, Joan stood between Aaron and Dave, holding up Ida's plate with one hand, a serving fork poised in the other. Ida herself was still muttering: "*Meshuggeh*. It's too much to eat here."

"People send food because they don't know what else to do," Joan said. "Just eat what you want and I'll throw out the rest when you're finished."

"All right." Ida pointed a finger and wagged it like she was scolding somebody. "Give me a plain piece of chicken. White meat, if it isn't too dry. Not so big. Okay. And some kugel. Just a small piece, that's all." She straightened the front of her jacket by the lapels, as if, having sunk so low as to ask for some dinner, she needed to restore a semblance of respectability. When the plate was set down in front of her, she pushed it back a few inches. "People have to be crazy to send in all this food."

Joan bit her lip, and Danny knew that any minute she'd say something to Ida that she would regret. But Aunt Barbara broke in. "Try the kugel, Ida. It's mine. I had it frozen, but it keeps well. Buddy took it out for me before he went in to the office. Let me know what you think. This time I put in a little crushed pineapple, like my friend Sandy does."

"I used to make my own kugel too," Ida said, with a dismissive wave of her arm. "When Sam and Esther were little. When Moe was here. But why should I go to all that bother now? There's no one to eat it." She pushed with her fork at Barbara's pudding, but did not take a taste. "Henrietta makes a wonderful kugel."

"Ach." Henrietta scowled like Ida had insulted her. She was covering her entire plate with a visible layer of salt, jerking hard with the shaker. "You know I was never much of a cook." She banged the shaker down. "What did I have to cook for?"

When she said this, she gestured with her chin in the direction of Aaron, who just sat there across from her, eating the piece of her gray pot roast he'd dutifully requested with his arms tucked into his sides like he was afraid of elbowing somebody. He didn't say anything, didn't so much as flinch; he was used to his wife's belittlement, thoughtless as breathing.

"It's a good thing you got all this food . . ." It was Buddy, through a mouthful of kugel. His plate was loaded like it was his only shot around the buffet at an all-you-can-eat place. Danny had seen the pictures of the gangly kid in his varsity baseball uniform, but every year since Danny had taken notice, Buddy had visibly thickened from Thanksgiving to Passover, coming to look more and more like the flip side of his wife's compulsion. ". . . as long as the funeral's not until Thursday, and you've got this whole crew to feed."

Danny shot a glance across the table at Elisa and Dave. As of just before dinner, everyone knew about the postponement. The story about the rabbi being out of town until the following evening seemed to have them all satisfied. But still, the less it got talked about in front of Ida, the better. Danny studied his plate, the pastrami sandwich he'd assembled mostly to placate his mother, trying to think of something to say to redirect the discussion. But it was too late. Silence was a vacuum Ida always rushed in to fill. "And what's wrong with your rabbi, that Rosenbaum? Supposed to be so wonderful. He couldn't change his plans and come home a day earlier? You've only belonged to that temple for, what— twenty years? You haven't paid enough money, with those big dues every year these fancy synagogues out here charge you? Your children weren't Bar and Bas Mitzvahed there? He's so brilliant, with the politics and the fancy sermons and big ideas? If he was so smart, he'd figure out a way to be there tomorrow.

"Now, my Schwartz: that's a rabbi." She reached across Danny to poke a finger at Joan. "You've heard him on the High Holy Days. Am I right?" She didn't wait for an answer. "He'd do anything for me. And my children. Anything. You know how friendly he always was with Sam, when he came to sit with me at the shul on Yom Kippur."

A grudging sparkle lit Ida's eyes, and she turned to play to the larger audience. "He'd kiss me and shake Sam's hand and wish us *gut yuntiff* like everyone else. But then he'd stay and talk for a minute, no matter who he had standing in line. And there are a lot of big people in my congregation, that Flatbush Jewish Center."

She directed this to Buddy and Barbara at the other end of the table, just in case the reputation hadn't reached Long Island's South Shore.

"He'd ask Sam how his practice was doing, and ask for Joanie and you kids. Each one by name—he never forgets. 'How's that brilliant Elisa doing in college? She going to be a lawyer like her father? And Danny, the swimmer. Has he made the Olympics yet?' And then he'd tell me, 'Ida, that's some boy you got.' And the way the other people would look at us, like I was there with a movie star. 'Go on, Rabbi,' Sam would tell him. 'You've got people waiting.' "

Ida fished a crumpled handkerchief out of her sleeve and shook it out, though she wasn't even sniffling. It was more like a flourish, a magic trick, to punctuate her performance. You could tell she was just warming up; that before you knew it she'd be back to the clarinet lessons, the flight of Sam's airplane across Prospect Park.

"Mother." Esther, in her schoolteacher's voice, practiced to explain the laws of nature to simpletons, to sound in control even when chaos was erupting around her. "We don't need to do this now."

Ida grimaced as though she'd tasted something bitter, and wheeled around to Esther. "Stupid! I'm talking about Rabbi Schwartz." She turned back toward Joan. "He's only the president of the United Federation of Synagogues."

"Brooklyn Chapter," Esther put in.

Ida ignored the clarification. "But maybe that's not good enough for *my daughter.*" On this last phrase, she had an abrupt change of accent, rising out of the gutters of Flatbush into a speech she must have taken from some Hollywood version of aristocracy, the same way she answered the telephone with a stuffy, inflated "Heh-doo?" or was suddenly awash in refinement on words like "ballet" and "Italy."

"Maybe they got something better up there in the sticks where you live. It's a wonder they even got Jews up there. But you—the big genius, the scientist. You had to follow that *meshuggener* up there. That no-good-nik. Him and all his big promises. 'Mrs. Winger, I'll make your daughter a millionaire.' Look where it got you. Up there all alone. You call that a life? Two beautiful babies, my grandchildren . . ."

Joan shot up from her chair. "Can I get anyone some more pot roast?" She practically shouted it over Ida. "Buddy? Aaron?" She grabbed for the closest container, a carton someone had sent from the Chinese take-out place. "Rice?"

"Never heard such a thing among Jewish people— sending fried rice for a funeral," Henrietta contributed, clucking her tongue loudly enough she could have been taking lessons from Ida. "Before you know it they'll be delivering spareribs."

Dave stood up with his plate. "I'll take some, thanks."

"Me too, Joanie," said Barbara, though there was no way she'd actually eat it. "Nothing wrong with fried rice, so long as it doesn't have pork. We've got the cutest little Chinese place by the high school, so when I pick the girls up . . ."

But Ida had never stopped talking, to nobody in particular, and now her voice resurfaced above the others. "When a Jew dies, you're supposed to bury him the next day. I don't care—Orthodox, Conservative, Reform. It's supposed to be the next day. You're not supposed to leave them just lying around like the *goyim* do."

When he saw his mother's eyes roll up, Danny figured he'd better jump in. "Listen, Grandma, why don't we talk about something else?"

"So who's talking? All I'm trying to say is your mother should have told me, understand? I could have called Rabbi Schwartz. He does funerals out on the Island all the time. Now she says it's too late. Nothing got in the newspaper."

"I didn't think of it, Mom." Joan had put down the fork she'd been holding, even though she hadn't eaten a bite.

"Okay. So you didn't think. Nobody criticized. I'm just saying I could have got Schwartz, that's all."

"Mother." Esther was sounding less patient now. "They wanted to get their own rabbi."

"Sure. So they got. For the day after tomorrow. So we can spend another day sitting around this house like a bunch of *meshuggeners*." Ida stood, the handkerchief twisted around her fingers now. She took a couple of steps, her heels sharp on the polished parquet.

"Mom, please sit down." Joan had her hands at the edge of the table, like any second she would stand too. "We're still eating."

"I can't sit no more. I been sitting all day. I sit anymore, my behind will fall off."

Danny tried to hold it in, but he couldn't help laughing; it came out through his pursed lips with a sound like a kid making fart noises.

"Grow up already, would you?" Elisa snapped.

His mother looked at him, and he shrugged an apology. She pushed back her chair. "All of you finish up. I'm just going to go comb my hair and put on some makeup so I look presentable."

"Nice going," Elisa spat at him when Joan was out of earshot.

"Right. Let's make out like it's my fault now."

"Come on, kids. That's enough of that," said Aunt Barbara, as if they were a pair of small children fighting over some toy. Then Henrietta stood and started clearing the plates. Aaron made a feeble plea for her to let people finish, but she paid him no mind. No matter how much food they had left, everybody swore they were done when Henrietta bore down on them—everyone, that is, except Grandpa Irv, who'd been eating slowly and steadily all the while, his head pitched down toward his plate.

"Irv." Grandma Bea was pushing at his arm. "*Irving.*"

"Whaah?" He looked up crossly like she had woken him.

Bea squinted her eyes and pursed her lips together for a moment before she said, "Do something."

Irv looked around the table, bewildered, as if he didn't know why anything would need to be done. "I am doing something. I'm eating my dinner."

Barbara and then Dave and Elisa got up to help with the dishes, so Danny took his chance to slip off, to the stairway. He hung for a moment on the banister at the foot of the stairs, looking up at his mother's closed bedroom door. He thought of the time in high school he'd stood in the very same spot, wondering if she was okay in there but afraid to go up and find out. Elisa was already off at college. Sam had gotten home late, but they'd waited for dinner. They'd barely sat down to the reheated steak, the overcooked broccoli and shriveled potato, when Sam and Joan started fighting. "If you keep this up, you're going to land in the hospital," Joan shouted. And Sam: "You're the one that's going to put me there." The usual exchange, except the week before a lawyer in Sam's firm had dropped dead of a heart attack. So Joan, who got giggly on half a glass of chablis, who called out a plaintive, drawn-out "Good-bye!" on the second and couldn't finish the dishes, decided she was going to get drunk. She took out a bottle of gin and downed a glass and a half before disappearing into the garage. Danny and his father sat in silence while she was gone. She staggered back a few minutes later, swinging a rope she'd fashioned into a lasso. "You want to be a cowboy?" she was saying, like a record playing one speed too slow. "I'll show you a cowboy."

Danny thought this was all pretty funny. He was laughing and whooping and cheering her on: "All right! Get him, Mom." When she started swinging the lasso over Sam's end of the table, Sam ducked, then stood up and grabbed the edge of the tablecloth in both fists. "Two can play this same game," he said.

That set Joan to laughing, then coughing. "Who do you

think you are? Marlon Brando?" In between gasps for breath, she kept swinging the rope. "I've seen that movie already."

"Joan, I'm warning you."

She swung the lasso again, a couple of inches from his face. "I'm telling you, I've seen that movie."

"Okay. You asked for it."

Danny had no idea what movie his mother was talking about, but he knew how the trick ought to work: you whip off the cloth without moving the dishes. But when Sam yanked at the fabric, everything slid smashing into a heap in the middle of the table; with his next flourish—like a matador whipping his cape to the side and up to let the bull pass—he sent the plates, glasses, silverware crashing onto the floor. He cast one haughty look at Joan as if to say, "Now are you satisfied?" and stormed out of the dining room.

Suddenly everything went very still. Danny heard coat hangers clinking in the closet, heard the front door slam. When he heard his father's car start up in the driveway, he had a moment of panic. But she was just about out of her reckless stage. With her lasso, she managed to pull down one last salad plate, but then she dropped the rope onto the table and stood breathing hard. The only thing she managed to say before she wove out of the room toward the stairs was, "I'll clean up the dishes tomorrow."

Danny must have stood awhile staring at the shards of china and glass, the slick of gin covering the parquet floor that he and his father had sealed with six coats of urethane, because by the time he got to the foot of the stairs, his parents' door was already closed, and he could hear her up in their bathroom. He stood and listened until the noises stopped, and then for a long time afterward, when there was no sound at all. Later, when his father would ask why he hadn't gone up to help her, at least check on her, Danny couldn't explain. It wasn't as if he'd run away. He hadn't budged from his post at the banister; he'd suffered through every last heave and moan. He just couldn't bring himself to go up there and open the door. He was never sure whether it was more that he knew she wouldn't want him to see her like that, or that he himself couldn't bear to look at her.

Now, so many years later, he climbed up and stopped at her room, and put an ear to the crack along the closed door. He could hear her, moving around in the bathroom, opening and closing the medicine cabinet doors, clinking her makeup bottles and hairpins and combs on the Formica sinktop. He wished he could go in and sit on the lid of the toilet seat, the way he had as a boy, seeing her from behind but watching her reflection as she bent to the mirror, never tiring of that transformation that gave her skin a pink glow that seemed to come from the inside, that turned her eyelids shimmering silver or blue; amazed at the nests and tails of dark hair she'd lift from her top dresser drawer like mysterious pets, at the heavy black lashes she glued to her own, so thick her eyelids always seemed to be fluttering. He would never go for makeup on girls his own age; when he'd start to kiss them, he'd hate the taste and the oily feel of it. But on his mother it was different, magical. "Don't you have anything better to do?" she'd say, pulling a pin for her electric curlers out of her mouth. "Why don't you go on and play?" He never told her this was just what he wanted to be doing, but he never budged, either. Not until he'd breathed in enough of the heavy creams and perfume that he felt almost dizzy. Not until it was time for her to take off the old terrycloth robe with the stains from her dark foundation ringing the collar.

When he heard the floor creaking—his mother moving from the bathroom to bedroom—he jumped back from the door. It occurred to him that Joan wasn't the only one he had sat and watched from the toilet seat; he'd watched Sam too, though he couldn't call up why or when exactly. That was the funny thing about Sam's absences as a father. When Danny reckoned the account of his childhood, he always wrote his father off as basically not having been there. And yet Danny had all these memories. Now what came to him with surprising vividness was the scent of his father's ablutions, lighter and cleaner than Joan's, not at all mysterious. On the heels of the smell came a vision: Sam standing at the sink with a towel wrapped around his waist, his chest covered with the mat of brown curls that Danny could never imagine sprouting on his own hairless chest, no matter how confident Sam sounded predicting it, lathering his face with the shaving brush and cup of Old Spice soap Danny and Elisa had chipped in for one Hanukkah. He couldn't talk— he drew in his lips, then worked up the frothy lather right over them—so it was the only time Danny was alone with his father when Sam wasn't lecturing or explaining or teaching him something. He ran the blade down his cheek, making skin-colored stripes where Danny watched for the tiny springs of blood Sam would later dab at with the styptic pencil. Maybe that was the mystery: how the blade was so sharp and the blood so close to the surface, Danny could never believe there were just those few drops, or that the little white wand made them vanish so easily.

13

*B*Y SEVEN O'CLOCK, Grandma Bea and Grandpa Irv
were out the front door, heading back to the Manhattan
apartment they thought they had closed for the winter. By
seven-thirty, the house started filling. By eight, Danny
found himself wandering room to room, hovering briefly at
the edge of one conversation after another: the tennis game
where Sam had passed out a week ago Saturday, how good or
bad Sam was looking at the Friday night bridge, the incompetence of the medical profession; his mother, patiently explaining the details of the past days to each new arrival, and
Ida cornering whoever she could, bending their ears with
tales of Sam's childhood, or with her—a mother's—claims to
maximum misery.

All of that was hard enough to take, but what was worse
were the furtive little groups that gathered in all of the rooms
eating cake and chocolates, drinking coffee, talking about
their own petty tragedies: the partner who was always late to
the Wednesday afternoon doubles game, the cheese store
that had mysteriously disappeared overnight, the ups and
downs of the futures market. Everyone was nice to Danny.
The women tattooed his cheeks with lipstick and gagged
him with perfume; the men pumped his hand or pulled him
roughly into their sides, throttling him with that kind of
gruff physical affection men show to younger men, like a
parade of self-appointed surrogate fathers.

At first, he was worried they'd hit him up with the usual questions—about his plans, and where he was living, and what he was doing for work. But nobody asked. They must have known it was a sore subject, having been regaled over cocktails and between hands of bridge with the story of Danny playing lifeguard at a dilapidated YMCA, doing the same thing he did during summers in high school for crying out loud, after all the thousands of dollars Sam and Joan had shelled out for an Ivy League education; of his apartment in some obscure Mafia stronghold, two blocks from the stinking sewer of the Gowanus Canal. Danny didn't doubt that his stumbling backward to Brooklyn, and his parents' lament, made for an engrossing topic of conversation, since everyone else's kids were safely in law or business or med school, on Wall Street or out in Hollywood, making their way. The most disturbing aberration Danny had heard about was the Epsteins' son, who didn't want to be an orthodontist like his father or even a regular doctor but had somehow gotten it into his head to be a veterinarian, in Vermont of all places.

Art Felstein and Morty Bass, Sam's law partners, came in around nine, having driven straight from the office, where they'd been sorting through the first string of crises the death had set into motion. When Danny was a kid, the pair had always put him in mind of a cockeyed Laurel and Hardy: Felstein the thin man, serious and refined, and Bass the heavyweight, good-natured blowhard. But after the initial round of greetings and explanations, the almost embarrassed shedding of mufflers and overcoats, even Morty Bass seemed unsure what to say. The men moved into the living room and settled uneasily at the edge of the couch, heads down and lips pressed together. As they accepted coffee, no cake, it struck Danny that they looked more genuinely, intently grieved than anyone else who'd come in all night. And why shouldn't they? Wasn't it true what his mother had said any number of times: that Sam spent far more of his hours with

Art and Morty than he'd ever spent with his family? That every morning when he left for the office, however much he might put on that martyred look and complain about the backlog or hours or pressure ("You think I work like this because I enjoy it?"), you could sense his excitement, like he was heading off to join the other two Musketeers.

Art and Morty loosened their ties and spoke to Joan in hushed tones—something about the partnership agreement, Sam's share of the firm, about her and the family never needing for anything. But from his outpost in the hall, Danny was only half listening. He was watching the third, younger man who'd come in shortly after them and sat to one side in a chair gazing pointedly at his polished loafers, as if to take in the details of the room, of Sam's domestic life, would be disrespectful; whose expensive-looking suit didn't disguise his flabby physique; who'd probably give his eye-teeth for some cake but said no because Felstein and Bass weren't taking it.

Even before Joan called Danny in to introduce them, Danny knew who he was. The guy who worked with Sam through all those late nights, who was there to hear Sam's last half word, who'd sat at Joan's side in the hospital waiting room. The idea of Jeffrey Skinner had bothered Danny all day, and as he took the soft, sweaty hand in his own, he couldn't figure out if the fact that he looked like a dork made it harder or easier. He was trying to think of what to say, of something to ask the guy, but then Dave was there, stepping between the two of them, patting Skinner on the back with a sober but familiar "Jeffrey," leading him off toward the dining room as if they had things to discuss.

What came to Danny, watching them walk away together, was Nathan's voice, the way his cousin used to make fun of the law firm—calling it *Stinger, Belchstein & Crass*, saying that when he grew up, Stinger, Belchstein & Crass was going to take him on as a partner. Everyone used to laugh—even Sam, when he got wind of it. Nathan didn't mean it to be nasty, shudder the thought; he was just being clever. But it always got Danny mad, and more than once he'd socked Nathan for it—Nathan who would never fight back, but would never cry either, only sneer harder back at you. It only struck Danny now that it wasn't so much the insulting pun on the name that had gotten him. It was the suggestion that Nathan—Nathan, not he—would someday be a partner.

Danny decided it was just as well he and Skinner did not really speak; Danny wasn't about to punch the guy out, but he didn't trust himself not to sound bitter. It was Skinner who cornered Danny sometime later by the coffeepot, as Danny was getting a refill. "I guess these days you don't have to worry about the caffeine. About it affecting your training."

Danny just looked at him over the rim of his cup.

Skinner poured a cup for himself. "I heard all about it at the office. Your swimming, and how you trained for it."

"At the office? You did?"

Skinner nodded matter-of-factly, as if he were surprised that Danny wouldn't have known. "Your father talked about it a lot, to the younger associates. When we'd complain about rotting in the library or spending all day wading through documents, he'd tell us to toughen up. That it wasn't all flashy negotiating sessions and court dates. 'Look at my son,' he'd say. And then he'd talk about how you'd swim up and down the pool for hundreds of hours before you ever got close to a race. He always said if we wanted to do the big public stuff, we first needed that kind of stamina."

"He actually said that?"

Skinner nodded again, slipping a couple of spoonfuls of sugar into his cup as if Danny might not notice him doing it. Danny just stared, and probably would have kept staring, except Art Felstein appeared at their side. "Excuse me, Danny. I'm going to have to steal Jeffrey a moment here."

Danny spent the rest of the evening trying to imagine his

father speaking about him with that kind of pride, holding him up as a paragon to fellow lawyers. But what about all the times Sam had made out like Danny's swimming was a worthless exercise, an excuse to avoid buckling down to any kind of *real work*? How could he reconcile *that* with what Skinner had told him? The partners and friends and the last of the relatives had gone home, the coffeepots were unplugged and the plates of cookies and candy encased in Saran Wrap, but try as he might, Danny still hadn't managed to square the two.

Elisa and Dave retired to Elisa's old room, and Esther and Ida headed up to the guest room soon after, Esther dragging her mother along, telling her if she didn't get to bed she'd be good and sick in the morning. Once their bickering had trailed off up the stairs, Danny looked at his mother, who'd be going to bed alone, tonight and maybe all the nights after this, and he knew that tired as he was, he had to try to outlast her. It didn't take his mother long to catch on to his game plan. When she realized he was sneaking cups of cold, sludgey coffee, following her through the house like a child you couldn't let out of your sight, she showed him the bottle delivered that afternoon by Middle Neck Pharmacy. "It's just a mild dose, but the doctor says it will get me to sleep. So you don't have to wait up with me."

"I wasn't waiting up," he lied. "I just wasn't sleepy yet." He eyed the bottle in his mother's hand, the prescription label: HALCION. "Why don't you take the pill now?"

She looked at him from under raised eyebrows, but got a glass of water and swallowed the pill. "If you want, you can go on up to bed. Really, I'll be okay. My friend Rhoda has the same prescription. She says you take one and don't think it's doing anything and then in about fifteen minutes it knocks you right out."

"So I'll wait fifteen minutes."

They set themselves up in the living room, as if to embark on a vigil, and sat in silence for a couple of minutes, listening to Sam's clock, to what sounded like Ida or Esther walking the hall to the bathroom. Then Joan shook her head. "I have no idea what he'd want," she said, as though in answer to some question that had hung in the air. Danny must have looked back at her blankly, because she clarified: "About the funeral. He never said what he wanted."

Danny nodded. Everyone knew what his mother would want: she'd been a long-standing and vocal advocate of cremation. Whenever they drove the parkway to Ida's house, she'd manage to get in a diatribe about the great tracts of land being wasted on cemeteries. Sam would shake his head and wink around at the kids, clutching the backs of their parents' seats to get a better view of those rolling green meadows run over with gravestones in precise rows, like a battalion of soldiers advancing: "Hmmm. It's a shame. All that prime New York real estate."

"I'm serious," Joan would say, and he'd answer, "I know you are," but never let on one way or another what he thought about *this barbaric practice* of burying people. Danny guessed that Sam might not even have an opinion; that it was one of those issues his father simply did not entertain, since it touched on intangibles like life after death, the relationship between matter and spirit—anything Sam couldn't get his hands on and make or fix.

The existence of God, for example. Danny had never forgotten the day he came home from Sunday School after arguing with the rabbi and asked Sam if he believed in God or not. Sam told him he didn't know, he'd never given the question much thought, and Danny looked back at him even more mystified than disgusted. How could you not wonder? How could you sit in synagogue all those years and listen to all that bullshit and not try to figure out if any of it were true?

As an adolescent, Danny's religious and metaphysical inquiries got focused by what the rabbi termed, in a letter to Danny's parents, "the working out of hostility against authority figures." But from the time when he was a boy, outside alone to rake leaves or gather stones for his father, or up on the sailboat's front deck, his face hanging over the side, watching the waves and the path the hull cut through them, these were the kinds of things he would think about: if God existed or not, and whether the universe was finite or infinite, straight or curved; if everything was just random or planned out ahead of time. It wasn't anything about the answers that kept him occupied with these thoughts. It was the way it made him feel that there was this big space around him, and his own head had gotten bigger by taking some of that in; it was the hum he felt inside his head, the trance like the one he'd later get going up and down a swimming pool. "Dad never was much for philosophical questions."

"I don't know about that," she said, with the tone she used whenever Danny said anything to suggest that his father had limits—as if she possessed some special, redeeming information Danny wasn't privy to. "But that's not what I mean. I'm talking about on a very practical level. How he wanted to be buried, and where. What kind of service he wanted. He'd never discuss it—all the times I tried to pin him down. It wasn't like the idea of dying frightened him. He just wasn't interested. He didn't believe in it. Even after his heart attack."

As she was saying this, her voice grew slower and quieter, as if it were getting harder and harder to draw the words up from the well of her sorrow and wonderment. Before he could think of something comforting to say, her eyelids succumbed to their weight and her mouth dropped open.

"Mom?"

She shuddered and hoisted her lids, but they only held for a moment.

When Danny was a boisterous sixteen, he'd once picked his mother up in his arms, like a groom about to transport his bride over a threshold, and carried her out of the Manhasset Triplex (kicking but not screaming—that would have drawn even more attention) at the end of *Gone With the Wind*. To-night he pulled her up by her hands and hefted her up the stairs with his arm across her back and under her armpit, like he'd do with a drunken fraternity brother. He managed to work her up onto the bed and laid an extra quilt from the closet over her. She groaned once as he pried off her eye-glasses, then went still.

Now it was past one o'clock, Cindy's plane was due in at eight-thirty, and he still couldn't sleep. Through the window across from his bed, leaking in around his shade, he could see a glow of the same orange he saw from the brownstone on Sackett Street. He'd never realized until he was fourteen or fifteen that the orange light was only the city—Manhattan—off to the west. No one had ever explained it; he'd just assumed a trace of the sunset lasted all night, like an after-burn.

Danny found himself wishing he'd slipped one of his mother's sleeping pills for himself. Then he remembered his parents' liquor cabinet. He crept downstairs and stopped at the light switch just inside the den, but he didn't flip it. Between the streetlamp and all the outdoor fixtures the neighbors kept burning, the room was plenty light to sit in, to pour a drink. From the shapes of the bottles on the shelf he could pick out Sam's Chivas. He splashed a healthy shot into a rocks glass and mimed clinking the glass against some-body else's, his father's. When Danny was swimming, there were times Sam seemed genuinely peeved that the kid wouldn't drink with him, as if Danny's training were a caprice, an excuse to stand aloof from a little normal father-son camaraderie. But since he'd stopped, Sam jumped all over him every time he picked up a beer. *What's that? Your second, or third? You better watch out, it's going to catch up with you. It's the same with all these former athletes. The minute they hit their mid-twenties, they go straight to hell in a handbasket.*

Danny poured in another shot for good measure and screwed on the cap. He heard the noise on the stairs as he was setting the bottle back. He stiffened and listened as the steps got closer, but still, when the hand reached around the corner and felt for the light switch, he couldn't help jumping.

"Who's down here?" The question croaked out in Ida's voice and then she appeared, one hand shielding her eyes, the other clutching her housecoat. She stepped into the room without seeing Danny. He froze, thinking that if he didn't move or breathe, maybe she'd just turn back around without having noticed him. She put a hand on the wall to steady herself. "Samuel Isaac?"

Danny stared. Her eyes were open, but her lids were half lowered over them, giving her a squinting, suspicious expression. Her hair was set with twisted bits of toilet paper held in place with clips, the same way he'd seen her do it when he was a boy and had to sleep over at her and Grandpa Moe's place off Flatbush Avenue. Back then, when he asked her about it, she scowled: "You won't catch your grandmother throwing money away on none of those fancy hair curlers." Then she bent her head down and toward him, as if he would want to put a finger to the white twists.

Now she took another step in his direction, pushing her leather wedge slipper. "Answer me when I'm talking. Sam? Is that you?"

"No, Grandma. It's me. It's Danny."

She cocked her head as if she were listening for something from the next room. "Where you been?" A step closer, twisting her ruffled collar, the flesh of her upper arm swinging free from beneath the short sleeve of her housecoat. "I told you not to stay out so late. You been running with those *shiksas* again? Wait till your father lays his hands on you."

"Grandma." He said it a little bit louder, not wanting to wake anyone else but hoping to startle her.

But she was turning, scuffing back toward the stairs. "*Meshuggener.* Just get yourself up to bed. You got school yet in the morning."

14

*H*E *COULDN'T MAKE OUT* what the voices were saying but he knew they were Ida's and Esther's, even before he opened his eyes. He never got that temporary reprieve he sometimes had in the morning, when for a moment he wasn't sure where he was, what part of his life he was waking up into. He had often found himself in that hazy zone in the early months of his battle with the tendonitis: he'd catapulted himself out of bed imagining he was still on the blue streak, and only with the first shot of pain through his shoulder would he remember. It happened again on Sackett Street, maybe because the place and its morning noises were so unanchored to the rest of his life, and so he was free, as in dreams, to swim across its whole length, and come up wherever he wanted.

If he could do that now, it might be as a boy six years old, before Parkwood Pool was even a hole in the ground, long before Grandpa Moe died and Grandma Bea had her accident, years before the first heart attack, when the sun coming through the window was the sun that he and his father would walk through to Steppingstone Park, where they'd lean against the rails of the dock and look out at the sailboats, and Sam would point out the big, fancy yachts, and the smaller boats like the one he was hoping to buy. Squinting against the glare off the water, Danny follows his father's outstretched finger to Steppingstone Light, the red brick building set atop a crown of rocks halfway across the Sound to City Island. He wants to know if there's a lighthouse keeper who lives there, but his father says no, it's all automatic now. Danny doesn't like that answer, so he asks if, when they get their boat, they can sail all the way out to the lighthouse. "Well, you can't sail right to it," Sam says. "There are rocks all around it—the Stepping Stones." He sees the disappointment on Danny's face. "But that's nothing. We can sail farther than that. A lot farther."

"We can?"

Sam turns Danny's face away from the lighthouse and points him eastward. He explains that the Sound keeps going out that way, all the way to the end of Long Island, that's shaped like the tail of a fish. He says that a few peninsulas over—he's been studying the navigational chart—is another, much bigger lighthouse: Execution Light, named for the sailors who died when their ships got wrecked on the rocks the light marks now—rocks that must have been much more jagged and treacherous than the playful-sounding Stepping Stones. "We can sail all the way out *there*."

Danny shades his eyes like a pirate, peering out where his father has pointed. The idea of Execution Light both excites and frightens him; he turns from the water and runs back down the dock, across the park and up the hill toward the swing set. His father doesn't run on the dock, but once he hits the grass he comes after Danny, charging the way he never did again after his heart attack, despite what Joan said about him never learning that he had limits—running and laughing without even gasping for breath, without reaching for the little brown vial, so before Danny can get to the swing set Sam catches him. Danny hoists himself up to the regular, big kids' swing and Sam pushes, until, in the air, Danny's toes can touch the strip of land on the other side of the Sound—the horizon his father has brought so much closer.

Danny held on to the image, then shook his head clear. Had a moment like that ever existed between them, or had he just concocted it? Anyway, he had no time for that now. If he was going to meet Cindy's plane, he had to start rolling.

When he was dressed, he took a breath at the top of the stairs, where the tones of the argument traveled up to him. First it was Ida: "There's enough cars here and plenty of yous to drive. I'll even go in that Nazi car if I have to."

Then Joan: "That's just not what we're going to do today."

Again Ida: "So what do I care? I'll take the town bus. It's got to bring you somewheres near there. This head of mine don't remember so good—where did you say it was? Right up there on Northern Boulevard?"

Esther: "Mom, we're trying to explain to you. It's not a matter of how you'd get there."

When Danny walked into the kitchen, Esther stopped and they all turned around to look at him. "How she'd get where?"

Esther glared at him and threw up her hands, like he was the one making trouble.

"What did I say?"

His mother let out a sigh. "Grandma wants to go see your father at the funeral chapel."

With that, Ida jumped up. "I want to go see him, sure. Tomorrow, with the help of That One Upstairs, they're putting him into the ground. We got a day to sit here, we may as well make it good for something." She rubbed her hands together in quick little jerks, as if to keep them from shaking.

"Mother, I want you to sit down right now," Esther told her. "After the night you had, this aggravation's no good for you."

Esther had planted herself in front of her mother, putting her hands on her hips like she was in charge, but Ida was still a good head taller and stood her ground, brandishing a trembling finger. "The night I had? And whose fault is that? Who could sleep? With you in the bed there tossing and turning and pulling the covers off of me."

"Tonight I'll sleep on the couch if that will make you happy," Esther said. "Now will you please sit down? And stop rubbing your hands like that."

But Ida wasn't paying attention. "What's wrong with a mother wanting to see her son?" She swung back around to face Esther. "It isn't my fault you didn't have a son left to look at."

Esther stared a moment, as if waiting to be sure she'd heard right, then lunged at her mother. Joan dropped her coffee measure but Danny got to them first. He took hold of Esther's hands, that were flying up toward Ida's neck. "She doesn't mean it. She's just all worked up." He looked at his mother, who'd rushed to their side. "Why don't we just tell her? This isn't going to stop till we do."

Ida spun around toward Esther, then Joan. "Tell me what? What don't I know? What are yous, keeping a secret now?"

Joan was shaking her head, saying, "Nothing, Mom. Really, it's nothing," but Esther cut in.

"Okay, fine. This is the way she wants it. Have a seat, Mother, so you can listen and listen good. I'm only saying this once."

Joan stepped toward Esther. "I don't think—"

But Esther waved her quiet and turned to her mother, who'd taken a chair and was leaning into the edge of the table, her mouth open, sucking in shallow breaths.

"You can't go see Sam today at the funeral chapel because he isn't there." Esther spoke the words slowly, with an emphatic, pitiless enunciation. "According to the law they had to perform an autopsy to determine the exact cause of death. His body was on its way to the morgue from the hospital . . ."

Later, when he'd play the scene back, Danny wouldn't be sure if Ida ever even heard what Esther had said—if she wasn't already going before that. Because her expression never really changed when Esther stopped speaking, except that her mouth opened a little wider and her eyes started rolling up in her head. It was the rolling he'd remember most clearly, because it happened as if in slow motion, so he could see her consciousness wavering, deciding, then leaving her face. He got to her side just before her neck snapped back. He looked once, quickly, at Esther—her own mouth open, all color drained from her face—before he lifted his grandmother. He moved her to the center of the kitchen floor, her feet by the refrigerator, her head at the stove, where he could lay her full out and have room to kneel alongside her. He gave the order: "Call an ambulance." Then he started working.

In all Danny's years as a lifeguard, he'd never actually saved anyone. He'd taught the little kids to stick their heads in the water, and blown his whistle when he caught the older ones running across the pool deck or goofing around too much on the diving boards; he'd sat there on the lifeguard stand in his racing suit and his shades and waited for the high school and college girls, the young mothers, to come by and flirt with him. He'd never administered mouth-to-mouth in any real emergency, just on the dummies with the hinged jaws they used in the water safety class, and on Andrea Cerilli, who belonged to Parkwood but went to the Catholic high school in the next town, who lay there on the mat with her eyes closed and her lips parted as if she were waiting for him to kiss her, who slipped her tongue into his mouth when it was her turn to do him. He pushed away the thought of crazy Andrea in the back of the bus on the way home from swimming meets and spread open his grandmother's housecoat.

The skin at her collarbone was freckled with brown spots and clammy with sweat, and so fleshless, translucent, he could see the pattern of veins running green underneath it. He gave a half dozen quick pumps on the bony cage of her chest, that didn't spring back like Andrea's had but felt like it might crack beneath that slight pressure, then considered her face. He moved quickly, yet not so quickly that he didn't have a moment to feel the revulsion, like vomit, climbing his throat, to swallow down on it. He ran a finger around inside her mouth to look for what the water safety manuals called *obstructions*, and what surprised him was how dry it was, almost dusty. He pinched off her nostrils and bent to the lips, dry also, and blew the air in, but didn't move away fast enough, so the breath flooded back sour in his face. A few more pumps to the chest, and the breath again—blowing in, then watching it leak back out: just doing it, figuring he could keep it up until the ambulance came, trying not to let himself think about how she might not come back but not expecting anything either, just the rhythm of pumping and breathing, the terrible taste of her lips, Esther and his mother and then Elisa and Dave in their bathrobes hovering over him, Esther chanting under her breath, "Mother, *please.*"

He almost didn't realize what was happening when he bent to blow in the next breath and the cough spat out in his face. He sat up and wiped his sleeve across his mouth, then bent again. But now her eyelids were fluttering, and just as he'd watched her go down, he could see her floating back up toward the surface. Her eyes opened, though they were still cloudy, dull; the movement was slight, but her chest rose and then fell again under the nightgown. He closed the housecoat over it. "Thank God," Esther said. "What do we do now? Should we—"

"Shhh," Danny told her. Ida's vision was clearing, until she was looking right at him, and knew who he was. She went to move her arm, as if to lift it up to her forehead, but he touched her on the shoulder. "Stay still."

"What do you got me down on the floor for?"

"You passed out for a minute," he said. "But don't worry. Everything's fine. We've got an ambulance coming."

"Ambulance? What ambulance?" A look of panic sharpened her features. She tried to sit up but she couldn't lift herself. "I don't need no ambulance."

Danny looked up at his mother for help.

"Mom, you've got to go to the hospital. Even if they only keep you a couple of hours. They're going to have to make sure everything's all right."

"All right? So what do those doctors know from all right?" She tried to sit again, and this time succeeded. "They get you into those hospitals and they kill you. I saw what happened with Moe. Just get me up off this floor. I'll catch my death of a cold down here."

Esther opened her mouth to answer, but Danny cut her off with a wave of his hand. "Someone run upstairs and get a couple of blankets." He bent back toward Ida. "Grandma, you've got to lie down and keep still." He put one hand behind her head and the other on her shoulder, to ease her back down.

She let him, but when her head was back on the floor she looked at him with a distrustful glint in her eyes. "So you're the big boss now? You and your father. Always—two bosses."

"Look, Grandma, I saved you once. I don't want to have to save you a second time."

"Now you're saving people? What is this—one of your swimming pools?" With that she flashed a crooked smile, and looked around to see if anyone appreciated the joke.

Elisa came back with two pink blankets and Danny spread them over Ida.

"That's a good boy," she said, and winked at him. Then softly, as if only he would hear: "Don't let them put your grandma into that ambulance."

He almost wished he could help her, make them leave her right there, but in another minute the men from the rescue squad came. There were three or four of them, storming into the kitchen in big green parkas and high winter boots, talking into radios that buzzed at their hips, brandishing

135

clipboards with official release forms. When they came in with the stretcher, Ida pulled the blankets up to her chin. "Yous ain't taking me to no hospital."

"Shhh," Danny told her. "It's going to be okay." He brushed back a lock of hair that had fallen onto her forehead, stiffened with hairspray into the form her toilet paper curler had given it.

Two of the men lifted Ida onto the stretcher. Another came in with a couple of heavy green blankets, and went to peel the pink ones off her. But now she held fast. "Keep your hands off these bedclothes." She gave the man a shove with one hand and gripped the pink wool for dear life with the other. "I know those hospital blankets, that yous never wash. And scratchy—they make my skin break out."

Joan stepped in. "Let her take these. We'll get them back at the hospital."

The man shrugged, and lay the green blankets over the pink. "It's cold out there, lady." Then he had the straps run over her and fastened before she had time to protest. The transmitter coughed from his belt, and he spoke into his handset. "We're bringing her out."

"Don't let them keep me there," Ida said, straining up from the shoulders as they lifted the stretcher into the air. "They get you in there and then they don't let you go." Now they were fitting the stretcher through the doorway out to the hall. "You can't bury my Sam without me there to see it."

"Danny," his mother said. "Throw on a jacket and take your dad's car. You better follow that ambulance. By the time she gets to the hospital, she'll be carrying on something terrible."

He looked at the clock, at the rest of them standing there in their bathrobes. From the front hall, the radio spat static, and then the door closed. "I was supposed to pick Cindy up."

"Someone will get her," Joan said, pushing him toward the

back closet, and then the garage. "Hurry. And call us as soon as you know something."

Danny had only driven his father's Mercedes a couple of times in his life, and always in some kind of emergency. When he got into the seat, he checked to make sure he remembered where all the important controls were. By the time he'd backed out of the garage—slowly, in spite of the rush, because his mother stood in the doorway watching him—the ambulance was already closed up and pointing out toward the main street, the last rescue guy climbing into it. When the siren came on, Danny whipped out the driveway, and swung right behind them into the road. He stayed with them for a couple of miles, but then they took a sudden left he wasn't expecting. He just kept on toward the hospital the way he would usually go, driving as fast as the traffic allowed him, feeling the engine's hum accelerating up through the gears, knowing his father would have had a shit if he saw him driving the car this way.

By the time he got to the hospital and found a parking space, Ida had already been wheeled into Emergency, and the woman at the desk told him E.R. patients weren't allowed any visitors. "I'm not a visitor," he said. "I'm her grandson. I *came* with her. I followed the ambulance."

"That's fine," the woman said. "I'm afraid you'll have to take a seat. Mrs. Winger was very excited."

"I know she was excited. She's a total nut case. That's why I came."

The woman agreed to go check with the doctor, but returned with the word that no one would be let in to see Mrs. Winger until they had her calmed down and stabilized.

"That could take a decade," Danny said under his breath.

The woman extended her hand toward the waiting room.

It was more than an hour before they let him in to see Ida. She was still in Emergency—they didn't have any regular rooms available—but they'd pulled a plastic curtain around her bed, probably to keep her from driving everyone crazy, or worse, killing somebody. They hadn't managed to calm her down, whatever megadose of sedatives they'd pumped into her; it had probably just taken them that long to accept the fact that this, for her, represented a *stable condition*. She had a tube up her nose and was wired to the chest and both arms, but she wouldn't lie still; when the nurse drew the curtain to let Danny in, they found her twisted around in the bed, trying to look at the monitors. The nurse settled her back down, but the instant the woman left, drawing the curtain closed, Ida was straining up again. "It's about time someone came. I thought yous was going to just leave me here."

He tried to explain that he'd been in the waiting room the whole time, but she didn't stop talking or waving her hands, the wires jumping and pulling at the tape that fixed them to her wrists and inside her elbows. "You got to get me out of here. They're making me crazy already."

He glanced up at the monitors, waiting for some kind of alarm to go off. "Grandma, you have to relax."

"Now she tells me she's bringing me breakfast. I don't want no breakfast. I told her I ate breakfast home. I need them to poison me with their lousy cheese omelet now?"

"Grandma, listen." He caught one of her arms in midair, laid it back down on the blanket and held it there. "You passed out. Your heart stopped. They're not going to let you go home until they think it's safe—however much of a pain in the neck you make yourself. I'm sure you'll get out a lot faster if you behave yourself and do what they tell you."

"I'm doing what they're telling me. I'm lying here, aren't I? I'm not taking the place apart. But believe me, if your father were here, he'd never put up with this."

Of course she had to drag Sam into it. "Put up with *what*?"

"With this." Her hand flew up out of Danny's grasp. "With the way they treat you here. They can't keep a person in here against their own will. It's not legal. And then if they're making you stay, there isn't a bed they can give you?"

"Mrs. Winger, I told you, your bed, she right here." A different nurse had pushed through the curtain, carrying a breakfast tray. She was pretty, and young, and when Danny stepped aside for her he shrugged, as if to apologize for his grandmother's conduct.

"I told you I don't want no breakfast," Ida said, peering with a look of disgust into a tin of grapefruit sections. "You ever been to Maimonides?"

The girl looked back at her, not understanding.

"Mai-mo-ni-des." She pronounced it one syllable at a time. "In Brooklyn. Now there's a hospital. That's where you get the good food. Not the *chazerai* like they serve you here. And all the money they're charging you."

"Grandma, she's just bringing the tray. She doesn't cook the stuff." He tried to catch the girl's eye, but she just smiled at Ida, as if they'd been making pleasant small talk, and disappeared through the curtain.

"You're hungry? You want to try some of this *dreck*?" Ida pushed the tray toward him. "Come. Do me a favor. You eat it."

"That's okay." The omelet was the dull, rubberized yellow of airline eggs. "I'll get something back home."

"You see?" Her arms flew up again. "So you know what I mean. Your grandmother hasn't lost all her marbles yet."

She leaned over and pressed the bell for the nurse, and a blinking light went on over her head. She waited about five seconds before she pressed it again, and another five before she started jabbing it. He was about to grab her hand when the nurse came in, still another one Danny hadn't seen before. This one was older, small but stern-looking, and spoke English. "Mrs. Winger, please. We're getting to you as soon as humanly possible. Don't forget this is an Emergency Room. Believe it or not, we've got other patients here who are in much worse shape than you."

"If I'm in such good shape, then what am I doing here? While you're at it, take this tray away, would you? The smell is enough to make a person throw up."

"I'll have somebody pick it up right away," the nurse said. Then she looked at Danny. "Maybe you better leave her alone now and come with me, so she can get some rest."

"Okay. Let me just talk to her one more minute."

He waited until the woman was on the other side of the curtain, then bent over and pinned Ida's two hands to the blankets. "I mean it. Don't give them any more trouble. And keep your hands still." He bent closer, to give her a kiss on the cheek, but she turned her face toward him, and puckered her lips out. He brushed them quickly with his own, but then stopped and looked down at her: how pale her skin was beneath the brown spots, how frail and even frightened she looked when she shut her mouth for a moment. "I love you, Gram."

"Okay. I love you too. Now go on, get out of here. Before that nurse starts giving you the business also."

Danny slipped through the curtain just as the fourth nurse arrived. He could hear Ida regaling her halfway out to the exit: "See, sweetheart, I can't stay here all day. You look like a smart girl. Maybe you've got some pull with the bigshots."

Danny called his mother to give the report; she said she'd send Elisa and Dave to take his place in the waiting room. He drove back home slowly, even skirting the high school to take the long way around. When he walked in from the garage, the house was so quiet he stood for a moment wondering where everyone had gone off to. But then his mother called out, "We're in here," from the kitchen. It was just she and Esther, sitting with untouched cups of coffee in front of them. Joan's hand sat on the telephone receiver, as if she'd just hung it up, except the two of them looked like they hadn't moved or spoken for several minutes.

He scanned the kitchen for some sign of his cousin's arrival. "Where's Cindy?"

140

"Upstairs," Esther said. "She's showering. She had a terrible flight."

His mother didn't look up when she spoke. "Abrams called right after Elisa and Dave left."

Jesus, Abrams: in all the excitement over Ida, Danny had managed to forget about the hunt for his father's body. Judging by her tone, he figured it must be bad news. "They still haven't found him?"

"No. They *have* found him."

"Well, it's about time. That's great." He looked back and forth between their grim faces. "Isn't it?"

"Sure," Joan said, her expression not lightening. "Assuming it's actually him."

"What does that mean?"

Esther stood. "They've located a body they're relatively certain is your father's. But before they'll ship it out to the funeral place, they need someone from the immediate family to give them a positive identification."

He turned to his mother, but still she didn't raise her eyes to meet his. "In other words," she said, "someone has to go look at the body."

15

*D*ANNY KNEW as soon as his mother said it: the someone was going to be him. It was a kind of code that had developed over the years whenever there was an unpleasant chore to be done. *Did anybody take out the garbage? Could somebody climb down the hatch and pump out the bilge?*—and everyone would look straight at Danny. But that was okay. The trip to the Medical Examiner's would at least get him out of the house. He could drive the Mercedes. And though the circumstances weren't exactly the ones he'd have chosen, he realized he did want to see Sam. He still found it hard to believe what his mother had said, about it being only the body. And there was something else too—something he wanted to look for; it went back to a suspicion he'd had ever since his grandfather's funeral.

He didn't remember that much about the funeral itself, except how amazed he'd been to see his father cry, and how, before the service, there was a room where Grandpa Moe's coffin was open. None of the cousins, except Nathan, were allowed in to see; Danny, Elisa and Cindy were stationed on a wooden bench in the front room of the Flatbush Funeral Chapel and told not to budge. The grown-ups and Nathan stayed in with the coffin for what seemed to Danny like almost an hour. He couldn't sit still that long.

Elisa hissed out a series of warnings, then threats, but Danny ignored them and went to stand by the closed wooden doors to see if he could hear anything, if they were in there talking, saying good-bye to Moe. Danny hadn't visited his grandfather during those last weeks of his illness, but his mother had told him that by the end, Moe was terribly pale and thin, not at all like himself. That was her excuse for not letting Danny in with the grown-ups to look, even though he had wanted to. She said it was better for him to think of Moe the way he always had; not to have this other picture stuck in his head, getting in the way of his memories. But Danny knew that wasn't the real reason. He was convinced there was some mystery about death that revealed itself when you gazed into the coffin, some secret and dangerous truth that kids were protected from. Listening at the crack between the carved double doors, he'd figured he must have been right. Grandpa Moe had never been much to look at even when he was alive, but from what Danny could hear, no one was saying a word. They were just looking and looking.

The bathroom door was closed when he went upstairs, but the water was no longer running. He hesitated a moment, then knocked. "Cin? It's me."

At first there was no answer. When she did speak it was with an irritation she didn't work too hard to disguise: "You better go downstairs or something. I'll be in here another few minutes."

"I don't need the bathroom. I just want to talk to you."

Again she didn't answer, but in a minute she cracked the door open and stuck her face out. Since he'd seen her last, her face had thinned out, grown more angular, and she'd chopped off most of her hair. Even though it was still dripping wet he could see she'd colored it with something that turned the brown an unnatural burgundy. "Hi, baby cousin."

That name had always been a term of endearment, but now it seemed to carry a shade of condescension, dismissal. "You look great," he said. What he meant was that she looked different, weird.

"I feel like shit." Her mouth screwed up into a pout. "I forgot they call those flights red eyes for a good reason. This little brat in the next row kept me up the whole time. I'm just going to crash for a while."

"You're going to crash now?"

"Yeah. Elisa said I could use her bed. Why, what's the matter?"

"You just got here, that's all. And actually, I was coming up to see if you'd take a drive with me."

Now her face lit up, and he thought of all the times they'd sat in a car staring into the mouth of his or her family's open garage, scheming about trips they could take together when they got older. "Listen, I should warn you: it isn't exactly a pleasure cruise."

When Danny explained the mission that would be taking them to Manhattan, Cindy got a nauseated look on her face and rolled her eyes: *There's always got to be some catch in this family, doesn't there?* "You're not getting me into any fucking morgue," she said.

"Nobody said you had to come in with me. You can wait in the car. That way I won't have to worry about where I park. You can even sleep on the way if you want to."

Her expression wasn't softening.

"It's not like I can't go by myself. I wouldn't mind the company, that's all."

She rolled her eyes again, but then shrugged her shoulders and flipped back a wayward burgundy spike. "Okay, what the hell, I'll drive in with you. I came all this way for a funeral, right? I may as well get the full treatment."

Danny went downstairs to the kitchen to wait for her. He was standing by the refrigerator, taking a swallow of milk, when he heard Esther say, "You're not going in that." He tipped the carton down to look at his cousin. She was wearing skintight black jeans tucked into black, ankle-high lace-up boots, and what looked like an old man's gray cardigan sticking out from beneath the leather bomber jacket she'd gotten in high school.

"What's wrong with it? I've got the right color scheme, haven't I?" She stood with her hands on her hips and her feet together, so you could see how much her skinny legs bowed. "Anyway, Danny said I don't have to get out of the car."

Joan stood and said, "She'll be fine," though Danny knew she'd never let Elisa step foot out of the house like that. "They'd better get going."

While Danny strapped himself into his safety belt, Cindy settled her boots up on Sam's leather dash. He started to say something, but held himself back. He glanced at the boots and then up at her hair as he pulled out of the driveway. He'd wanted her to come with him, but now he wasn't sure what to talk about, where to begin. It suddenly struck him that here was this person he barely knew, and who barely knew him; after all, he'd been seventeen when she'd moved out to Portland. The silence was starting to weigh on him when she broke it by clicking in the cigarette lighter. He turned to look at her: she'd never smoked. But it was a joint she was holding. "You're smoking that now?"

The lighter popped out, and she sucked at the joint until it sparked. "I'm not lighting it up to save it for later."

When the first curl of smoke bloomed, he used the electric controls to lower her window.

"Oh, I forgot," she said. "We wouldn't want to stink up the Mercedes."

He didn't answer, but kept his eyes on the road; they were almost up to the Bayview Avenue speed traps. He only turned to her again when the smoke burned his nostrils. She was dangling the joint right under his nose. "Go on. Have a hit."

He waved it away from his face. He liked to drink all right, but he'd never done more than dabble in pot smoking; he'd always figured it would be bad for his wind. Paradoxically, it was precisely his swimmer's pristine, hyper-developed lungs that had won him the pool of fifty bills the spring before in his fraternity's annual Bong-a-thon, that he'd entered for the first and only time on Greg's dare. He could hold more smoke for more seconds than anyone, but he couldn't handle the effects like the more seasoned dopers; Greg wound up pocketing his winnings for safekeeping, because Danny never made it back up to his room.

Now Cindy squinted at him through the twisting veil of smoke. "I heard your jock days were over."

She heard: that was about the extent of their contact since she'd gone out west—second-hand reports from each other's mothers. He'd sent her a few cards, at birthdays or Hanukkah, but she'd never once written back. "You heard right. I just don't think this is exactly the time, that's all."

She took another hit. "Oh, but it *is* the time. That's why I brought it. I thought it would help take the edge off your errand." She flashed him her *Go on, it will be all right* smile, the one he had always succumbed to when they were kids, that she'd used to cheer him on to the edge of the waterfall at the end of their stream, to lure him into her parents' liquor cabinet.

Danny only took a few hits, but by the time he eased out onto the Cross Island Parkway he was feeling funny behind the wheel of his father's Mercedes. The traffic seemed to be zipping along much faster than usual, and the cars in the other lanes to be slicing in, like they were about to sideswipe him. Cindy didn't appear to notice anything different about his driving, though; she was looking out the window, pursing her lips on the end of the joint. Along the parkway to her right lay a jogging path, a band of marshweeds, and then Little Neck Bay, iced over now, all the boats put up for the winter. When the parkway swung west, the Throgs Neck Bridge stretched out into view, and Danny caught a quick glimpse of Steppingstone Light. "Cindy?" She was staring out her window, maybe following the spans of the bridge. "You ever see a dead person?"

"Not in real life," she said, recrossing her boots on the dashboard. "I mean—you know what I mean."

"Remember how they wouldn't let us see Grandpa Moe?"

"Yeah. And I also remember that you were the only one who wanted to."

Her tone was impatient; he kept quiet for a few minutes. Then he was merging and shifting lanes as the road bent toward La Guardia Airport. He tried to keep his eyes from sneaking across to Shea Stadium, but couldn't help thinking of the '69 Series he'd gone to with Sam. Of November Saturdays huddling under the stadium blanket, watching Joe Namath go back for the pass, praying the other team wouldn't sack him. "Did you ever wish you could have seen Nathan?"

She jerked her head toward him. "Give me a break." Her face was set as though he had slapped her. "I came along because you said you needed the company. I thought getting high would help us both to relax. But I don't intend to engage in a whole morbid exercise."

"I'm sorry if you find it morbid. It's kind of hard to avoid. I *am* going to the city morgue to identify my father's body. A couple of hits of a joint aren't going to *take the edge off* that."

"Let's just change the subject, okay? I mean, the first thing out of the baggage claim and my mother has to treat me to a detailed description of Ida passing out, and you doing mouth-to-mouth on her. That image really made my morning, let me tell you."

There was the taste of Ida's lips again, but also the feel of her skin, fragile and papery, when he'd touched her. "What your mother probably didn't tell you was that it was her fault."

"No. As a matter of fact, she said it was your fault. But she said you made up for it playing lifeguard."

"That's the biggest crock I've ever heard in my life."

"Well, if it's out of my mother, anything's possible."

"She actually said it was my fault? Jesus Christ." He slammed down the heel of his hand on the steering wheel.

"Take it easy, would you? It wasn't me that said it." She shivered and zipped her window closed. "I should have known better than to get you stoned."

"Yeah, you should have."

He smacked the wheel again, though it didn't help. She twisted back toward her window. He didn't break the silence when he turned off the parkway, following the route Sam had always taken to go to his office—the back way to the Queensboro Bridge. He didn't even say anything when he drove onto the upper roadway and, off to their left, the lower half of Manhattan rolled out like a carpet. He waited to get that sense he'd had the morning before on the Promenade only he didn't feel anything, except the ache behind his eyes from the pot and the tightness in his chest—that dread—as he turned off the bridge and headed down Second Avenue.

The Medical Examiner's Office was on First Avenue and 31st Street, along Hospital Row. That whole strip was a tow zone: AUTHORIZED MEDICAL PERSONNEL, EMERGENCY VE-HICLES ONLY. He found a space a couple of blocks west. He pulled up the parking brake before he turned to her. "This is legal. You don't have to stay in the car."

She looked out the window at the featureless, residential block. "It doesn't look like a very interesting neighborhood."

"It isn't the Village, if that's what you mean." He hadn't been proposing that she go out sightseeing. He waited a moment to see if she would catch on, but she was feeling along the side of her seat for a lever. When she found it she pressed the seat back to recline. "I think I'll snooze out while you're in there." When he opened his door and stepped out, she added, "I hope it's him."

He stuck his head back through the door. "What?"

148

"I hope it's Sam. That's what you're here to find out, right?"

He shut the door without answering and stood there a moment. Yes, that was why he was here, though he'd almost forgotten that side of it—forgotten that the body they'd wheel out or pull out to show him, however they did it, might not be his father's. And then his job would be to stand there alongside the corpse of some complete stranger, shaking his head. "No. You've got the wrong guy. That's not Samuel Winger."

Cindy knocked on the window and mouthed, "You all right?"

He nodded, put a hand up and turned away from the car. Maybe it would be okay if that happened. Maybe that should even be what he was hoping for. If the body they thought was Sam's was some other guy's, then the whole thing could be just a close scrape. Somehow, somewhere, Sam could still be alive; he could have come back to in the hospital after they'd closed the book on him. Of course it was crazy, but no more crazy than that his father would be the stiff wheeled out on a gurney. He quickened his step. The sign was flashing DON'T WALK, but he trotted across Second Avenue.

Danny's idea of a morgue came from movies, from detective shows on TV, and in translation got a little mixed up with the image of a police precinct. He pushed through the doors of the squat, thirties-style municipal building expecting to step into the drama of blue-shirted cops rushing about with radios crackling and nightsticks dangling from their belts, of greasy-suited homicide dicks pacing the floors and grinding cigarette butts with the toes of their wingtips, of hysterical women dragged in to identify husbands or lovers or sons who'd gotten on the wrong side of some dealer or two-bit hustler, shot or stabbed or shoved under moving express trains. He never figured on the silence of the large waiting room, the stony patience of the men and women who sat on benches, alone or in twos and threes, faces not so different from the ones he'd see lining subway cars to and from Brooklyn. No one even glanced up at him as he scanned the room, then spotted the gray-haired receptionist stationed at a large desk against the far wall. The woman wasn't in uniform, but wore a plastic-covered ID tag pinned above the pocket of her beige blouse. She took Danny's name and wrote it down on a list, and told him to have a seat on one of the benches. "When there's a clerk free, you'll be called to take care of the paperwork."

He found a place on a bench near the front, between a middle-aged black woman knitting a square of bright orange yarn and an older white man, who must have been a mechanic or plumber, judging by the work-soiled hands sitting limply in his lap. Danny had to wait fifteen minutes, long enough to appreciate how, quiet as the place was, it supported a steady flow of traffic: someone coming out of the doorway behind the receptionist, the next person being called up to go in; another woman with an ID tag and clipboard appearing at a door to the right and calling a name, someone standing up from a bench and advancing toward her; two or three new people walking in from the street. Some of the people rushed across the room when their names were called, while others moved like they weren't in any hurry at all, a little like sleepwalkers. Most of them left that door to the right with the same deadened expressions that they had worn in, but a few came out looking shaken, confused. One man flew out after less than a minute looking as though he'd witnessed a miracle; he scurried back toward the exit in quick little steps, checking over his shoulder every few feet and crossing himself, like he didn't trust his good fortune.

When the receptionist called Danny's name, he fell into the pattern of traffic, following the woman's finger through the doorway into a smaller room lined with filing cabinets, with a dozen gray steel office desks, a dozen men and women bent over typewriters. Danny took a seat across from the clerk who was free—a beefy-shouldered man who looked around Sam's age. His tag read Bob Vernon. "Your name, son."

"Daniel Winger."

Vernon typed it onto a form. "Legal address."

He started to say 383 Sackett Street, but instead gave his parents' address.

"Telephone."

He gave his parents' phone number also.

"Social Security number."

He stumbled over a couple of digits, but then got it right.

Vernon typed it in, then hit his carriage return several times. "I'll need to see your identification." He pushed his lips out as Danny produced his blue nylon waterproof wallet. "Got to make certain you are who you say you are."

Danny fished out his license, and handed it over the desk. Vernon looked it over and squinted back at him: brown hair, brown eyes, five feet eleven inches. Danny felt like he used to at the door of the local bar where the high school seniors hung out as the eyes of the bouncer darted between the fake license one of Danny's teammates had rigged for him and his whiskerless face. "I need to see some picture identification."

Danny blinked down toward his wallet, then back up at Vernon. He didn't have any; he'd stopped carrying around his expired student ID a couple of months ago. He opened his mouth to give Vernon an argument. They had to let him in to say the guy they had found wasn't Sam. If Danny wasn't who he said he was, what would he be doing there in the first place? But then he remembered his new staff ID from the Y. He pulled it out and shoved it over to Vernon. "Here. See? Daniel Winger."

Vernon studied the tiny photograph laminated onto the card, then looked back at Danny with a frown, like he wasn't convinced.

"It's not the world's greatest picture."

Vernon nodded gravely, but finally passed the card back, and zipped the form out of the typewriter. "Do you claim that the above information is accurate and true to the best of your knowledge?"

Danny nodded.

"Sign here."

Danny signed.

"Okay, son. You can go back to your seat now and wait till you're called."

"How long will that be?"

Vernon shrugged, putting Danny's form on a pile to one side of his desk. "Fifteen minutes?" he asked more than answered. "Half hour?"

Back in the waiting room, the seat Danny had occupied was now taken up by a couple of birdlike, frightened-looking Chinese women. He found another place two benches over, on the end, next to a Pakistani or Indian reading a newspaper in his own language. Danny scanned the columns for something recognizable, but then gave it up. For a while he monitored the waiting room's stolid human machinery, the shuffling and reshuffling of people on benches, the exits and entrances. It was like one of those movie versions of the processing centers for heaven or hell, the places where souls get assigned to new bodies, and all the applicants are doing what they've been told, waiting on line as if they have all the time in the world to wait, and they do. Danny seemed to be the only one around him who had trouble waiting. The Pakistani lowered his paper and gave him the eye, and only then did Danny realize he'd been shaking his legs, the way he used to under the dining table, until Sam would slam down his fist and swear the whole room was vibrating: *What's wrong with the kid that he can't sit still long enough to get a meal into him?*

He said sorry, and the guy disappeared again behind his paper, but a few people from the benches in front of them turned to glare. The only other sounds were the footsteps, clicking or scuffing along the worn marble floors, the hushed murmur from the receptionist's desk, and the calling of names—names for paperwork and names to go into that door to the right, which must take you to where you looked at the bodies. Name after name, but no Daniel Winger.

When he thought about it, Sam wasn't exactly one to point a finger about sitting still; he was even worse at waiting than Danny. They'd sailed from Martha's Vineyard to Nantucket in a fog so dense they couldn't see the cabin of their own boat from the cockpit, because Sam got tired of waiting for it to lift; they'd threaded rocks into dangerous harbors in the black of the night, because Sam wouldn't anchor outside and wait until morning; they'd braved thirty-knot winds with a dangling mainstay, because no one in that particular port could repair the rig the same day. Sam couldn't wait, and he didn't like to go slowly. Even if they were just out for a quiet afternoon on the Sound, he'd be clocking himself against every other boat on the same point of sail, making sure nobody gained on him. Sometimes Danny thought his father would go crazy when there was no wind—pulling in one sheet, then the other, then letting them out, even though both sails were just flapping, scanning the horizon for any boat that was moving better than they.

Danny liked to race, sure; there was nothing he'd loved more than swimming the anchor leg of the relay when his team was behind but he knew he could beat the time of the other team's anchor, and he'd stand there shouting and dancing on the block until his number-three man was close enough Danny could gamble on a big flying start. And then he wouldn't look. *Never look:* he'd even learned that from Pete and Tommy at Parkwood. Just haul it for all he was worth, seeing nothing but the black stripe and his own churning sea underwater, until he slapped the wall and heard the other slap, a split second after his. Danny had loved to race, and to win, but nothing compared to his father. In the end, Danny never forgot it was all a game, that tenuous streak of his luck.

But with Sam, you could never be sure. Like the time Sam and Joan sailed up to Bar Harbor, Maine, the summer after Danny's junior year, and he drove up the coast to spend a few days with them.

There was a stiff wind the afternoon the three of them sailed up into Somes Sound, a finger of water, like a fjord, up the middle of Mount Desert Island. They had to beat a tight zigzag between the rock cliffs that made a sheer drop into either side of the Sound; another sailboat was zigzagging in ahead of them. With each tack Sam drove closer in to the cliff before he'd shout the command: "Ready about. Hard alee," and after a couple of tacks Danny and his mother realized what he was up to. When Danny was a boy, he would have been just scared shitless: Joan shrieking, "Come about! What are you, crazy?" as the rock loomed up and sped toward them; Sam yelling back, "No. Hold your sheets. We can get ten more yards"; Danny clutching tight to the jib sheet, then whipping it off the winch when Sam gave the shout, dropping it like a snake so it wouldn't rip through his fingers when the sail slammed across the bow in that wind, Sam shouting, "Now! Let it go!" if his timing wasn't just perfect. That summer he was old enough to be scared but to be pissed off also.

It took eight or nine tacks' worth of those extra kamikaze ten yards before they cut behind the competing boat and then sliced back over in front of it. Sam waved at the other crew like anyone out for a friendly recreational sail, but when Danny asked if they couldn't ease off, now that Sam had gotten his kicks, his father said no, tighten up on that sheet. "I don't want the sons of bitches sneaking back up on us." Sam would say the other guys lost because they didn't have enough nerve, but Danny always thought it was that they got caught looking: they couldn't believe their eyes when they saw that maniac driving up to them.

Another name was called from the door to the right, and a big woman with teased yellow hair, two benches up from

him, stood. She draped a ratty fur jacket over her arm and
waddled off toward the woman who'd summoned her, a
dignified rigidity to her broad, fleshy back. Danny hopped
up himself and started to pace the aisle between benches. A
few heads turned, but he didn't care. If his father walked
into the room at that moment, Danny would tell him what
an asshole he was. He'd accuse Sam of reckless endanger-
ment. He'd take him by the shoulders and give a good shake.
What do you think you're doing, pulling this shit on us?

When Danny's name was finally called, it almost didn't
register. His hands were clenched into fists shoved deep in
his pockets, and he was pacing back almost as far as the exit
door, like if they didn't call him soon he'd pace right out onto
the street. A few seconds passed before he realized the name
was his own. Then something froze up inside him. He
turned and measured the space between where he stood and
that door. He started across the room with slow, deliberate
steps, trying to stretch out the distance. The woman repeated, "Daniel Winger," when he finally reached her. She
had stiffly sprayed, reddish brown hair and cracking lipstick
that looked almost purple against her brown skin. She
opened the door and motioned him in. "Right this way,
child."

When Danny had looked at the door from his seat,
watched the ones who were called being ushered in through
the doorway, he'd assumed it led into a corridor that took
you back to where you needed to go: that world of refriger-
ated air and long chrome tables with white plastic sheets he
imagined in the morgue's inner recesses. Now he was surprised to step through and find himself in a small cubicle,
painted the sickly green of junior high classrooms, facing a
wall of plate glass. Through the glass he could see another
bare half room, with an opening in the floor, a kind of shaft
the shape of a rectangle. There was nothing like the rows of
metal drawers in the wall that they always showed on TV.
He scanned the bare walls through the glass and on either

side of him. They would have to wheel the body in on a gurney, but there was no place for it to come through. In confusion, he turned to the woman. She had taken her clipboard and stepped to the side of the glass. Before he could ask what was happening, she was speaking into an intercom on the wall: "Ready for Samuel Winger."

He stared at her for a second, but her eyes were turned toward the glass. He followed them, in time to become aware of the sound—a dull buzzing like a motor, an elevator hum—and to see that something was coming up in the shaft. Before he'd really started to race, to pore over his splits on a stopwatch, to fight for every hundredth shaved off his best times, Danny had never realized how long a second could be. This was a couple of seconds, before the slab rose up to the top of the shaft and stopped, flush with the floor, in full view. It was about three feet by seven feet, just slightly wider and longer than the body that was laid out on it, wrapped from head to toe in what looked like white waxed paper.

If he'd realized what was coming, he could have turned away, but it was too late. The only thing not covered was the face. At first he just stared; he couldn't have said yes or no one way or the other. No hair was visible, no ears, not much of the chin. The skin was pale, almost gray, and riddled all over with broken blood vessels. But that wasn't what startled him most. It was how the face looked blown up, like it had been pumped full of air. Like someone had taken his father's face and made a balloon of it. Because, yes, he could see it now: it was Sam.

He spun around toward the woman, who was gazing down, away from the glass. "What makes him look that way?"

"How's that?"

"All blown up like that."

He watched her eyes as they traveled to the slab, then back over to his. "He's not going to look like his usual self. They've just finished the autopsy. When they work from the back of the head, the face always puffs up some."

"But why would they be going into his head? The man had a heart attack."

"They've got to check everything." She stepped back to the side of the glass, by the intercom. "You just take your time. You make sure we've got the right person."

He was sure, but he wasn't going to say so, not yet. He got his balance by holding the grabrail that he noticed now in front of the glass. "Can you leave me alone for a couple of minutes?"

She nodded, and clicked her heels to the door. "I'll be right outside. You just give a holler whenever you're ready."

He stood pressing into the rail for a minute before he knew he wasn't going to look up again, that there was no need to. He opened his mouth to say something, maybe I'm sorry, but it just came out like a gasp. *Forget the face. The face doesn't matter.* He tried to still his breathing enough that he might wait to sense something flowing toward him from his father's body. But all he could feel was the wracking of his own chest. He swung away from the glass, swallowed hard. "Okay. Come back in."

The woman shut the door behind her and walked back to the intercom. She picked up the handset and spoke, more softly than before: "We're all through."

In a moment there was that hum again, and he turned to watch the slab sinking, the face that was his father's yet wasn't, three feet down, four, then five, until it slipped out of view, back down to that other level. Then there was just the black of the empty shaft, like before. He didn't take his eyes from the glass. "Yeah. That's Samuel Winger."

16

*W*HEN DANNY GOT BACK TO THE CAR, it was idling—the heat on full blast, a jazz station screeching some crazed alto saxophone. Cindy was facing out the passenger window, her knees hugged in tight to her chest. She didn't move when he snapped off the radio, cut the fan. It was just as well she'd passed out; now he was the one who didn't want to talk, answer questions. He swung out into the street, and didn't think about where he was driving until he found himself at a red light, looking across First Avenue into the mouth of the Queens-Midtown Tunnel. He could turn up First and head back uptown to the bridge, but it made a grim sort of sense that he should go this way, under the river, through the whooshing, dim-tiled passage that had made him queasy when he was a boy, so he'd have to ask once, twice, three times were they almost to the other end yet, until Sam said, *Sit back and relax, pretend it's only a road*, but he couldn't; all he could think about was the weight pressing down on them, all those millions of gallons of river. Cindy shifted in her seat to face him when he started up through the light. He drove slowly, as if he wanted the tunnel to go on forever, as if it were a passage through the tiled underworld of the M.E.'s Office, and at the end was not daylight, weightless sky, but the dark shaft, the slab, the body that had belonged to his father.

Cindy slept until he nudged her, a mile from the house.

She woke up enough to make it inside and back upstairs to bed, but not enough to ask him how it had gone. When he walked in from the garage, his mother did not ask him either—just held his face with both hands and then took him into her arms. "I shouldn't have asked you to do that." He squeezed his eyes shut over the picture. "Someone had to go. It's okay."

"I should have gone myself."

"No, you shouldn't have."

Elisa and Dave came back from the hospital with the word that Ida was restored to peak form—regaling everyone within earshot, conscious or unconscious, with Sam stories; grilling the doctors about their medical pedigrees, then insisting she knew all the big men in Brooklyn, who'd studied at Harvard and Yale; moving without skipping a beat to broadcasting Elisa's and Dave's accomplishments ("I have only smart grandchildren") until the two of them didn't know where to look and the doctors were smiling and nodding, backing out through the curtain. For all that, the doctors planned to keep her there overnight; barring any new downturn, they'd let her out first thing in the morning, in plenty of time for the funeral.

When Elisa made this announcement, Danny surreptitiously crossed himself. It was a gesture in which he always took a secret and perverse satisfaction, maybe because of its foreign, forbidden quality, maybe because Jews didn't have any equivalent, and so he'd had to resort to all his shaking and snapping and lung-ballooning, when the guys from the other teams, the *goyisher* towns, whose jokes about the dirty kikes could sometimes be heard from across the partition between the two locker rooms, who made a big, beefy, muscular splash whether they were any good or not (*their* mothers didn't have them on skim milk and low-cal margarine)—those guys had only to stand on the block with the crucifixes dangling between their pectorals, bow their heads and perform that ritual touching of points, like the four points of the compass, the winds, to attain that aura of special protection.

Esther the masochist left in the rental car to take up her post at the hospital, and Joan wrote out a note for Cindy, in case she woke to find everyone gone: they were driving to Crestwood Funeral Chapel, to meet with Abrams, to confer on *details*. Danny tried his best to get out of going. He told his mother he was tired, he'd trust them. But she said no, she wanted everything right, they had to all do it together. She came downstairs with her hair combed and her makeup on, in a fancy sweater and matching corduroy jeans, and wouldn't let Danny or his sister or even Dave drive. She seemed almost awake again, directed, now that the waiting was over and there was something to do, as if the mix-up with the body was already ancient history.

Crestwood was just up Northern Boulevard from the gold, pink and turquoise edifice of Leonard's, the local Bar Mitzvah mill, where Danny had spent half his Saturdays in junior high, eating stuffed derma and Chicken Kiev and dancing the fox-trot—first as a legitimate guest, and then, in ninth grade, as a crasher: floating from reception to reception in that palace of receptions too big for a couple of extra guys to draw much attention, posing as long-lost Cousin Jeff or Peter's old buddy from summer camp (the name of the Bar Mitzvah boy was conveniently posted on an easel outside each reception room), staying just long enough at each one to get a handful of hors d'oeuvres and sometimes even a cocktail, to find a partner for a slow dance and inhale a whiff of perfume from behind a jeweled earlobe, feel a brush of stocking against suitpant, a light crush of bosom through satin or taffeta.

In its way, Crestwood was the Leonard's of funeral parlors. Danny had never been inside the place, but he'd driven by countless times, so the stucco facade with its quartet of fake marble columns was one more part of the neighborhood landscape familiar enough you didn't even bother to scoff at it. The large entrance foyer carried forward the same crassly executed pretensions, with its forest green and gold patterned carpeting, that looked like a plusher version of what his friends' parents laid down in their basement rec rooms; the molded concrete urns guarding either side of the heavy oak doors with their clumsy medievalesque hardware; the pedestal fountain, that might have even been real black marble, spouting its pitiful trickle of water. Maybe they turned up the juice for the actual funerals.

A short man who turned out to be Abrams appeared through a door to the left of the fountain. He wasn't exactly obese but carried his solid, considerable bulk like a suit of armor, and walked with his thick little hand already outstretched. "Mrs. Winger. Children. My most heartfelt sympathy in this time of your loss. I know how anxious you've all been to get the ball rolling. Let me take you right back to our showroom."

Behind the fountain was a second pair of oak double doors that must have led into the chapel itself. Abrams ushered them through a single door to the right and back along a corridor carpeted in the same green and gold, into a spacious parlor lit by crystal chandeliers and lined in burgundy Ultrasuede. It looked like a glitzy furniture showroom, only instead of sofas and cocktail tables there were caskets, elevated on Ultrasuede-covered pedestals. Danny had to admit the dark red set off the woods—brilliant cherry, black walnut, clear maple, all polished until they reflected like mirrors, not a smudge or fingerprint anywhere: Sam would approve—rather nicely, so you almost started to look at the caskets as pieces of furniture, fine cabinets, divorced from their purpose.

Danny slipped away from the others and wandered the aisles. Some of the caskets were heavy, ornately carved affairs with multi-tiered moldings, designed to carry conspicuous consumption into the grave. But there were others with simple, clean lines that were actually beautiful, that Danny caught himself thinking Sam would have liked, might have chosen. He sneaked a look around to see that no one was watching, then ran a finger along one knife-sharp edge, across the silk finish. That particular model was closed but others were open to show off their linings: pleated or tufted or tucked in varying degrees of gaudiness or simplicity, in satin or velvet or, in the low-budget version, a thin velveteen.

Elisa and Dave were standing off to one side—Elisa was crying again, and Dave was servicing her with a handkerchief—but Joan was in the middle, two aisles over from Danny, her back to him, stopped in front of an open box with an unfussy lining in a rich-looking velvet of a middle, boy's blue, not ostentatiously bright but still cherry, nautical. When he came up alongside her, she didn't turn her head, but kept staring into the velvet interior. "I don't want red. That was never his color."

"No. This one's right," he said, and pictured his father lying there, how sharp he'd look against that shade of blue, as if his eyes would be open. The wood was right also—darker than the one he had touched, rich-grained; he guessed a mahogany. The handles were sturdy, plain antiqued brass, that looked like they could have come off an old captain's chest. He walked around to the other side, facing his mother, to see the lid. Even Sam would have to admire the workmanship.

Danny himself was a passable carpenter. The summer after his junior year he'd built a pair of bookcases for his room at the frat house; that fall, while he was still at home, he'd made a chest with a couple of shelves and a drawer to put next to his bed—he was using it now on Sackett Street. They'd come out all right—good enough that people didn't guess right away he had built them—but he knew they'd have come out better if he'd let Sam help. Sam would never have made the stuff out of pine; he wouldn't have just recessed the nails and used wood putty, he'd have drilled holes and set plugs; he would have probably dovetailed the drawer,

162

which certainly wouldn't jam whenever you tried to open it. But Danny had insisted on doing the projects himself, and making his own mistakes if it came to that. Just to make sure, he'd only worked when Sam wasn't there—which wasn't too hard to arrange. The last place he'd wanted to be was down at the workbench with his father breathing over him, picking apart his design, taking the tools right out of his hands to show him how something ought to be done—*Don't worry, I'll give it right back, just look a minute and learn something*—the job as good as finished before Danny got hold of the hammer or plane again: all those evenings and week-ends when he was a boy down in the basement at his father's command, even when there wasn't really anything for Danny to do except stand around and watch and listen and now and then hand something over.

Sam is building a stereo cabinet, and has to drill a hole into an expensive piece of molding, a delicate strip of wood that could easily split if the drilling is not done just so. He makes his pencil mark with that precise, almost imperceptible flick of his wrist. The strip is too fragile for the vise grip, and he asks Danny to put a hand on either side of the pencil mark, to press down hard until he tells him, not to let the thing move. Sam's goggles and hairline are sprinkled with saw-dust. "Understand?"

No, Danny wants to tell him. *I don't understand. I'm an idiot.* He just nods.

"So what are you waiting for?"

Danny presses down two fingers on either side of the pencil mark, willing them rigid.

"You'll never hold it like that. Get your hand on there. Put your body into it."

Danny adjusts his grip and his stance, pushes down and closes his eyes. He hears the drill slice the air before he feels the vibration. His eyes are squeezed tight now, he wishes he could cover his ears, the bit of the drill is his father boring into him. He redoubles his grip—its force is the press of his hatred—but it isn't enough, or it's too much: beneath the rasp of the drill he can't hear the squeak of the wood as it slips, but can feel it, just before he feels the crack, the split opening. His eyes are open, the drill rearing up in his face.

"Son of a bitch."

"I didn't move it, I swear. It just broke." He steps back, as if his father might slap him, might come after him with the drill. He imagines his mother, upstairs puttering in the kitchen, or off somewhere reading a book. His mother, who cried out whenever his father raised his hand to Danny: "Not that face. Please, anywhere but that face." Who sometimes even put her body between them.

Now his mother was stepping back from the blue-lined casket, looking at Danny. "I don't care what Ida says about a shroud. I want him dressed in his tux. The new one. With the fancy cummerbund I got him at Bloomingdale's."

"In his tux?" He peered into the mahogany, but the picture that filled it was Sam on the slab, rising up as if from some netherworld; Sam in his waxed paper mummy's wrap, with that ruined face.

"I know it sounds crazy, since I don't believe in any of this stuff. But I want him looking his best when people see him."

"*See him?* You mean— The casket isn't going to be *open*, is it?"

"Why? You mean for everyone to file past? No. It'll be opened just for the family, for a few minutes, privately."

He looked down at his feet, to block out both her face and his view of the casket. He'd almost gotten carried away with the fantasy, the showroom illusion: velvet the color of twilight over Long Island Sound, impeccably crafted mahogany. "I don't think we can do that."

"Sure we can. That much is allowed. That's how it was done for Grandpa Moe, you remember?"

"Yes, I remember. But that's not what I mean. I'm not talking about Jewish observances."

164

"Oh." She cracked a little, grimacing smile. "You mean, the way he looked when you saw him."

He nodded, holding her gaze, hoping she'd understand without his having to go into details.

But she shook her head in a tiny, dismissive motion. "Don't worry about that. That's what these people are here for. They have their ways of fixing things up."

"But even if—"

"Shh." She patted his hand. "That's one thing we don't have to be concerned about. Haven't you ever heard Grandpa Irv tell that story about the funeral for Grandma's friend Ruthie? How Ruthie had never looked that good on a single day of her life? How all the women got together and drafted Ruth's cousin Jean to ask the mortician where he bought his foundation?"

Joan summoned Elisa and Dave to approve the selection of the blue-lined mahogany. Once they'd admired the velvet, Danny eased the lid shut, so they could consider that view. He didn't like the feeling of shutting it, the finality, and the others must have sensed it too; they all stood there not speaking, staring at the box which suddenly wasn't a box any longer, wasn't a piece of furniture they were pricing. Once again, or for the first time, it was really a coffin, and not just any coffin but Sam's: the vessel that would carry his body to its ultimate port. The silence was only broken when Abrams stepped back into the showroom, having left them alone for what he must have deemed the respectful interval. "I see you've zeroed in on one of our handsomer models."

Abrams showed them back up front, then through the door where he'd first emerged, and into his private office. He installed himself behind a vast walnut desk that gleamed like a casket, and motioned for them to take seats across from him. There were a number of forms to fill out and decisions to cover: what kind of flower arrangements, and where they should be placed; precisely who should be directed to the room where the family would gather and the casket would be on display; how many limousines should be sent to the house in the morning; whether cards with directions to the cemetery should be available in the chapel foyer. There was a painstaking debate about the wording of the obituary Abrams would call in to the *Times*: whether Sam should be listed as *faithful husband, loving son and dutiful father*, or *loving husband, devoted father and dutiful son*, or some less orthodox variation on the accepted adjectives (*neglectful husband, argumentative son, alternately absent and tyrannical father*), and in what order, because Ida might have another attack if being her son wasn't the first of Sam's attributes.

After a certain point, Danny tuned out the words, until it was just Abrams' solicitous drone; his mother's voice pitched up to sound businesslike, in control, the way she talked with repairmen or on the phone to people from credit card companies; the occasional counterpoint of Elisa's nasal vibrato. There was no way even the fanciest Great Neck mortician could bring back Sam's face from the state in which Danny had seen it, could make it presentable. He thought of his mother's reason for keeping him from Moe's open coffin, how that deathly image would get in the way of the picture he should preserve in his memory. He tested himself with the dueling mental pictures he had now of Sam, willing his mind to flip back and forth between the face on the slab and the face of his living father, like flipping back and forth between two slides on a screen. He complicated the game with slides from different eras: Sam of the hospital bed and the tubes; the beaming, tuxedoed Sam of the Bar Mitzvah album; Sam at the tiller with a sandy, week's growth of beard; snoring away on the living room floor; on the slab again.

Next he played the game with pictures of himself, as if he were another person he was trying to find or define, a series of different persons: the reigning champion of the refrigerator snapshot, the newspaper clippings; the Bar Mitzvah boy with that sickish curl of his lips, when the photographer told him to smile and he didn't feel like it; the chubby little boy made chubbier by the orange life vest, screwing his eyes up into the sun, the light exploding around him off the cockpit's white fiberglass. All the times that boy had wished himself dead, and now he worked to picture that also: the ski jacket he wore the day he dove into the Sound lapping around a pair of arms that had given up treading water.

"Hello? Earth to Danny."

Elisa. "Yeah?" They were all looking at him, even Abrams. "You ask me something?"

His sister gave a magisterial roll of her eyes; no amount of puffiness would render them incapable of that gesture. "We asked if you'd given any thought to delivering a eulogy." Her tone was impatient, as if this was a subject he'd been assigned to consider and his time was up.

"Elisa and I decided we'd each like to deliver one. We talked about it this morning, when you were off at the hospital with your grandmother." Joan's tone was gentler, as though they'd been doing something they shouldn't have behind Danny's back. "Dave said he'd like to deliver a third, if you didn't feel up to it."

"We figured four would be a bit much," Elisa said, not looking at him but at Dave.

"Of course, you've got first dibs," Dave said, with his square-jawed, man-to-man Harvard expression, the kind of look you beam the guy you've just beaten while pumping his hand.

"Maybe Danny needs some time to think it over," his mother said.

"But, Mom, it's tomorrow morning. Dave needs the time to prepare."

Danny imagined his brother-in-law with a legal pad, preparing as if for a law school examination, a court brief;

imagined Dave at the pulpit giving his speech, while Danny himself sat like a dolt in the pew in his grown-up Bar Mitzvah suit. "No, he doesn't. I'll deliver the eulogy."

When Danny said that, he only knew he didn't want Dave usurping his place; he hadn't begun to imagine what he might actually say up there. But when they got home from Crestwood, and his mother and Elisa retreated into their rooms to work on their drafts, Danny got himself a pad from Sam's cache in the study and shut himself up in his bedroom. He set himself up at his old corner desk and studied the calm yellow sea, the blank pad, as if something might rise up to ripple its surface.

He could see the afternoon fading fast out his windows but he felt the kind of paralysis he'd gotten in high school facing the night's pile of homework, the clean slate of his social studies essay or book report, and the words didn't come, only numbers: the leading times, complete with splits and down to hundredths of seconds, of every decent free-styler in the county, the state, the eastern division, parading before him in precise columns, like rows of swimmers lined up for their heats (Grandma Ida had said more than once that with the head for figures he showed in his swimming, he should grow up to be an accountant like Moe), until his mother came in to check on him. He'd tell her he had it, how he needed to bring down his first and third splits to make it into the finals. She'd say that's great, but what about *The Sun Also Rises*? Isn't that what your paper's about? I want that page filled before your father walks in here for dinner.

Danny would get the paper done, even if it meant sitting up long after he should have on a night before practice—he needed to keep his grades up to have even a prayer of swimming for one of the Ivies—but he rarely got As. His mother said his problem lay with logic and organization, but what he'd written always made perfect sense to him. He wished the schoolwork could be like his swimming, where he could see plainly what lay in front of him, the guy he needed to

168

catch; where it was all in the numbers. His father said he should look at some of Elisa's old papers (they were saved in accordion files in her closet, year by year, subject by subject, as if they were sacred documents), but those weren't any use; they sounded too much like Elisa. Danny got by with his Bs (what slipped down to B minuses or Cs when he finally got to his Ivy League college) but he always felt like he was missing something, some trick of the game, a secret code that the better students had learned while he was running splits in his head for his hundred-yard freestyle.

Now Danny listened to the silence of the house, but underneath it he could imagine the fluid scratching of his mother's and sister's pens as they glided over the pages. No doubt Elisa was painting Sam as a model father, an inspiration to excellence. And it wasn't hard to envision what his mother would write. She'd stand up at the pulpit and tell everyone how much she'd loved Sam, what a wonderful husband he'd been, how exciting he'd made every day of her life—as if she hadn't spent half of it sitting up waiting; as if she hadn't flung dishes, slammed doors; as if, the night she broke the wedding china, when Danny was supposed to be fast asleep, he hadn't stood at their door and heard that tone of sober menace he scarcely recognized: *I'll take you at your word just this once. But if you ever so much as give me a reason to suspect again, I swear to God I'm divorcing you.*

Again Danny studied the blank yellow pad, and in the upper right corner drew a doodle of a stopwatch. He penned a lightning bolt across it, as if the glass over the watch face were cracked. If he was going to be honest, without schmaltz or idealization, what would *he* say? He could talk about the fraternity paddle, or all the nights he got sent up to his room, so often over the years it began to seem like the only time he could breathe was when his father was gone. But no one wanted to hear that shit. The eulogy a son made for his father wasn't supposed to be an exercise in self-pity, or a complaint. And anyway, those things alone didn't get at the truth of it, any more than the family's store of seagoing legends, or Ida's old ditties, or the romantic version Joan was bound to portray. The truth, like the stories, was slippery. What difference did it make now that at least once, on every day of his life that Danny could remember, he had hated his father? He wanted him back alive. He didn't want him to be that body wrapped in waxed paper.

17

BY THE TIME his mother called him for dinner, Danny had drawn some more doodles and printed his father's name a few times but hadn't written anything. Joan and Elisa had each finished drafts of their eulogies before they'd gone down to set out the food, another smorgasbord of stuff sent in from the local caterers and delicatessens. No doubt, as they'd worked, they had also talked about Danny, how Elisa didn't think he was up to this, because when his sister asked him over dinner how it was going, and he said it was coming along, don't worry, he had the whole evening, she shot Joan and then Dave an unmistakable *I told you so* glare.

"Anyway, what's it to you?" He sounded as irritatingly casual as he could, pitching his fork into a pile of cole slaw. "You weren't counting on having the chance to edit it or anything, were you?"

"That's not the point," she said, her nostrils fanning out in their trademark, self-righteous flare. But Joan pronounced her name once, in that tone that brooked no further discussion.

Now Elisa was sulking, and Danny took some pleasure in that; he glanced over at Cindy, who was busy munching out on a combination of vegetarian eggrolls and potato knishes, to see if he couldn't rekindle some of their ancient, anti-Elisa-and-Nathan alliance. And yet, a part of him wished the whole thing hadn't turned into such a big issue. Wished he could just say forget it, he hadn't come up with anything; Dave should go ahead, take his place. But it was too late for that. He'd have to sit at his desk all night if that's what it took to put something together.

The minute dinner was over, everything got whisked away: the rabbi was due to make his appearance at eight, and Joan wanted the place respectable. At quarter to, she ran upstairs to comb her hair and freshen her makeup, and asked Danny if he didn't have a nice sweater he could put on. He didn't, but he said he'd look, and when she went back downstairs to brew some coffee, he sneaked into her closet and borrowed one of Sam's cashmere V-necks.

Danny's father had never been a big fan of Rabbi Rosenbaum. After his childhood in Brooklyn's Conservative shuls, he never felt quite at home in the Reform temple, with its two High Holiday shifts, its Louise Nevelson altar that looked like pieces of dismembered bodies; with so little Hebrew used in the services. Still, it wasn't so bad in the early years, under the steady hand of old Rabbi Herzberg, whose English didn't sound quite like English anyway, who had an air of Brooklyn and, beyond that, of Eastern Europe, about him. But when Herzberg retired, they brought in a young replacement fresh out of the seminary, from California of all places. Sam and Joan and their friends immediately took to calling him the Boy Wonder, even though he was only a year or two younger than Sam. Rabbis were supposed to be gray-haired elders, not of this world, almost biblical creatures, like the Talmudic scholars Ida insisted had distinguished her family for generations, men who devoted their lives to study and prayer, who you wouldn't run into at the indoor tennis courts or shopping for shirts at the Abraham & Strauss men's counter. But the Boy Wonder did play tennis—three times a week—and he did shop for shirts. In fact, he was quite the sharp dresser. Underneath his robes you could see collars that were light blue or yellow or, God forbid, *striped*, and one Rosh Hashanah he even showed up in a pink one.

Danny didn't see why that should offend Sam, since he was surrounded by a congregation whose principal incentive to prayer seemed to be showing off their mink coats and diamond jewelry and haute couture evening wear. But he could see how the sermons got to his father. Rabbi Rosenbaum talked about the Vietnam War, the *moral scourge* of Watergate, the senseless destruction of the environment; he advanced the radical view that Palestinians were also human beings who, one day, sooner or later, would have to be afforded a piece of God's earth; he talked about the sex and drugs that were *rocking the lives of our young people*. After services, most of the congregants would stand around nodding their heads, saying, "He gives an interesting sermon," or, "He's provocative, you have to admire him for that." But Sam didn't have to admire him, or pretend that he did. He'd come right out and say for anyone within earshot that the sermon had been another one of the Boy Wonder's stinkers: where did he come off mixing himself up in politics, trying to tell them what they ought to think? And he'd only get more irate—even threaten to stop paying his dues—when Joan would remind him, "That's what a rabbi is for, sweetheart."

Danny usually thought the sermons were pretty cool, as long as he was able to keep them tuned in, and more than anything he appreciated the way they steamed up his father. He liked the fact that Rosenbaum was a bit of a jock, and decent-looking enough to figure in local cocktail party gossip as some kind of ladies' man. He just never understood why Rosenbaum never liked *him*, why he seemed to assume that Danny was wising off whenever he asked him a question. Danny himself would have been the first to admit he was no Hebrew scholar. How many hundreds of times had he gone over the *Haftorah* portion for his Bar Mitzvah, and still he blew it on those last couple of lines. They wouldn't have wanted him in the new Hebrew High School even if he had signed up along with Elisa. And he wouldn't have been caught dead at a function of the Temple Youth Group. But none of that meant he wasn't sincere in his spiritual grapplings. Okay, so he could have phrased it to come off as less insolent, but he really *had* wanted to know what kind of a jerk would gamble his whole existence on something you could never *prove*. Rosenbaum could have answered him; he didn't need to boot him out of the class, and make him spend a month of Sundays in the religious school principal's office. The question wasn't so off the wall, as Danny was pleased to discover years later, in Introduction to Western Philosophy; it had driven whole schools of thought as recently as the nineteenth century.

Cindy said she'd pass on *the clergy* if nobody minded, and headed upstairs with a book. But everyone else was assembled in the living room when the doorbell rang at precisely five after eight. Rosenbaum wore a dark suit and tie and a white shirt with only a super-fine pinstripe, as if he'd known Sam's views and deferred to them for the occasion. He nodded gravely and gave a smile that looked more like a grimace when Joan introduced him to Esther. He unbuttoned his suit jacket before he sat down, and said, "Only if it's no trouble," to Joan's offer of coffee and rugelach. It struck Danny that he looked very tired and, up close like this, no longer so terribly boyish: a bona fide rabbinical gray had filled in at his temples, and he was pale (he would have been better in a pink shirt), like he hadn't gotten his usual couple of weeks in the Caribbean after Hanukkah.

For a long moment he didn't speak, but glanced from face to face, as if he were looking for some inspiration. Finally he inched the cup and saucer away from the table's edge and refolded his hands in his lap. "When I think of all the years we've known one another, all the joyous occasions and milestones we've shared"—the words were stiff, ceremonial, but it was his natural, real-man's voice, not the rabbinical voice he used at the pulpit during his sermons—"it's hard to imagine we'd be sitting here like this . . . I've been remembering your Bar and Bas Mitzvahs, your confirmations, the wedding, what, just a couple of years ago . . ."

Joan nodded. "Two years this June."

The rabbi looked at Elisa, then Dave. "I remember he was very proud that night."

Elisa looked down at her lap as if she might burst into tears. Very proud and very relieved, Danny thought, but didn't say anything.

"I have to tell you that I've presided over a lot of funerals since I came to Beth Israel, but this one strikes especially close to home for me."

Danny studied the rabbi's face, the furrow etching itself between his dark eyebrows. There was no way to tell if he really meant that or if it was part of his spiel, what he said to all of his grieving congregants. When he started to talk about how Sam's death brought up thoughts of his own mortality, Danny drifted off like he inevitably did during a Rosenbaum sermon. Only now he wasn't daydreaming about swimming times or girls. He was thinking about the eulogy, remembering back to when he'd had to write his Bar Mitzvah speech.

It wasn't bad enough he had to perform the reading of the *Torah* and *Haftorah* portions for that particular Saturday morning in June, and make the blessings before and after each passage; to stay late after Hebrew School two afternoons a week all winter and spring for practice and coaching sessions with old Cantor Leibovitz, who shouted his Yiddish insults right into your ears, and rapped you on the skull with his gold, imported-from-the-Holy-Land pointer when you were especially thick-witted. He also had to compose and memorize and deliver an original speech on the subject of his entry into Jewish manhood—Rabbi Rosenbaum's innovation.

Danny had already sat through enough Bar Mitzvah services to know that all the speeches sounded the same; you'd practically think the rabbi himself had written them. The opening was always something along the lines of, "Today, I am a man," which even to Danny's twelve-year-old ears had sounded ridiculous in those breaking, just-barely-thirteen-year-old voices. Every kid went on to say how much his religious education had meant to him in preparing to take his place as a Jew; every kid thanked his parents and brothers and sisters and grandparents, and whatever other friends and relatives he could throw in; they all said something to the effect of how, though they were finished with the arduous program of study that had brought them to this momentous occasion, it wasn't an ending but a beginning: all the same bullshit.

Leading up to the Thursday when Danny was scheduled to present a draft of his speech to Cantor Leibovitz, he spent hours imagining different, outrageous things he could say. In his head, he concocted a kind of Rabbi Rosenbaum–style, agitational sermon about how the *real* purpose of a Bar Mitzvah was to give your parents a high-sounding excuse to blow several thou on a party; how all the momentarily pious Bar Mitzvah boys were blessing the *Haftorah* all the way to the bank, because what was on their minds wasn't the community or the People of Israel but how much their total haul in checks would be, and if it would beat their friends' haul from last weekend; and how, if it wasn't that, it was whether the girl they had the hots for would let them go to second the next night in the service parking lot out behind Leonard's, because everybody knew that even the most stalwart of Great Neck princesses had a soft spot for Bar Mitzvah boys—it must have been all that talk about manhood.

Of course, thinking all that, picturing himself up at the pulpit reciting it, was just a way of putting off writing the actual speech. He could never say that stuff, his parents would kill him, and anyway he wanted the party, the checks, as much as the next kid. Coming down to the wire, he actually had a vision of a serious speech that wasn't meant to offend people but to say something he wanted to say, something about what being a Jew really meant to him: how he wasn't nuts about Hebrew School and had a hard time sitting in temple, but how sometimes, in the smaller, original chapel where they still held Friday night services, he could shut off all the hormones and let himself just go still inside. And then, when he looked up at the stained glass windows, the ark, he'd feel some kind of spirit swelling inside him, some kind of love—maybe even God, how did he know?

When he finally sat down to write, he couldn't exactly put that into words he would actually stand up and say. He no longer remembered the specific act of composing the speech, but he'd done it, and learned it by heart, and that Saturday morning he'd gotten up and delivered it, not looking at anyone. He didn't say, "I am a man," but he did use the words *manhood* and *entrance into the community;* he thanked Sam and Joan, and even Elisa, and the rabbi and Cantor Leibovitz and the whole congregation to boot. And what difference did it make, he only stumbled over a couple of words, everybody *kvelled* about what a fine speech it was, his mother cried and his father shook his hand, pumped it hard, and it was over, over. And no one but Danny himself would ever think of it as a betrayal.

Tonight, in the living room, he snapped back to attention when Joan picked up her legal pad and started going over the family's concerns. She told the rabbi that she and Elisa and Danny would be delivering eulogies, in that order. She asked that the service at the graveside itself be kept to a minimum, and confirmed that she'd purchased a family plot at Knollside Memorial in eastern Brooklyn. She also asked that the rabbi recite a brief prayer at the grave of Sam's father, Morris Winger, who was just two rows over—she'd give him the Hebrew name in the morning, once she'd gotten it from her mother-in-law. "Which brings me to the next issue."

"Yes." The rabbi nodded his head, still with that solemn expression. "I remember Mrs. Winger."

Esther barely suppressed a guffaw; the couple of glasses of wine she'd drunk with dinner, and her mother's absence, had put her in a much better mood. "I don't imagine anyone's ever forgotten her."

Rosenbaum allowed his face to brighten a shade. "An outspoken woman."

Emboldened by the momentarily lighter tone, Danny said, "That's one way of putting it."

But his mother was in no mood for clowning, even about Ida; she shot him a quick, sober glance before she continued. "The woman is difficult under the best of circumstances, but right now she's beside herself, and there's no telling what kind of shape she'll be in by the morning. Just be prepared for the fact that whatever you do—however lovely it is, which I'm sure it will be—she'll find something to make a fuss about. So be polite with her, humor her as far as you can, but understand that no matter what she says, it isn't your fault, or your problem."

"If it's anyone's fault, it may as well be mine—always is." Esther's words were slurred, but not enough that the rabbi would notice. "Anything she doesn't like, just tell her I put you up to it."

Rosenbaum cracked a wooden smile, like he wasn't sure if she was kidding or not. "We'll do our best to keep Mrs. Winger satisfied."

Fat chance, Danny thought, but kept the crack to himself this time. "Does that cover all your concerns?" The rabbi looked first to Joan, who nodded and squared the legal pad on her lap. Like a good student, Elisa nodded in turn, as if she'd received a complicated set of instructions and understood them completely. Then his eyes lighted briefly on Danny, who could already see the rabbi letting himself think of the short drive home to Great Neck Estates, his wife and maybe a shoulder rub waiting, the fact that Sam Winger might have dropped suddenly and tragically dead but he, Richard Rosenbaum, was alive.

Danny cleared his throat. "I've just got one question."

"Okay. Shoot." Rosenbaum was trying to look imperturbable, *Sure-my-son-that's-what-I'm-here-for,* but Danny could see his cheek muscles twitch.

"Do Jews believe in an afterlife?"

He looked at Danny and blinked, surprised; who knew what the hell he'd expected. He even took a sip of coffee to stall. "That's a good question. I assume that at this point you want the short answer."

Danny shrugged. "Whatever answer you've got." He widened his gaze to show he hadn't meant to sound disrespectful.

"You see, Daniel, the problem is that different rabbis and scholars have touched on the question in different ways in their writings over the years. And there are some parts of the Jewish tradition with well-developed discussions and speculations about life after death. But what's most interesting is actually how little the subject comes up in Reform Judaism today, especially when you compare it with other religions. The idea of an afterlife has never been a focus of Reform Jewish thought. We've always been more oriented toward *behavior,* toward this world and this life, and doing the best we can with that. Which is not to say that there aren't mainstream Jews who, in one way or another, believe in some kind of ongoing spiritual life, even if it's only through the living memory of our loved ones. And of course that's important in Jewish teaching—honoring the departed through memory, saying the Kaddish."

Danny thought of all the years when he was a boy, those eight long days between the New Year and the Day of Atonement, when he racked his brain to come up with every white lie he'd told, every punch he'd thrown, every nickel he'd fished from the lining of his mother's pocketbook, so he'd have time to feel badly enough that God would take notice and inscribe him for another year in The Book of Life, which he took quite literally as an enormous ledger, like

Grandpa Moe's accounting books. He supposed that in some childish way he'd imagined a companion volume, a Book of Death or of Spirits, where the souls of the departed good would be registered. "So it never says anywhere that the soul doesn't die—you know, with the body?" He didn't look at his mother or sister, just at the rabbi. "Eternal life and all that?"

"Well, the liturgy speaks of God as 'implanting within us eternal life.' Whether you choose to take that literally is up to you. For most of us, I think it's more of an idea, a yearning toward God. But that's the thing about Judaism—there's no centralized spiritual authority that says, 'You must believe *this* or *that*.' And this is one of those elements of the faith that's left more or less up to the individual."

"Pretty vague religion," Danny said.

Rosenbaum slapped his hands on his knees, as if in self-congratulation, and stood. "That's one of the reasons it's lasted four thousand years, I guess."

18

*B*ACK UPSTAIRS IN HIS ROOM, Danny was disappointed to find the blank yellow pad still awaiting him, as if, while he was downstairs with the rabbi, his corner might have been the site of a miraculous visitation—the angel of undisciplined students, of ambivalent sons, descending through the dark to his desk to bestow upon him the perfect eulogy. It was strange, this new preoccupation with spirits he'd developed since the news of Sam's death. Angels weren't the sort of thing he'd given much thought to since the tendonitis, when his own guardian spirit deserted him. And they weren't the sort of thing that had much connection with Sam. What use did the self-made man have for angels? And what was the sense of bothering over an afterlife, when you had the hubris to think that your own, earthly life would go on forever?

Hubris: the word had always been linked, in Danny's mind, with his father, from the first time he heard it in Mrs. Goldfarb's tenth-grade English class in the unit on Greek mythology. The association had earned him the only A he ever wrung out of old "Goldfart." It was on a surprise in-class essay test, which Goldfart was famous for: *Use a contemporary event to illustrate the concept of hubris.* Almost everyone else in the class ranted on about Nixon and Watergate but Danny wrote about Sam, the time they'd sailed through The Race and Plum Gut while Sam tried to barbecue.

At the end of Long Island, where the Sound met the Atlantic Ocean, and the waters with their different currents and tides came together, sailors were confronted by a pair of obstacles, like some twin perils from out of *The Odyssey*. First came The Race, where the water swept in or out in swift, tall waves that were nothing like what they had in the Sound, or what you'd find in the ocean for that matter either; you could see them running ahead of you from quite a distance (Elisa was nearsighted like Joan, so Danny always served as the lookout) and wanted them moving in your direction. Once you got through The Race, if you planned to cut over to Montauk, there was Plum Gut to cross. You could spot that from a distance too, but it wasn't anything as surreal and beautiful as the waves of The Race skimming like some invading, alien sea across the surface of the regular water. Plum Gut was chaos, all roil and chop and slap, perpetual Small Craft Warnings. To get through safely in a boat the size of the Wingers', you had to plot and time your passage precisely. So on the sailing trip, after dinner, when the kids were tucked into their bunks and Sam sat out in the cockpit reviving his Eagle Scout skill of spotting the constellations, Joan would hunch over the charts and current tables by the cabin reading light.

It so happened the day of their crossing they were running behind schedule; while Joan had planned to enter The Race by late afternoon, it was almost dinnertime before Danny called back from the bowsprit that he spotted the waves in the distance. Sam had picked up two fat sirloin steaks that morning when they'd gone ashore, and saw no reason not to proceed to barbecue. He had a miniature sailboat hibachi that fit on the narrow piece of stern deck, just outside the guardrail. Joan said absolutely not, you've got to be out of your mind, but when had that ever stopped him? The coals were glowing nicely by the time they entered The Race, and you would have thought from Sam's grin that he'd scheduled it that way on purpose, and perfectly: any idiot with a chart and a current table *got through*, but how many did it while grilling a sirloin?

They were running before the wind, the waves were at their stern, picking them up and soaring them, so Sam decided to throw on the steaks. Joan started screaming and hollering: *You're going to set the boat on fire! I married an imbecile!* The steaks started sizzling, they smelled great in the middle of all that salt air, and Danny was laughing along with his father—*Come on, Ma, don't be such a chicken*—until the first slam of Plum Gut sprayed up cold in his face.

The boat started pitching port to starboard, the bow reared up and crunched down hard on the waves, and Danny could see his father's eyes darting from the water to the sails to the grill, which was bucking and sliding. "Take the tiller," he called out to Joan, and reached for his barbecue mitts. "I'm going to bring the grill down into the cockpit."

"Over my dead body. You want to burn us all up for two lousy steaks?" She had to really shout now over the crash of the water.

"That's some of the best-looking sirloin I've ever seen. And it wasn't cheap."

"I don't give a damn."

Just then, the boat jerked to starboard, almost pulling the tiller out of Sam's hand. He'd been standing, bracing his feet on either side of the cockpit, but now he fell back, just in time to reach across and grab the sliding hibachi.

"That's it," Joan shrieked, stumbling toward him. "Give me that tiller. It's going. Every last piece of it."

There was no arguing with her, just as after a certain point there was no arguing with the force of the Gut. Danny thought his father was going to throw the grill itself overboard, but he grabbed the steaks and flung them out one right after the other, like a desperate offering to an offended god, then lifted the grate in one hand and tossed the burning charcoals out after them. Looking over the stern, Danny could see the patch where they'd been swallowed up,

183

belching a puff of smoke or steam amidst all the sea spray. And it really was like an offering: the gods were appeased; within what seemed like a matter of moments the slamming stopped, and they were out of the worst of it. Suddenly they could look back and see the whole of Plum Gut as if it were hatched in on a chart, how small it was really, and then Sam let Joan have it. "I had to listen to you. Another five minutes and those steaks would have been charred but bloody in the middle, just like you like them. I should have sent someone down for a plate. We could have saved the damn meat at least, and built a new fire to finish it." Sam would never admit that he himself had been scared, that it wasn't just his *hysterical wife*, though Danny liked to think he had seen the fear in his father's eyes, at least for that moment.

Danny was wondering if he could somehow work the story up for the eulogy when the knock sounded. He quickly covered over the pad so they wouldn't see he didn't have anything written yet. But it wasn't his mother and sister coming to check on him. It was Cindy. "Sure, come on in. I could stand a bit of break."

She stepped up behind him. "Working hard on the eulogy?"

He pushed the pile of magazines that was hiding the pad toward the window. "I'm trying to."

"So what are you going to say? I sure as hell wouldn't want to get up there. But then again, standing half naked in front of hundreds of people prepares you for this kind of thing, right?"

He watched as she picked up a paperweight with his college seal, turned it over in her hand like it was some peculiar tribal artifact, then set it back on the desk. She had always made fun of swimming, ever since he'd started to win, as if she'd felt more at home with him when he was a loser. "How about we change the subject?"

"Okay. What should we change it to?"

He pushed his chair back so he could prop his feet up on the desk. "How about you. Your life out there."

"*Out there?* I love that. That's just how my mother says it. Like the place doesn't have a name. Or like that poster—you leave New York and step off the edge of the known world."

"I'm sorry. I didn't mean it like that. Your life in Portland, okay? I don't give a shit where it is. Your life, period."

"So you want to know what I'm doing."

"Sure."

"I'm waiting on tables."

There was a bullying defiance in her tone that dared him to disapprove. He wasn't going to fall into that trap. It wasn't as if this were *Sam* she was talking to. He nodded neutrally. "What kind of restaurant?"

"Actually, it's kind of a dive." She was sitting up on the desk now, dangling her legs. "Nothing nouvelle or anything. Pretty blue-collar. But they get great bands on weekends, and the tips aren't bad. It's right near my apartment."

"Sounds cool," he said.

"It's okay." She pulled at her jeans. "Me and the bartender are lovers. Well, kind of lovers."

He nodded again. He didn't know if he wanted to get into the details. As far back as junior high school, when Danny was still just trying to get inside a girl's bra, sex had been like drugs for Cindy: something to try in all its variants, something to use to get back at the world. "So, you're working at this restaurant. Are you into something else on the side? Everyone who waits tables in New York is actually something else, you know. An actor, a writer, some kind of part-time student . . ."

She hopped off the desk. "So waiting on tables isn't enough, I guess. It's just what you do to get by while you groom yourself for something worthwhile and respectable."

"Did I say that?"

"No, but you must have been thinking it. Otherwise why

185

would you ask? Anyway, don't you know it's *your* family that succeeds in life? Everyone in *my* family is a failure. Or they fly out a window first, just in case they might have succeeded."

"Jesus." He swung his legs to the floor. "Talk about being morbid."

She put her hands on her hips and stood over him. "Isn't it true, though?"

"Well, what about me? What's so different about what I'm doing? Okay, I went to college—to swim. And I got into this great school because of my freestyle times. But look at me now. Working at the YMCA pool, hanging out. I'm not exactly tearing up the greater metropolitan area."

"But for you it's only temporary. Failure is like a game you've been playing, to get back at Sam."

"What the hell makes you say that?"

She shook her head. "Give me a break, okay? It's so obvious. I'll be generous: I'll give you a couple of years. You'll take your Ivy League diploma and get into law school or business school, something Uncle Sam would approve of."

He stood up himself now. "Bullshit."

"Yeah, right. Just you watch. You won't be able to help yourself."

"So I guess that's why you never answered my cards. God forbid you might be caught corresponding with some *Future Lawyer of America.*"

"Come on. You sent me a couple of postcards. Big deal. I didn't realize I'd incurred some huge obligation. I just didn't get around to answering, that's all."

"Right. Like you never got around to answering your mother. Or Ida. I'm glad to be in such distinguished company." He turned away from her, toward his reflection in the window. "I wasn't just some other relative hounding you. I thought we were friends."

"We were friends. I mean, we are."

186

"Yeah. I noticed."

"Look, I'm sorry. Maybe I did throw you in with the rest of the family. I think you can understand why I wanted to get as far away from all of them as I could. Anyway, about this other thing: it's not like I'm insulting you. I'm just saying, you'll do something. You'll make something of yourself. And that's right for you. Nobody who went at that whole swimming thing like you did—"

He spun back around to face her. "The swimming was different."

"You think it was. Because it was something separate from Uncle Sam. But it was just your way of showing him."

"I wasn't showing him shit. I was just doing this thing I could do. I was showing *myself*, okay?"

"What's the difference?"

That stopped him a moment. "The difference is—look, just forget it, okay? I don't need this right now. I'm supposed to be writing a eulogy. Maybe we can continue this discussion some other time. Like in another five years, on your *next* visit."

"Jesus, I don't believe you. You're really pissed that I moved out west."

"I don't give a flying fuck where you moved. I just want to get through this night, okay? I just want to get through this funeral."

When Cindy left, she didn't shut the door all the way, so Danny walked over to slam it. As he did, a twinge shot up into his bum shoulder. But then, as suddenly as it had come, it was gone. The pain, like his speed, was a phantom. And so was that sense of himself, his *blue streak*—as if none of it had ever been part of him. It made him think of all the biographies he read when he was a boy, how it had always bothered him that the famous man's childhood, even his early adulthood, was usually dispensed with in a brief summary, a chapter at most, as if all those years that to Danny were his whole existence so far scarcely counted, were just a kind of holding period, a prelude to the real life. Much as he liked the stories, the parts when the real action started, it had made him wonder: Weren't all the elements of the great man's early years, however apparently unrelated, a crucial part of what he'd become? Or was childhood in fact the kind of blank, the mistake the books were suggesting, where you were just waiting for your real destiny to kick in, to catch up with you? If Cindy was right, and in five years he'd be a law clerk, a stockbroker, would all the years of his swimming—his victories and defeats, his exhilaration and pain—be swallowed up as if they'd never existed? Would the skin of his life heal over them like old scars, until he hardly noticed them?

By the time Danny went back downstairs to find his mother, to tell her he had no eulogy to deliver, she had already retired with her sleeping pill. Elisa and Dave were up in Elisa's room, and though Danny saw a light coming from under her door, he didn't bother to knock. He didn't want to tell *them*. It would have to wait until morning. He thought he would be too riled to sleep, but when he lay down it all hit him. The next thing he knew, daylight was flooding in through his windows—he'd never pulled down the shades—and he was shaking himself free of the dream, like you'd swim up through a pool and shake off the water.

In the dream, Danny's shoulder was killing him. Not the way it had at the beginning, when he'd only lose a few tenths of a second on his hundred and could manage the pain, but the way it had at the end, senior year, when he'd leave the pool in the middle of workout, pretending he just had to go take a whiz, and crouch down in the toilet stall where no one could see him, breathing hard and pressing his fingers into the shoulder, as if causing himself pain from without could cancel what was coming from inside. In the dream it was hurting like that, and it was the day of some big meet, like the Easterns. Danny went to find Coach Lowery, to tell him he had to scratch Danny out of his heats. There was a long, dimly lit hallway that Danny had never seen before, with little offices like catacombs down its length. When Danny finally found the one that was supposed to belong to Coach Lowery, the person sitting at the desk was the woman from the Medical Examiner's Office. She motioned Danny to a seat, as if she'd been expecting him. "We can scratch you, if that's what you really want. But there are a lot of people coming to see you swim today."

His shoulder started burning hotter. "Like what people?"

"I don't know," she said. "Let's see who we've got."

Just then Danny noticed the glass wall behind the desk where she sat and the small, rectangular pool on the other side of it, just big enough for a single swimmer to float in. She picked up the handset of her telephone and Danny was seized with a panic. "That's okay," he said. The pain in his shoulder was suddenly gone but he thought he was going to be ill. "Please. I'll take your word for it. You don't have to call anyone."

Now, awake, Danny checked his clock: seven-thirty. The limousine wasn't scheduled to get them until nine. He couldn't scratch himself from this race, and he knew what he needed to do to get ready. He shook out his arms and legs to loosen them, and went to his sister's door. "Elisa? You up?"

"Yeah. Come in." She was at her old desk with the princess telephone, already dressed in a black wool suit and white blouse, copying over what must have been her eulogy with large, precise letters.

"Listen, I know this is going to sound strange. But you've got to do me a favor."

"What's that?"

"You have to help me shave down."

"What?"

"You heard me."

She looked down at her paper, then back up at him. "In case you hadn't noticed, this is no time for pranks."

"Yeah, I've noticed. I'm serious."

"You're out of your mind."

"Listen, cool out for a minute. If I could explain it to you, I would. It's just something I have to do. Please, for once, be a pal. I'll never ask you another favor as long as I live."

He could see she was thinking it over, her eyes darting between his face and the door, as if he were asking her to do something that could get her in trouble. "But it takes forever. We'll tie up the bathroom, and everyone's got to get ready."

"Is Mom up yet?"

"Yeah. She's already gone to the hospital to get Ida. She wanted to have plenty of time to deal with all the red tape. Dave went with her."

"Okay. You go tell Esther and Cindy to use Mom's bathroom if they need one right away, and then meet me in ours. I'll go in and get started."

Shaving down wasn't ever something he'd rushed; it was part of the whole, drawn-out, exacting process of getting psyched up, rife with superstition and ritual, where no one could talk to him, and he'd always listen to certain songs, and all he'd eat for breakfast was one of the individual filet mignons Joan stocked in the freezer for Sam, since the doctor told her those had less fat and cholesterol than Sam's usual sirloin. He didn't go through all that for every meet, just the big ones, and he only shaved down at the end of the season—for the Counties and States, and the Eastern Divisionals, when he made it that far.

The first couple of years he'd done it, Elisa had still been home and she'd helped him. Joan put her up to it; she said she couldn't bring herself to mutilate her own son. It didn't make Elisa squeamish, only impatient, since she had to submit to Danny's rules, and to silence, though afterward she liked to go on about how disgusting it was. Danny had an answer for that. If it was so disgusting, then how come she shaved her own legs and, worse than that, armpits—the one part of his body not covered by his racing suit that he *didn't* shave. And he'd always throw in the threat: if he ever made it to the Nationals, he was going to shave his head too, and then she'd really have something disgusting to look at. He never did get around to shaving his head, but every March from ninth grade on he'd shaved the rest of his body, even before he had all that much hair. He could get his legs, his arms, his stomach and chest by himself; he mostly needed help with his back and shoulders, and touching up the backs of his thighs. After Elisa left for school, he'd had to enlist a teammate; in college he'd gotten his girlfriend or, in a pinch, Greg. Every spring he wore long shirts and pants until well into June to cover the stubble, and itched like a sonofabitch. But it was all worth it for that moment he entered the water, and every follicle, every pore of his skin, was open and shocked completely alive, every surface and plane of his body charged with the new electricity. It was like a reenactment of that first freestyle race—sneaking up on himself, shocking himself into becoming a different person.

He'd forgotten how much the electric razor pulled at the hair on his calves, but he didn't stop. By the time Elisa stepped into the bathroom, he'd finished both legs. She didn't say anything, as if, because they were shaving him down, she was bound to observe his old code of silence. She sat at the side of the tub until he'd gotten his arms, and held the buzzing razor out to her. He had a lot more hair on his back than the last time she'd done this—all of a sudden the past year or so he seemed to be getting hairy like Sam; it pinched like mad when she started running the razor over the back of his shoulder. If only she wasn't moving so quickly, it might not have hurt as much, but he didn't tell her that. She must have just sensed it from the way his muscles jerked and tightened at the razor's touch, because she slowed down then, and even placed her free hand on his shoulder. She kept the hand on him as she shaved in stripes down his back, more carefully than she ever had when they were in high school, as if somehow she understood that it really did matter now. He was glad that she was behind him, that he didn't have to see her face, but just feel her touch, the fingers pressing into his skin alongside the burning pull of the razor.

In the end, for all the time she took, it wasn't a spectacular job—definitely not championship caliber. The light in the bathroom wasn't so great—a couple of the bulbs needed changing—and Danny's shaver head had gone a bit dull. But it was good enough for his purposes. Good enough so that when they were all done, when he'd thanked her and she'd slipped wordlessly out of the bathroom, the shower water stung his open pores like the Jesus. Good enough that when he pulled on his suit pants and the shirt his mother had pressed for him, he felt the strange, naked tingling over every inch of his skin, and knew there was no backing out of this.

19

THE LIMOUSINE WAS WAITING outside the house at ten minutes to nine, but it took another twenty minutes to get everyone organized—Ida sending three different people to different parts of the house to find the same hairbrush or prayerbook or purse because she was under strict instructions to run around as little as possible (those *meshuggeh* doctors, what did they know? knock on wood, there wasn't anything wrong with her, not that they were smart enough to find anyway); Esther circling round and round Ida on her throne in the den, "Mother, can I get you something to drink?" "Mother, do you need an extra handkerchief?" as if, on this morning she was to bury her son, Ida might wake up to the fact that God had given her a daughter also; Cindy oversleeping and then taking ten years in the bathroom applying eye makeup; Elisa standing in the living room as if at a pulpit reading her eulogy, silently but moving her lips as she went; Joan running back and forth across the kitchen pulling out platters and baskets and serving spoons (two of her friends were coming over straight from the service at Crestwood to set up a buffet), every minute or so calling out, "Two more minutes," dispatching Dave to the driver to say please hold on, we're just about ready.

Danny floated among them, helping to straighten the back of his grandmother's collar, grabbing a pitcher from a shelf that was out of his mother's reach, not speaking any more than he needed to just to avoid seeming strange. In the inside pocket of his suit jacket he'd put three folded legal pages so he'd have something to walk up to the pulpit with. His mind wasn't scrambling for what he would say when he got there; his mind had gone still. With his resolve to shave down, something had gone calm and sealed over inside him, so all the pictures and stories and battling truths, the Plum Gut of what he felt about his father, himself, was now like the even, pale blue of an empty swimming pool, waiting, shimmering in its skin of light, not to be shattered until the gun goes off.

There was only comfortably room for six in the back of the limousine; Danny volunteered to sit up front with the driver. Through the plexiglass divider he could hear his mother telling everyone they looked beautiful (handsome for Dave); hear Esther say she wished Cindy wouldn't wear that mauve eyeliner, it made her look like a ghoul, and Cindy answer, "It happens to be the style, Ma. I don't *manufacture* it"; vaguely make out Ida muttering to herself, to the doctors, to That One Up There. The rest of them just let her talk; no one dared to try and break in, or to answer her.

When they pulled in at Crestwood, the parking lot was already filling with cars, and inside, the foyer and the chapel itself were buzzing with people—some that Danny recognized, many he didn't, in the moment it took for Abrams to appear and whisk them off through a door to the left, down a hallway they hadn't seen yesterday, and into the private room, where Bea and Irv, Henrietta and Aaron, Buddy and Barbara and their two girls (Danny's other cousins, the "babies," still in high school) were waiting. Danny greeted everyone, then pulled aside to catch his breath. It was then that he noticed the alcove at the far end of the room, just big enough for the mahogany box on the platform draped in blue velvet. They'd made the right choice: the wood glowed—it must have been polished one last time that morning—and the lines of the box were graceful, dignified. He looked around for Ida, who had noticed the coffin too;

she was stooped over, dangling a handkerchief from one trembling hand, stepping shakily and slowly but definitely *toward it*. He didn't rush out to stop her, he just watched her go, wondering in his immobilized dread what she would do when she got to it.

The doctors had told Joan that Ida was in delicate shape; the sight of the coffin up close like that or, worse yet, the sight of it open, might well prove too much for her. But just before she reached the alcove, from either side of her, Esther and Henrietta sped up, grabbed her by her elbows and wheeled her around and away, with such coordination and efficiency they could only have planned the action ahead of time. While Esther sat her mother down on a chair facing away from the alcove, Joan pulled Henrietta aside. From where he stood, Danny could only make out some of the whispering, but he gathered they were plotting to get Ida out of the room when Abrams came to open the coffin.

The door kept popping open but it wasn't Abrams yet, only some friend or client or twice-removed relative the ushers hadn't succeeded in heading off, and who made a quick, embarrassed apology before ducking out again. Three sides of the room were lined with chairs, and Joan took one along the inside wall, halfway between the alcove and Ida. Danny sat next to her, and she reached out to straighten his tie. "Things got so crazy this morning with Ida and everything, we never had a chance to discuss your eulogy."

He patted his jacket pocket; the folded papers crackled reassuringly. "I guess it'll have to be a surprise."

"You know your father loved you very much," she said, taking his hand.

He felt his fingers ball up into a fist beneath her touch. "He sure had a weird way of showing it."

His mother looked like she had an answer for that, but just then the door opened again, and this time it was Abrams,

195

short of breath and flushed but looking pleased. He spotted Joan and came over. "We've got a full house out there."

"Maybe we ought to get started then," she said, though she didn't stand up.

"Whenever you're ready."

The signal went out to Esther and Henrietta, and Ida was surrounded, led from the room—actually less led than supported: she really did look weak, and glazed over, like she didn't quite know what was happening. There had only been a spotty, quiet murmur of conversation, but now a deeper hush fell as Abrams walked toward the casket. "For anyone who would be more comfortable, we have a second family waiting room, just one door down on the left."

Try as he might to hold it at bay, Danny flashed now on the image of Sam at the morgue. He leaned over so he could whisper into his mother's ear. "You're sure you want to be going ahead with this?"

"Shhh." She straightened the jacket of her black velvet suit. "It's going to make some people feel better."

Even after Abrams left the room, nobody moved right away, and at first Danny thought no one was going to look. But then Buddy and Barbara and the two girls walked over, and stood there for a long moment, all holding hands. When they turned to walk back, tears streaked both the girls' faces, Barbara was dabbing at her mascara, and Buddy looked humbled, like he might have peered into a mirror of his own death, but none of them seemed shocked, or sick to their stomachs. Bea and Irv went next, and stayed longer, but when they came back across the room they just looked tired and old with their parchment suntans; you couldn't tell if they had really seen anything. Danny didn't know why it surprised him to see Elisa and Dave step up, arm in arm like some old couple too but their backs straighter. After a minute Dave stepped back but Elisa stood there still looking, like she always did at the museums they got dragged to growing up, planting herself forever in front of one painting as if there were levels and levels of what you could see and she had access to more of them than Danny did.

He was starting to think she wasn't ever going to budge when the door was opened and quickly shut a couple of times, and from the other side the usher's voice rang out, tense. "I'm sorry, sir. This is private. You'll have to go around front." Danny couldn't make out what the other person was saying, but somebody was rattling the door. The usher again, more desperate: "No, you can't go in there. That's for the immediate family only." And then the other voice exploded. "For Christ's sake, would you get the hell out of my way? I'm his brother-in-law. How's *that* for immediate?"

By the time the door busted open, everyone was turning that way. Uncle George stumbled in with the look of someone late for a party but relieved he hasn't missed it entirely. Before anyone else could recover enough to open their mouths, Cindy stepped out from where she'd been standing. "Jesus, Dad."

George sidestepped her with a pained smile. Then his eyes lighted on Danny's mother. He cracked his mouth sideways like he was chomping on a cigar, his old Groucho Marx imitation. "How do you like that? I knew I'd find the place sooner or later. I heard we were having a funeral." He lurched about the room for a minute, nodding at the relatives as if it hadn't been years since he'd seen them, as if he hadn't been effectively excommunicated from the family. Then he spun around to the alcove, where Elisa was already backing away.

Danny felt his mother's grip on his arm. "We've got to do something. We've got to get him out of here before Esther and Ida—"

Danny stood. "I'll take care of it."

It wasn't hard to take George by the arm so it seemed like Danny was just there to help, being friendly. What was hard was getting him turned around toward the door. Especially because as Danny was trying he caught a glimpse of his father against the blue velvet backdrop, in the tuxedo as Joan had insisted, and maybe he wasn't seeing straight, maybe it was just that it was only a flash, but Sam looked all right—the house, the temple of Sam, whatever was lying there; looked a little pasty but remarkably almost himself again, an exceptional likeness, so Danny couldn't help staring back as he led George out, and barely saw all the people as he pushed through the hall, George saying, I'm sorry, and, I didn't mean to get your mother upset, and Danny dazed, shaking his head: No. Really. We're all glad you came. We just need to find you a seat, that's all.

There was a knot of people at the double doors; between and over their heads, Danny could see that the chapel itself was much bigger than what he had pictured, and packed like Abrams had said. It could take ten minutes to drag George through there and find him an empty place in a pew. "Listen, Uncle George, I'm just going to leave you here, okay? One of the ushers will help you."

George nodded. "Sure. Don't worry about me." He started forward like he was about to hug Danny, but checked himself. "Listen, kid, I'm sort of in a jam about this. Do you think anybody would mind if I came back to the house afterward?"

Danny glanced back over his shoulder through the crowd, to the hallway that led to the family room. He worked to hold his ground against the current pushing toward the chapel.

"Just to see everyone. Pay my respects. All those years in a family don't just get wiped out like that, do they?"

"Look, Uncle George, don't ask me." They were pressed close together now. "I really don't know what to tell you."

George clapped a hand on his shoulder. "Okay, kid. Forget I said anything."

Danny's back was wedged against the oak door; it seemed like any second George would be pushed or fall over on top of him. "Listen, I'm sorry, but I've got to get back." He fished down into the pocket of his suit pants. "Here. Take this." He held out one of the handkerchiefs his mother had given him before they went out to the limousine. "It was my father's."

George stared down at the pressed linen, the monogram, like it was some holy relic. He probably made too much of thanking Danny but he couldn't hear, he was pushing back through the crowd, the cheeks red from the cold, the chilled furs and camel's hair overcoats, trying not to shove anyone, just get through. When he got to the room marked PRIVATE, the door was partway open, and Abrams reached out for his arm. "Good. Here you are. Your mother's waiting for you at the end of the line. We're ready to lead the family into the chapel."

Danny blew past Abrams and into the room. There had to be time still. He had to get another look in the coffin, a real look, to see if the miracle, if that face . . . But the platform in the alcove was empty, Esther and Henrietta and Ida were back, and everyone was lined up in twos and threes like a grade school class, like his Confirmation processional. He stared at the alcove a moment, then fell in next to his mother. "I didn't think I was out there for *that* long."

"I thought we better not wait anymore." She motioned with her chin toward the front of the line. "Your grandmother's going downhill fast."

She was right. Danny realized that was what he was hearing in the background: Ida weeping and moaning and muttering incoherently, with Henrietta and Aaron standing on either side of her, holding her up. He stared again into the alcove, and tried to conjure the vision he had seen on the way out with George, the impossible restoration.

His mother must have caught him looking, because she touched his arm. "I know you didn't get the time you needed. It's just that Esther came back in and said that if we didn't get started . . ."

Danny might have gotten angry if his mother hadn't sounded so helpless—as helpless as she'd always been to get Danny what he needed from Sam. Danny hadn't gotten the time that he needed when his father was alive. Wasn't it only fitting that Sam should be snatched away now, in death, also? And he *was* dead—no less definitively than the disfigured creature Danny had seen in the morgue. What difference did it make what he'd been fixed up to look like?

Danny was saved from answering his mother by Abrams, who barked out a sharp little cough at the door. "Okay, folks. We're going to move now."

Danny sucked in and let out a deep breath, though his lungs weren't feeling very elastic. He breathed again, even deeper, and tried to pretend it was just like that moment in the locker room where the team was lined up, ready to make its entrance onto the pool deck. With Ida up at the head, their progress down the hallway was slow, and even before they got to the special side door Danny could hear the tones of the chapel organ. When Abrams opened the door, the organ swelled to meet them; Danny and his mother stepped into the music. They were coming in from the left at the front of the chapel, between the raised stage with the organ and pulpit and vases full of white flowers—gladiolus, yes, he remembered his mother requesting those in the meeting with Abrams—and the first row of pews, reserved for the family. They crossed the center aisle to fill in the nearest couple of places in the right pew. Now the coffin came into view, center stage but set back a way, camouflaged by the tall flower stalks. Danny swiveled away from it to look behind him at the row after row of full pews, and the people standing three deep along the back wall—more than he could size up at a glance, even though he was good at estimating a crowd: the sports reporters used to ask him for figures to print in the college newspaper.

Abrams closed the door they had come through, and then a movement on the right caught Danny's eye; stepping through a door that gave out onto the stage was Rabbi Rosenbaum in black robe and yarmulke. From his jacket pocket Danny slipped out the blue satin scullcap he'd brought from home, that he'd found in Sam's keepsake drawer. As he was setting it on his head, Rabbi Rosenbaum completed his measured processional up to the pulpit. The organist looked over his shoulder, played a few more of the mournful, trembling chords, then brought his hymn to an abrupt halt, the way the end of the music in temple had always sounded to Danny, like there was only one song—continuous, everlasting—that the organist was tapping into, and it was strictly arbitrary where he started or stopped. Rosenbaum lifted his head with his eyes closed, as if in deep meditation, as if he were ordaining the silence that fell over the chapel as the organ reverb faded away. His eyes were still closed when he started intoning in Hebrew, from memory, and Danny shut his own eyes too. Couldn't it just be some Friday night in the Beth-Israel chapel, or—better yet—in Ida and Moe's Flatbush shul, where everything got read in Hebrew, and so the words never mattered, not to Danny anyway, only the lulling, repetitive music, the pendulum sway of all those bodies *dovening*, keeping time, that made him drift outside himself, or deeper inside, to the seat of some ancestral memory that somehow knew, beyond language, what all the words meant, knew that prayer was not the words but that state of being hypnotized.

Without missing a beat, Rosenbaum slid from Hebrew to English, and Danny opened his eyes like it was a summons. *The Lord is my shepherd, I shall not want.* How to look at the rabbi without seeing the polished mahogany catching the light at the edge of his vision? *He maketh me to lie down in green pastures; He leadeth me beside the still waters.* To listen not to the words themselves but only to that deeper music. *He restoreth my soul; He guideth me in straight paths for His name's sake.* Danny sat up straighter against the back of the pew, and didn't shut his eyes again, but bowed his head. *Yea, though I walk through the valley of the shadow of death I will fear no evil, for Thou art with me; Thy rod and Thy staff, they comfort me.* He couldn't help himself; he pictured a broad, dim valley like something out of *The Lord of the Rings,* some barren tract beyond the bounds of known earth that the hero has to traverse to accomplish his journey. *Thou preparest a table before me in the presence of mine enemies; Thou hast anointed my head with oil, my cup runneth over.* He had to give it to the Boy Wonder, he read the stuff well. Or was it the words themselves that made the rabbi something other and more than he was, other and more than the man who'd spoken last night in their living room? *Surely goodness and mercy shall follow me all the days of my life, and I shall dwell in the house of the Lord forever.*

In the pause after Rosenbaum finished the psalm, Danny became aware of his mother sifting through her purse for a tissue, of Elisa sniffling, and his grandmother across the aisle, the thin, reedy thread of her weeping. He didn't have to turn around to sense the rows of people stretched out behind him, all their barely audible shiftings and snifflings. He tried to sense some presence of his father amidst all of that, some vibration or emanation, only there was none. But what did that mean? If you walk through the valley of the shadow, if you dwell in the house forever and ever . . .

Lord! what is man that Thou takest knowledge of him; or the son of man, that Thou makest account of him! Man is like unto vanity; his days are as a shadow that passeth away. In the morning he flourisheth, and groweth up; in the evening he is cut down, and withereth. Maybe Rosenbaum had just been trying to let him down easy, all that bullshit about believing whatever you want. Maybe he felt nothing because there was nothing, just a body like his mother had told him, and he was as stupid as everyone else who had looked. No, he was even stupider. Because he'd been to the Medical Examiner's Office, to the room with the corpse-sized shaft in the floor. He was supposed to have learned something. And still he was snowed by the poetry, by the makeup and tux. Didn't his father say it to him when he was a kid? Say it with the paddle in his hand, glinting in the light like the coffin wood: *I can't punish you for what you don't know, but only a fool doesn't learn from experience.*

Out of the depths we call unto Thee, O God, our Heavenly Father. In Thy hands are the souls of all the living and the spirits of all flesh.

It must have been that word, *flesh*, the way Rosenbaum lingered over it, because right then Danny saw the face on the slab in the morgue, saw it like the glass wall wasn't there, like it was plain as day right in front of him, and he felt like he had as a kid on the beach in Nantucket the summer they sailed there: he'd never seen waves so big, and he stood rooted, knee-deep, mouth open, watching one come, and just never moved, so he got slammed full force in the face and chest with that immense wall of water. What slammed him now wasn't grief, it was the impact of his father's betrayal. The rabbi hadn't tricked him, and neither had Abrams. Not even death itself had. He had been tricked by his father. The body was all that you had. And his father had behaved all those years like his body was indestructible.

Danny's eyes came back into focus when he realized the chapel was silent again, and Rosenbaum had just said something about the life of all life. The rabbi stood there a moment, then closed his book. He nodded down toward the pew where Danny sat with his mother and sister. Joan must have squeezed Elisa's hand first, because she squeezed his, then slid her pocketbook onto the pew and stood up with her sheaf of papers. But Danny never really heard her eulogy, or his sister's. He put his elbows on his knees and his head down, almost between his legs, the way he did on the bench on the swimming pool deck. He ran his hands up and down his calves so he could feel, through his suit pants, the shaved skin. He started to hyperventilate. *Twenty-five years of growth and adventure, the best partner and friend I could ever have hoped for,* but no: it was only the splash of kicking, the pock of hands knifing in, only the mixture of steam and chlorine that was stinging his nostrils.

He was dimly aware of his mother sitting back down, of Elisa blurring through his field of vision, of the tremulous voice in which she started speaking. Filling his mouth like a sour saliva was that old taste of fear; he swallowed down hard against it. He'd never been the kind of competitor who choked in a race; in his most important wins, the pressure, the crowds, the daunting odds had made him rise above himself. Now he couldn't think about the fact that he was once again swimming the backstroke—that he was going in blind. He'd have to trust himself to know what to do when he hit the water.

When Elisa sat down, Danny rose. Walking to the front of the chapel, climbing the few small steps to the stage, it was like he was alone, the way he'd always felt when he rose from the bench and strode, with his back to his team, to the starting blocks, because at that moment he *wasn't* part of a team, he was just one swimmer, and all the shouting, the cheers, the sounding again and again of his name, was just like the roar of the surf when you were facing the ocean. He took the sheets of paper from his jacket, laid them down on the slanted top of the lectern, and ran his hands back and forth a few times to smooth them. He gripped the lectern's sides as if gripping the edge of a starting block. Only then did he look up, to see his mother's and sister's faces turned up to his, waiting, and behind them the sea of faces all the way to the wall. It was a good thing he had the pulpit to steady him. He felt himself reel; a wave of something like nausea washed over him. He looked back down until the streaks of blue bleeding across his paper were lines again.

Most of you probably know that I didn't get along particularly well with my father. It wasn't easy being his son. And I guess I didn't do such a great job of it: the last time I saw him he was threatening to cut me out of his will. He paused and shook his head, as if to say, *Can you believe that one?* and heard a few chortles from the crowd—people who knew Sam well enough to see the humor, or thought they did.

He wouldn't let his eyes get pulled down to that first pew. When you dive, you set your sights farther, on the end of your lane, as if looking at it would actually get you there, get you closer. *All my life I couldn't hammer a nail without my father taking it out of my hands. I couldn't trim a sail without him knowing it could be brought in another eighth of a turn on the winch.* Now he had it—the rhythm, the roll of the litany. *I couldn't scramble an egg without him looking over my shoulder, picking at how I was doing it. And that's not even getting into the big things.*

He stopped and swallowed, but he couldn't look out at the chapel too long, or else the rows of faces started swimming in front of him. *It's hard having a father who's perfect. Especially when he expects you to be perfect too.* He felt the rage well up in him, snatching his breath. *But he wasn't perfect, was he?* He waited a moment, as if someone would call out an answer while he sucked at the air. *If he was perfect, then he wouldn't have died at age forty-five. So he didn't do everything right. But now I can't tell him that. Now I can't tell him anything.*

He heard his own echo, a reverb like the organ's, that warned him his voice was veering out of control. He ballooned his lungs and let the breath slowly leak out. Suddenly it was as if, with the breath, the anger had leaked out of him also; or like the wave of it he'd been riding had washed him up, spent, on some unfamiliar shore. He looked down at his mother, his sister, almost surprised to find them there, sitting in the pew in their simple, dark outfits. *There's probably a lesson in that. But I don't know what it is yet.*

Danny was always a sprinter, focusing on the fifty and

hundred, the two hundred tops, but every now and then a coach had needed to stick him into a four hundred. He remembered the feeling after he'd snapped his last flipturn, and it didn't matter how sloppy-tired he was, how pool-drunk, he only had one more lap. *I guess I'll have to figure that out on my own. Like I'll have to figure out a lot of things—without his help. And that's the crazy thing about all of this. Because that's what I've been wishing for my whole life: to be able to figure something out without him standing over me, already knowing the answer, or anyway being so cocksure he knows.*

His eyes were tearing over but he could still see the wall: just another stroke or two and the slap. *Only now it suddenly hits me how much I'll be missing.*

Danny didn't know how he got to his seat, it was like those moments during a race when time and distance evaporate, because the next thing he saw was the lap of his mother's black skirt, rising up to accept him. He must have wept, and then she wasn't holding his shoulders, she was gently shaking them. He sat up and looked around, almost expecting it to be like one of those classes in high school where they showed a movie and he fell asleep, and only woke up when the rest of the class had moved on to next period. But the chapel was full still, everyone was rising to their feet. *Al malay rachameme:* the rabbi was singsonging Hebrew, and from out of the jumble of syllables Danny recognized *Shmuel Yitzhak ben Moshe*, Sam's Jewish name.

O God, full of compassion, Thou who dwellest on high! Grant perfect rest unto the soul of Samuel Isaac Winger, who has departed from this world. Lord of mercy, bring him into Thy presence and let his soul be bound up in the bond of eternal life.

Danny wiped his eyes with the tissue his mother held out to him.

Be Thou his possession, and may his repose be peace.

So that was the catch. Eternal life was just the buzzword for infinite rest, for a nothingness so total it attained true perfection. He joined in on *amen*, but just in a whisper.

20

*A*T *SWIMMING MEETS*, after Danny had logged his last race, he could start to wake back up to the world around him—to things like the time, whether or not it was dark yet outside the milky pool windows, who was sitting with who on the bleachers, what girls had come. Now, leaving from the side door of Crestwood, before stepping into the limousine, that's how he felt—like his eyes were back open, and he could notice the day: the blue sky over Northern Boulevard, the incredible wintry brilliance, so even though it was bitingly cold out everything was flooded with light. When the limousine started rolling, he kept his eyes out the window (from the backseat this time) and tried to ignore Ida's running complaint, addressed to everyone and nobody in particular: "What kind of a rabbi is that? He doesn't know that the man had a mother? *Shmuel Yitzhak ben Moshe*, son of *Moshe*, that's right. But since when isn't a mother even worth mentioning? And, *nu*, the rabbi doesn't deliver a eulogy anymore in a Reform congregation? It's just these *cockamaimie* speeches the three of yous got up there to give? And my grandson, the Ivy League graduate, he gets up there to speak and you can't understand a word that he says. Some *bubbe-mayse* about scrambled eggs? That's what he has to say for his father?" He tried to ignore her, and his sister's soft weeping, and Cindy brooding on the opposite seat, so he could follow their progress through all that light along the old parkway into the meadows of eastern Brooklyn.

At the traffic signal after the parkway exit, on the narrow concrete median, a skinny old man shivered in a worn parka much too short and thin for the weather, with two plastic pails at his feet, half filled with bunches of carnations and roses wrapped in cheap cellophane. The hearse made it through on the yellow, but their limo got stopped at the light. The cars that drove by on the cross street were rusted old beaters, with motor oil decals and dragging mufflers and big Bondo spots, and except for a corner gas station and a few broken-down storefronts, all you could see was stone walls and cemeteries in every direction.

After they pulled into the front gates of Knollside they had to wait for clearance to proceed up the road that wound through the city of graves; the hearse had passed through ahead of them, but now the grave site preparations needed to be completed. Danny drew his coat around him and got out of the limo, in spite of his mother's warning that he'd be chilled to the bone before the service even got started. He couldn't listen to Ida, or to Aunt Esther trying to answer her mother as if she were conversing with a reasonable individual: "It's not the rabbi's fault if there's nothing specific about the mother of the deceased written into the funeral service," and, "This way the service is more personal, when everyone gets up and says what they feel," which brought the inevitable rejoinder down on their heads: "Everyone? Who's everyone? I only saw the three of *them* getting up. Nobody asked me to get up there and speak about my own son, may he rest in peace. And believe me, darling, I know him better than the rest of yous put together."

Outside, a line of cars had formed behind their lead limousine, each one puffing its cloud of exhaust into the chill air like the breath of a crouching animal. He couldn't go far—he had to be ready to hop back into the limo when they got the signal from the guy at the gate—but he did cross the road and stroll a little way in along the path that bisected the first quadrant of graves, trying not to pay attention to the gravestones themselves, the monotony of the gray granite, the names chiseled into it; pretending it really was just a meadow, as it had once been, a forgotten, pastoral corner of Brooklyn.

The ground was bare, a hard, crunching carpet of winter-dead grass, but Danny imagined the meadow blanketed by a foot of fresh snow, the kind of blizzard New York never seemed to see anymore but that they'd gotten when he was a kid, so when his father shoveled half of the driveway, the other half had snow piled above Danny's head. He had plenty of time to picture it, and remember the tunnels he'd dug into the sides of those mountains of snow, how Sam would take his big shovel and help him get the cave started, and later come back outside and stand right by the entrance and pretend to be calling and calling him—plenty of time, because as it turned out, there was a delay at the grave site.

The night before, the temperature had dropped below zero, and something had frozen up in the machine that lowered the casket down into the grave, the kind of screwup that would have driven Sam to distraction, so that when Danny heard the limousine driver calling to him from his lowered window, and the limo crept through the acres of graves until it pulled up to the path that was closest to the family plot Joan had purchased, when they all assembled and made their slow processional to the tune of Ida giving the rabbi what-for (she'd managed to collar him outside the limousine), what they found was not the mahogany casket elegantly levitated above the grave on its platform, as if it would never be sullied by earth, but the actual hole with the casket already lowered into it by some crude set of pulleys the Knollside management kept on hand for emergencies, and which had just been whisked out of view to avoid upsetting the relatives.

Danny found himself between his mother and sister, with both of them taking his arm. His face was numb with the cold, but he was glad of that. Glad too that his mother was crying now, really sobbing, and not muttering anything under her breath, not saying, "It's all my fault," or, "I should have done something to stop him," as if she'd finally fallen through all the layers of guilt and self-deprecation to arrive at pure grief. He was glad the plot they'd had available—close enough to Grandpa Moe to keep Ida quiet on that one point at least—was a corner office of grave sites, bordered on two sides by paths so it had only a single neighbor, and that on the edge of the plot stood a big, arching oak, that would give shade in the summer, and a windbreak in fall, and that even now in the dead of winter had a smattering of deep golden leaves to light up its branches—an oak like the one in Prospect Park where Sam's plane had landed some thirty-five years ago.

And it didn't matter that the rabbi was speaking: *The dust returns to the earth as it was. All flesh is grass, and the goodliness thereof as the flower of the field. The grass withereth, the flower fadeth.* Didn't matter that the sobs and lamentations rose up around him like a flock of starlings to roost in Sam's tree. You could see the blunt edge of the shaft dug into the ground, and the pile of dirt they'd use to fill the hole in again, but for now, the top of the casket reflected the sky like a mirror, a sea without a breath of air disturbing its depths, and made a rectangle of the most perfect blue light. And Danny was certain he could conjure that blue when he came to stand by the grave under any color of sky, to talk to his father.

Whither shall I go from Thy spirit? Or whither shall I flee from Thy presence? If I ascend up into heaven, Thou art there; if I make my bed in the netherworld, behold, Thou art there. If I take the wings of the morning, and dwell in the uttermost parts of the sea, even there would Thy hand lead me, and Thy right hand would hold me. And if I say, "Surely the darkness shall envelop me, and the light about me shall be night"; even the darkness is not too dark for Thee, but the night shineth as the day; the darkness is even as the light.

He lifted his eyes from the grave, and let them rest on the faces around him; in that moment all of them had gone still, as if frozen in contemplation of that same endless reflection of sky. The rabbi closed his prayerbook and his eyes, and his face was still too. Danny slipped his arm out from his sister's and reached into his coat pocket for the card he'd picked up at the funeral chapel, so he could join in reciting The Mourner's Kaddish. He thought of how, at the temple, he used to crane his neck around to see who stood up when it was time to say Kaddish at the close of services, as if they were publicly revealing some shameful secret, as if they would be somehow visibly marked.

Yis-gad-dal v'yis-kad-dash sh'mei rab-ba . . . Yis-bo-rach v'yish-tab-bach, v'yis-po-ar, v'yis-ro-mam, v'yis-nas-sei . . . They only spoke the words in a murmur, but Danny could imagine them drifting out like curls of smoke over the meadow of graves and beyond—drifting out over all of Sam's Brooklyn.

21

_I_T WAS TOO COLD to stand around very long at the graveside; the rabbi sped them through a second Kaddish by Grandpa Moe's stone, and then they led Ida away from the plot as she called feebly over her shoulder, as if speaking to Moe, "Not much longer, I'm coming. Just keep the place warm for me." No one spoke much on the ride back home, not even Ida. Danny was glad the subject of the eulogies didn't come up again. He didn't know what he'd say to his mother and sister, since he hadn't heard theirs; maybe later he'd ask to see what they'd written. For the moment, he tried to put the whole business out of his head, to not start running mental replays of his own performance, touching it up as he went, the way he'd always done after swimming meets, but especially when he'd lost a race. Had he lost this one? There was no way to call it yet. Much as he tried to brush off the impression, he couldn't help noticing that Elisa and Dave seemed to be avoiding his gaze. Had his speech embarrassed them? He hadn't exactly mouthed the usual platitudes, but he hadn't said anything so outrageous either. All the bad stuff he'd brought out in the beginning was just a setup for what he said in the end—finally, in so many words, that he needed Sam, in spite of everything, and would miss him. They had all understood that, hadn't they?

Danny looked to his mother, but she seemed to be miles away; he could see her already worrying about the buffet, wondering if the women put everything on the right platters, trying to figure from the crowd at Crestwood how many people would come, if there would be enough food for them. Danny decided he'd pull her aside when they got to the house, and ask if she thought people had taken his speech the right way. But the minute they stepped in the door, they were all swept up in activity. Before Danny had even gotten his coat off, people started crowding into the hall, clambering to get their own coats taken and hung, to be pointed toward a bathroom or telephone or cup of hot coffee, to be set up with a *shiva* stool.

It occurred to Danny that this was the *wake*, though the word sounded foreign to him, more appropriately Gentile. Everywhere he turned, someone was tugging at his sleeve, breathing into his face with their lame introductions: *You don't remember me. I'm your father's Cousin So-and-So. The last time I saw you, you were this tall.* None of them said a word about his eulogy either, except the president of the Beth-Israel Sisterhood, who planted her fat red lips on his cheek and gushed, "You spoke just beautifully. Your father would have been proud." That wasn't the kind of reassurance Danny was looking for. Clearly the woman hadn't actually heard the first word he'd said; as far as she went, he may as well have just gotten up there and delivered another kissass Bar Mitzvah speech.

He did his best to force a smile, then excused himself and headed into the dining room. The buffet might not have been just as Joan would have done it herself, but the table was laid out with the best of the allied forces of Great Neck delicatessens. He surveyed the spread but didn't feel hungry. He decided to go looking for Cindy, with the hazy intention of sharing another one of her joints, asking her what she thought of the eulogy. Before he found her, he spotted Elisa and Dave, huddling over a stuffed whitefish that must have been a yard long. When Danny got closer, he saw that it was just a platter of whitefish salad, with the head and tail stuck back on for effect. He paused, trying to formulate a suitable crack about fish eyes, one of the things, when they were kids, that he'd used to gross out his sister.

Elisa and Dave didn't realize he had come up behind them, but he was close enough to overhear what Elisa was saying in conspiratorial tones as she bent over the platter. "I still can't believe he actually threw that in, like it would get him some laughs. Can you imagine what he would have said if he only *knew*?"

Danny popped up between them. "If *who* only knew *what*? This sounds juicy."

Elisa dropped her plate into the whitefish and clapped a hand to her chest. "You scared me half to death."

Dave pulled himself up straight, but Danny thought he caught a guilty look flicker across his brother-in-law's face.

"Well?" He scrutinized Dave, then his sister. "Come on. I could use some distraction. You're not going to let me in on the hot family gossip?"

"The *hot family gossip*, as you call it, is none of your business," Elisa said. "Do you always go around eavesdropping on people's private conversations?"

"Real private." Danny retrieved her plate from the salad and handed it back to her. "I could hear you halfway across the room." That was stretching it, but he decided to push things a little, to fish. "You weren't talking about me by any chance, were you? About my eulogy? If I only knew *what*?"

Elisa let out an exaggerated snort. "Don't be paranoid. We were talking about a guy in Dave's office." She turned to Dave for confirmation. "Weren't we?"

Dave nodded matter-of-factly and served himself a spoonful of whitefish. He held the spoon out to Danny, as if the subject were as good as dropped. Danny looked from one to the other, but their expressions weren't giving anything away.

"You want some or not?" Elisa said. "Don't just stand there gawking like you're going to catch us at something."

"Okay, okay. No, thanks. You seen Cindy?"

Elisa said she'd seen her come down from upstairs a little while earlier, so Danny kept making his rounds. Wherever he looked he saw people stuffing their faces and chattering with a manic levity, so even though Joan was only serving soft drinks and coffee and tea, it was starting to seem like a party where the guests were getting juiced up on alcohol. Two of the couples from the yacht club were laughing about the summer Sam had taken his turn as commodore, and had all the launch boys terrorized. Skinner and a couple of associates from Sam's department were comparing notes on what happened the first time Sam got his hands on one of their briefs. Ida was waving off food so she could have both hands free for gesturing to the Flatbush contingent about Sammy the Eagle Scout. Relatives who hadn't spoken for years were filling plates of lox and pickled herring for one another, remembering their childhoods in Brooklyn or on the Lower East Side. Joan's second cousins and Sam's great-aunts once removed were noisily getting acquainted.

Suddenly Danny wanted also to be laughing and reminiscing, to shake off the anxious weight he was feeling. When he swung through the hallway into the living room to find Elisa and Dave sitting on the couch with Jeffrey Skinner, he took the armchair across from them.

"We were just telling Jeffrey about Ringer, Belchstein, and what was the last one?" Elisa banged the heel of her hand on her knee several times, like she used to when they watched TV quiz shows. "You know, what Nathan used to call the firm."

"Crass."

"That's right. Crass!" Whenever Elisa talked about Nathan, it was with that same reverence she'd had for him as a girl, like he was still the smartest and most clever guy going, like he hadn't killed himself.

Danny said, "Stinger."

"How's that?"

"The first name wasn't Ringer, it was Stinger. *Stinger, Belchstein and Crass.*"

Skinner shook his head. "Your father must have blown a fuse over that one. I'd like to have seen his face when he heard it."

But Elisa explained. "Actually, he didn't get mad. That was what our cousin always did—make these snide word plays. Sam didn't take it personally. I think he respected him for it."

"God, that reminds me." Danny sat up at the edge of his chair, rising to the mood. "What was that word Nathan said? You know, when he used to crack us all up." He fixed his eyes on Elisa. "And Mom and Dad and Esther and George would look at us like we were idiots."

He closed his eyes and could see the three of them—himself, Elisa and Cindy—rolling around on the floor, with Nathan standing over them like they were animals in some experiment he had rigged. "It was something incredibly stupid." He turned to Dave and then Skinner, because suddenly it seemed important that they understand—because you couldn't really know Sam, or any of them, if you didn't have the atmosphere of those years, when they were kids and the families were all together. "Something completely mundane like, I don't know—bullfrog."

"Foghorn!" Elisa jumped up. "It was foghorn!"

"No." They all turned and there was Cindy, standing at the edge of their circle, her hand on her hip. She squinched up her brow and pursed her lips into her best Nathan face, and spoke in a voice that was pinched and hyper-mature and slyly amused, uncannily like Nathan's: "Shoehorn."

She held in her laughter long enough to pull off the act, but then they exploded, all three of the cousins. Dave and Skinner just looked at them, shaking their heads. And why not, it was totally dumb, it was dumber than it ever had been, only they couldn't stop. Every time the hysteria started to ebb, Danny or Elisa would repeat the word in their own inferior imitation and they'd break up all over. At the point when the tears were rolling down their faces, Ida came marching through. She took one look at them and clucked her tongue several times, achieving a volume and conveying a degree of disgust of which she alone was capable. "Yous should be ashamed of yourselves! This is a house of mourning. Don't yous have any respect?"

They all held their breath until she passed, muttering, into the dining room. But then they burst out again. In another minute, Elisa wound down and wiped her eyes. "I feel bad."

"About Grandma? Why?" Cindy sat down on the floor by the couch. "She's going around putting on a performance and getting laughs wherever she can. She's just pissed that everyone's sick of her stories already."

"But still—"

"Come on." Danny jumped in to side with his cousin. "We were just having fun. I mean, we're mourning too. We're just not doing it in the same way that she is."

Dave put his arm around Elisa, whose lips were turned down like she was about to start crying for real, not laugh-crying.

"Hey," Danny said. "You want to sit around on a wooden crate all afternoon, be my guest. I've got another idea."

"What's your idea?" asked Cindy.

"There are a couple of six-packs in the back of the refrigerator in the garage. I saw them last night. One of us takes a coat or something and smuggles those suckers upstairs to my room. That old hi-fi Sam and Nathan built is still in my closet. I don't think it would take much to get it hooked up."

Elisa looked skeptical, but Dave put his hands on his knees like he was ready to take up the cause.

Cindy chimed in. "What have you got for tunes?"

"What have I got? Need you ask? I've got my extremely valuable collection of vintage 45s, that's what."

Cindy groaned. "That same shit you used to play in elementary school?"

"The very same. But hey, there's some classic stuff in there. You'll see, it'll all come back to you."

"That's what worries me."

Skinner bowed out of the family reunion, and Danny had to go after the six-packs himself, the other three having chickened out on him, but one by one, so it wouldn't look like too obvious a conspiracy, Elisa and Dave and Cindy slipped up to his bedroom. On one of Danny's closet shelves, Sam had built a pullout base for the hi-fi set, so it was easy to get to the wires. The turntable and boxy receiver and pair of burlap-covered speakers were anything but state of the art. With the brown metal platter, the gray-green plastic tone arm and knobby black dials, the whole system looked like some army-issue World War II number. But Danny could still remember the excitement that Hanukkah fifteen years back when Sam brought all the pieces home from the electronics shop, like the boy who'd saved his meager earnings from chores week by week until he could make the trip to Messer's on Avenue J and buy the components for his first Brooklyn wireless.

Danny didn't remember what had started the fight—why he'd refused to build the phonograph with his father, so Sam and Nathan had done it instead. He did remember that by the end he had wanted back in to the project, and watched from the door as they mounted the platter onto the base of the turntable, adjusted the tone arm and set the needle in place; he crossed the threshold when they put the first record on, and asked, "Can I listen?"

Now it took just a couple of minutes to resecure the wiring, Danny's cases of 45s were dusty but still on the shelves where he'd left them, though Joan had threatened every year to pack them off to the Beth-Israel Bazaar, and the plastic 45 adaptor was waiting on the phonograph spindle. When Danny pressed down his first selection and set the tone arm in place, the homemade speakers crackled to life as if begrudgingly from their long sleep. The static grew so loud Danny didn't think they'd be able to hear any music, but when he turned the volume down, it rumbled out: the whine of a fighter plane that served as the opening riff of "Snoopy Versus the Red Baron."

It was a stupid, childish song, but one that Danny had always enjoyed, because it told a story he could act out along with the lyrics, and because it was about an underdog having his day. But Cindy groaned, "Jesus, take that shit off," and Dave and Elisa booed, and they all got so rowdy he couldn't even play it through to the Baron's demise. He got better marks for "Summer in the City," and Gary Lewis and the Playboys doing "This Diamond Ring." The mood turned silly enough that when he found "Last Train to Clarksville," he pulled his sister up to dance with him. At first she resisted, but he tugged on her arm, and then, from the recesses of a carefree, frivolous girlhood he hadn't remembered her having, she hauled out *the pony*. Before the song was through the second verse, they were all dancing it, even Dave, and laughing and shouting the chorus.

When it was over, Elisa, Dave and Cindy collapsed and popped open their beers. But Danny was on a roll; he stood on tiptoe to reach the top shelf, where he'd stashed the really egregious bubblegum tunes, the ones he wouldn't be caught dead playing by the time he hit high school. He couldn't believe what clattered down at the back of the shelf when he pulled out the last case. "Sonofabitch." He set the records by his feet and just stared for a moment.

"You okay?" Cindy said.

He didn't answer. He didn't lift his hand either, as if he were afraid to touch the thing.

Elisa nosed in behind him. "What did you find in there?"

Now he did reach up to the shelf. He swiveled to face them and held up the paddle, as if to ward off any interlopers.

"Holy shit." Cindy jumped up from his bed. "The instrument of torture! But check out how small it is."

Danny turned the paddle over a couple of times in his hand. He hated to admit it, but she was right. The slab of wood he remembered was so much broader, and at least twice this thick. And maybe it was just the action of time, but the shellac looked so dull, when back then it had practically thrown off sparks when Sam brandished it.

"Oh. I've heard about this." Dave approached to examine the paddle. "Nineteen fifty-two. Phi Beta Upsilon." He flipped it over and read the smaller letters. *"To Samuel Winger from Marcus Greene*. Who was Greene?"

Danny shrugged. "Some fraternity brother, I guess. Maybe his pledge brother." He'd never given much thought to the name, or what the paddle had signified for Sam before he'd turned it to its more ignoble purposes.

"So this is what the old man used to spank you guys?" Dave waved the paddle like a baton, making a figure eight in the air.

Danny didn't want to seem uptight—he'd brought them up there to have fun—but it bothered him, seeing Dave swinging the paddle around like that. "Listen. Like Ida said, show some respect. That was a major formative influence on our childhoods."

"Oh, was it now?" With that, Dave did something Danny would have never expected: still gripping the paddle with one hand, he bent over and looped his arm around Elisa's waist and hauled her off to the bed, where he draped her, a little clumsily but effectively, across his lap. He held the paddle over her as she covered her ass with both hands. "I'll kill you! Leave me alone!" Finally he just gave her a *potch* on one cheek with the end of the paddle. He flashed Danny a triumphant grin. "At least it hasn't impeded the growth of either one of your *tuchases*."

Danny wasn't grinning back. "Let me have the paddle, okay?"

The other three were still laughing.

"Damn it, just give me the paddle."

Elisa caught her breath and stood up from Dave's lap. "What's your problem? Who says all of a sudden it's yours?"

"You better believe it's mine. Unless I'm remembering wrong, *I'm* the one who got spanked with it. It's my rightful inheritance."

A sudden, haughty chill passed across Elisa's face. "You might just be right about that one."

Dave grabbed her wrist. "Come on. You're not supposed to be—"

She pulled her arm free. "I can say whatever I want. I'm sick of his shit already. I'm surprised he didn't complain about getting spanked in the eulogy." She spun around on Danny. "You've always felt sorry for yourself, haven't you? You had such a terrible father, poor kid. You never think about how miserable you made *him*. All the trouble you were always causing."

Dave tried again to grab hold of her. "She doesn't know what she's saying. It's just all the stress coming out." And then to Elisa herself: "Cut it out, okay? It's going to be hard enough on him."

Danny felt his fingers pressing into the paddle. "What's going to be hard? What the hell's going on here?"

Elisa was suddenly still, a guilty, abashed expression replacing her fury of a moment before. Dave let out a long breath and shook his head with his eyes half shut. "Now you've done it."

Danny stared at one, then the other. "Done what?" Then he remembered their conversation from earlier. *If he only knew* . . . A guy in Dave's office, his ass—it was Danny they'd been talking about. They knew something he didn't, something about him and Sam. Then it hit him: his line about *rightful inheritance*. "No, don't tell me. It's the will, isn't it?"

Neither of them said anything, but they didn't need to.

He could tell by the way they couldn't look at him. Danny's father hadn't been bluffing the night of the fight. He'd actually gone ahead and cut his only son out of his will. Gone ahead and made it so Danny was not his son after all.

"Where are you going?" It was Elisa, reaching out to stop him.

But he was moving too fast. "I'm going to speak to Mom, that's where."

Danny barreled downstairs and whipped through the living and dining rooms. He found his mother in the corner by the coffeepot, standing with two of the women from the Friday night bridge. "Can I talk to you alone for a minute?"

He didn't wait for an answer, but pulled her by the arm into the kitchen, where one of the friends who'd set up the buffet was refilling a platter of cheese. "That's okay, Audrey, thanks," Joan said. "I can get that."

Audrey took one look at Danny's face, wiped her hands on a dish towel, and scurried back to the dining room.

Danny swung the door closed behind her, then went to shut the sliding doors on the other side. "The big secret is out."

She stared back at him, not understanding.

"I found out about the will," he said. She opened her mouth to speak but he cut her off. "I know we had problems. That wasn't anything new. But disowning me? Isn't that a little extreme? I mean, when I felt really paranoid, I imagined him going ahead with it. But I never actually believed that he would." He shook his head, scarcely believing it even now. "How the hell could you let him do that?"

"I didn't let him do anything. I didn't even know about it myself until yesterday afternoon, when Morty called from the office."

"And when were you planning to let me in on the news?"

"Next week sometime, when things settled down. When Morty had a chance to see if anything could be done. You've got to understand, it was all a mistake. Morty said Dad was always pulling that—going in and rewriting his will, then changing it back a week later. He said your father wrote him and Art out when they had that argument about merging with a bigger firm. He didn't mean anything by it. It was just a way he had of blowing off steam."

"I guess I won't take it personally or anything then. It's just my rotten luck he has to drop dead before he gets around to reinstating me."

"Don't start thinking that way. Morty said we have a good chance of getting the whole thing reversed, since nobody would be contesting it. On the basis of your father's *intentions*, rather than the current letter of the will itself. On the grounds that it was just a short-term disagreement."

"It was a long-term disagreement. It's been going on my whole life."

"Listen, sweetheart, I know how this makes you feel. But we'll get it straightened out. And even if it can't be changed, I'm here, as the executor of the estate. I'll make sure you've got everything you need. And then there will be my will . . ."

"Everything I need? I guess you don't understand. I don't give a shit about the money. I won't starve, with or without it. What I need is a father."

"You had a father, and he cared about you very much. If he didn't, he wouldn't have given a damn about what you were doing with your life."

"Swell. That makes me feel really loved. He cared enough to say I wasn't his son because I rented some lousy apartment."

"It wasn't just the apartment. *Or* the job. Even you have to realize that."

"Yeah. And even *you* have to realize—"

But he never got to finish his sentence, because just then Henrietta burst through the door and ran to them in short, scuffing steps, both hands clapped over her mouth. "Joanie, you've got to come quick. Because now we've really got *tsuris* here."

Danny and his mother dashed after Henrietta into the hall, and Danny's first thought was of Ida, passed out on the floor again. But Ida was standing there, on her two feet, even though it looked like Aunt Esther was practically trying to wrestle her down to the ground from behind. Facing off against Ida, waving Sam's handkerchief like a flag of surrender, was Uncle George. "I'm sorry I killed your grandson. I'm sorry I ruined your daughter's life. My life is miserable too, if it makes you feel any better."

"That's touching, George." Esther had gotten a grip on Ida for the moment, and craned around her to spit out the words. "Why don't you save it for your therapist or your girlfriends, and just leave us alone today."

George made a little mock bow, brushing the floor with the handkerchief. "I'll be more than happy to leave you alone. I didn't come here to see you, or your lovely mother for that matter. I came here for Sam. He *was* my brother-in-law of twenty-five years. It so happens I loved the guy."

Ida lunged, and broke free of Esther. From off on the sidelines, Henrietta pushed Aaron into the fray. Aaron managed to grab hold of both Ida's wrists, but he couldn't keep her from shouting. "You loved him? What do you know about love? He was my son. My son, do you hear me? You never deserved to be in the same room with him. He had more good in one little finger—"

"I'll show you a finger," George said, and held up his middle one. But it didn't seem funny now, the way those kind of antics had when Danny was younger. Danny had edged in close enough to smell the liquor—scotch, it seemed like—on George's breath. As Ida was shouting, his uncle's expression had gone from genteel, if sarcastic, to menacing. "He was your son, all right. And you want to know how he talked about you when you weren't around? His darling mother? How much he loved *you*?"

Danny looked to Esther for some kind of response, but she had dropped back to the wall as if she'd been struck. Aaron too had stepped back, and was suddenly doubled over, clutching his chest. For an instant it was just the two of them, George and Ida. In the old days, they had been a good matchup, but now Danny could see Ida's jaw falling slack the way it had the morning before; see the glint in George's eyes as he took a breath before his next onslaught. Danny made his decision in a split second, like everything that had happened that day converged, and some starting gun went off inside of him. He grabbed George's right arm to swivel him away from Ida and then took his swing. He didn't mean to hit him square in the face like that, or that hard so he felt the impact, like a rifle kickback, right through his shoulder, and heard the sickening crunch of bone. He pulled his arm back and froze, as surprised as anyone else, to see George sink to his knees, blood running down from both his nostrils.

When the ambulance pulled up, Danny thought he recognized two of the guys who had come to get Ida. They took Aaron out on a stretcher first; he swore he was fine—short of breath, that was all—but Henrietta insisted that he be hooked up to a monitor. She kept repeating, "The man isn't well." Danny muttered, "Then why did she push him into the fight?" but no one was listening. George said he would ride sitting up, it hurt less that way, and he shook his head when the rescue guy asked if he wanted to call the police. "It's just my nephew, the hothead." He did his best to wink at Danny and crack a smile. "I was out of line myself. You know how it is: tempers always run high in families."

Danny laid his arm lightly on George's shoulder and flashed a grin at Elisa, who'd been shaking her head in disbelief ever since she'd seen what Danny had done. Before he spoke, he made sure Dave was listening. Danny didn't know, in the end, exactly who he'd gotten back at by punching George, but now he had the chance of a lifetime to get back at his sister. "Uncle George was always jealous of Elisa's nose job, anyway."

Elisa turned crimson and shot a quick, terrified look at Dave.

Danny gave George's arm a squeeze and raised his eyebrows in Dave's direction. "Weren't you, Georgie?"

22

AFTER THE AMBULANCE PULLED AWAY from the house, the wake thinned out fairly quickly. Elisa and Dave disappeared upstairs, and Danny would have given his right arm to eavesdrop on that one. Cindy had vanished too, probably to go smoke a joint. Ida sat on a *shiva* stool and mopped her brow with a handkerchief. She waved away Esther's offers of water or tea with muttered bits of abuse: "*Meshuggeneh*, to marry a guy like that in the first place. Your father and I both said from the start it would come to no good." She only wanted Danny to stand by her side, so she could pat his hand and shake her head, chuckling softly: "Now it's twice you saved my life this week. That was some punch you threw. Knock on wood, I'm glad I lived to see that at least. You're a good boy. That's what I was always telling your father. 'He's a good boy. Leave the poor thing alone for once, would you?' " Ida had her stool set up in view of the hall, so as each group of relatives or friends stepped up for their farewells, she called out to them: "Did yous get a load of my grandson here? Should have been a boxer instead of a swimmer. Am I right? Every grandmother should be so lucky. I lost my son, but my Danny here, he looks out for me."

When Bea and Irv appeared in the hall, Danny pried his fingers from Ida's grasp to go say good-bye to them. Bea took both his hands in hers and got that look she had when she was struggling toward speech. There was a long pause before she came out with, "The eggs."

Danny turned to his grandfather for a translation. Irv looked to Bea. "What? *The eggs?*" He shrugged. "Your grandmother's tired, that's all."

But Bea gave him a jab in the side. "Irving, shhh." Then she turned back to Danny, taking his hands again, squeezing them with more urgency. "The eggs," she repeated. She sounded definite, like it was no mistake, those were the words she was after. "You have to boil the eggs."

Danny was about to shrug it off too, but then he remembered. "*Eggs.* You mean like I said in the eulogy?"

Bea smiled and nodded, triumphant. "You have to boil them yourself now."

"Scramble," he corrected her, though he didn't know why he was quibbling.

Vindicated, she beamed at Irv. "You see? Danny knows what I mean. Now he has to scramble them."

Once the door was closed on the last of the guests, Danny helped Ida upstairs so she could lie down and rest—doctor's orders. He came back down to the den to find Esther sitting alone. "Where's Mom?"

His aunt motioned toward the kitchen. "There was a phone call and she took it in there."

"You know from who?"

"The Medical Examiner's Office. Some assistant to the M.E."

"What about?" Danny was suddenly seized with a panic, as if it had something to do with his identification: they'd found another body that *really* was Sam's; he hadn't looked closely enough at the one they'd sent up on the slab, and had blown it.

But Esther didn't sound worried, just tired, matter-of-fact. "It must be the preliminary results of the autopsy."

Danny mouthed a silent "Oh" and dropped back into his chair. Since his trip to the Medical Examiner's Office, he'd

228

thought about the autopsy—to the extent that he'd let himself think about it at all—as a senseless, routine disfigurement, performed by the anonymous ghouls that practiced their art on those unseen, lower levels of the morgue complex. He'd forgotten there were reasons for doing it, beyond the legal requirements; forgotten that it would yield information.

It seemed like several minutes before his mother emerged from the kitchen with a dazed expression, like she'd been wearing when Danny first saw her, the morning he'd traveled home. She recruited him to run upstairs and ask Elisa and Dave to come join them. Elisa greeted him at her door with blotchy cheeks and a scowl that said she'd get him back for this, but both she and Dave fell in behind him without an argument when he said he thought Joan had word of the autopsy.

When everyone was seated around the coffee table, Joan glanced from one to the next with an expression Danny couldn't size up. "I don't know if the news is good or bad. It isn't what we were expecting."

Danny's mind raced back to the murky suspicions he'd felt when his mother had first recounted the tale of the death and the events leading up to it—what seemed so long ago; the sense that things weren't right somehow, or weren't what they appeared. "So he didn't die of a heart attack after all."

He phrased it like a statement, not a question, and for an instant everyone stared at him. Then his mother shook her head. "No, he didn't." She swallowed before she went on. "The autopsy indicates he died of a massive cerebral hemorrhage."

Danny stared at his mother. Elisa was saying, "Can they know that for sure?" but Danny was thinking about Sam's face at the morgue, what the woman said about working from the back of the head.

"The doctor said the results were pretty conclusive. Apparently your father had an aneurysm, at the base of the brain. In the ring of arteries that supplies the brain with blood. The doctor called it the Circle of Willis."

Danny knew he'd heard the word "aneurysm" before, but he wasn't sure where. He waited for someone else to ask, but they didn't. "So, an aneurysm: what is that, exactly?"

Esther, the science teacher, jumped in. "It's a weak spot in an arterial wall."

Dave, who'd been uncharacteristically quiet, piped up next. "What causes it?"

Joan answered. "Nothing causes it. It's just there, from birth. Like someone might have a congenital weakness in a particular knee, or"—her eyes paused on Danny—"a shoulder. The doctor said it's not uncommon for a person to have one somewhere along his bloodstream and never know that it's there. It's only a problem when it happens to be in a high-volume area."

"Like the brain," Danny said.

His mother nodded. "In those cases, at some point, sooner or later, the weak spot begins to give way. More often than not it will happen sometime during childhood. The spot balloons out and fills with blood, until it bursts from the pressure. The doctor said it had probably been leaking blood for several days before it finally went."

Suddenly it all fit together—the ache at the base of Sam's neck, the whooshing sound in his ears, the word he only got through a part of. The way they had his heart beating, but no vital signs. Danny couldn't help thinking aloud: "Instant death."

Joan tilted her head in assent. "This Dr. Richardson who called said he wouldn't have felt any pain, any more than he'd already been feeling. Or maybe just for a split second."

Danny knew more about a split second than anyone else in the room, maybe even more than the esteemed Dr. Richardson. When his mother fell silent, he imagined that final instant not as a sudden blackout but an explosion of light, the last, fierce streak of his father's consciousness.

He was still holding on to the vision when his mother started to speak again. "Richardson said they would have spotted it if they'd done a CAT scan after Dad's fall. But even then, there's nothing that could have been done. He said they can't go in and operate on that part of the brain without turning the person into a vegetable."

Danny saw his sister flinch at the same moment he did.

"Those aren't the words he used, but that was the general idea."

Joan was quiet then, and Danny could sense his sister trying to picture it too: the impossible image of Sam like that, dead as Sam but alive still, the lie of a body.

Danny shuddered. "Well, at least you can say one thing: it sure lets you off the hook, Mom."

His mother looked at him like she didn't get it.

He jumped up from his chair. "Don't you see? It means no one's to blame. No one could have done anything. I mean, here's something even you can't find a way to feel guilty about. Now you don't have to spend the rest of your life believing deep down that you killed him."

His mother stared at him for a long moment with a face that seemed to be pulling in two different directions: part of her lifting with the dawning truth of what he had said, another part wrestling to hold on to her guilt, because, good or bad, it was something that tied her to Sam. Finally she stood. "I don't think I can sort through that one today. I guess we've all got some new things to think about. For now, we better get going on this disaster area."

With that, everyone stirred, and started taking cleanup orders from Joan. Danny pitched in too but moved as if in a dream. He still couldn't quite digest the fact that his father had had this thing—this random, minute imperfection, this time bomb ticking away at the base of his brain all those years, his whole life. It was like a freak accident, like what had happened to Grandma Bea, only the bolt of lightning didn't come from nowhere, from out of the blue. It was planted inside; it was an inseparable part of you.

He tried to put it out of his head, to tell himself it made no difference: heart attack or whatever, his father was still just as dead; he'd disowned him just as completely. And yet the fact of the aneurysm somehow changed everything. You could no longer say Sam's death had been premature; it was a miracle he'd lived for almost forty-six years, and at such a pitch of intensity. And it wasn't like Nathan's death— stupid, completely avoidable. Sam's death was more like a force of nature, something you couldn't argue with. It wasn't just rotten timing, bad luck; it was destiny. Danny was still puzzling over it when he got ready for bed that night.

He was sleeping downstairs on the couch in the den, so Ida could sleep alone and Cindy and Esther could use the two halves of his high-riser. Joan had taken a pair of Sam's plaid flannel pajamas and laid them across the pile of blankets she'd set out for Danny. He snickered to himself when he spotted them. Wasn't it just like his mother to leave them there, like an unspoken consolation prize for the lost inheritance? But still, he lifted them gingerly, with a certain reverence. The pajamas had a ring of light blue paper around them, the tops and bottoms each had a sheet of crinkly paper inside the folds, and the flannel bore the exotic but familiar smell of the Chinese laundry by Danny's old elementary school. They felt even softer than they would have otherwise against his shaved skin, and the stack of quilts enveloped him in a comforting warmth, but still he couldn't sleep, on account of the memorial candle.

They'd lit it earlier that day, after they got back from Knollside—a glass cylinder filled with seven days' worth of milky wax, as if that were a fitting interval, and after seven days you'd be prepared for the fact that the flame would go out, always did, none of the magic that came to the rescue of

Judah and his band of Maccabees, one day's oil that kept burning for eight. They'd set it on top of the bar in the den, where it had burned through the wake with nobody taking much notice—a tiny flame lost in the brighter light of the day. Now, in the darkened room, the reflection of the glowing cylinder danced and grew, spreading up the wall behind it and onto the ceiling, even sending spots and pulses of light across the room to the wall behind Danny's head, playing and shifting to the rhythm of some indetectable breeze, to the stirring caused by Danny's own breath maybe.

He almost wanted to go shake everyone out of their beds and bring them down there to see it: how that little candle was filling the room, making the walls pulse and shimmer, that dancing, breathing light that seemed so alive. But he didn't move from under the quilts; he decided to keep the show for himself, as if hoarding what little of his father's was given him.

At some point he must have slept, because when he heard the footsteps it seemed that he was resurfacing, that his father had been in the room with him—not speaking, just sitting there in the flickering shadows. He shut his eyes and listened to the slow footfalls descending the last several stairs. Damn if his grandmother wasn't up on the prowl again. He didn't know if he could bear the sight of her filmy nightgown, her cloudy, half-opened stare, in this light. But when the footsteps sounded on the stone floor of the den, it wasn't the click and scuff of Ida's house slippers. There was a long pause, during which he could have even drifted off again, and then the steps were coming toward him, so lightly it seemed he might have been dreaming them.

The whispered sound of his name didn't startle him; neither did his cousin squeezing in next to him on the couch. He moved sideways toward the wall to make room for her. There was light enough from the candle to see her eyes, the anger flashing. "I wish it was my father that had died and not yours."

"George isn't that bad," Danny said. He pulled himself

up to a sitting position. "He was a pretty good sport about what happened today."

Cindy snorted in spite of herself. "I still can't believe that you decked him."

Danny laughed too. "What I can't believe is that Elisa didn't deck *me* after that nose job crack."

"And right in front of Dave. That was bad."

"I know. But I couldn't help myself. I've been waiting for a chance like that ever since she met the guy."

Cindy tried to smile, then hung her head. "Listen. I'm sorry for the way I was treating you. For the stuff that I said. I didn't mean anything by it."

Danny shook his head. "Forget it. None of that matters now. We've got a fresh start. Just don't fucking cut me off this time, okay? My father cutting me off is about all of that I can handle."

She nodded. "You must be pretty pissed about that—the will and everything."

"Well, I *was* pissed, when I found out. I was so pissed I could barely see straight. I mean, I punched your father for Ida and everything. But I also just needed to punch someone, I was so furious. And it was quite the punch—like someone nailed *me*. It cleared my head right out. Then the M.E.'s Office calls up with this aneurysm thing. It's kind of hard to stay on the same track after hearing that. It's like, either nothing makes any sense at all, or you have to figure there's some underlying reason for all of it. Like somehow it was meant to come out this way. Like my life will wind up taking a certain direction because he died before we had a chance to make up. Like getting cut out of his will is some kind of test, or a lesson."

"So what are you going to do?"

"What can I do? I'll go back to Brooklyn. I'll see if I can take on some extra shifts at the Y, and start saving some bucks again. I'll look around for this girl I met in the laundromat the night that he died. And, shit, I don't know—I

guess I'll try to figure out what I want to do with my life."
He sighed at the enormity and simplicity of it. "I'll scramble
the eggs."

"You'll what?"

"Never mind. It's just a manner of speaking."

He thought Cindy would press him to explain, but her
gaze had slipped past him to the wall behind his head.
"Jesus. Check that out."

He turned to look but knew what he'd find: with the
hours, as the pool of melted wax in the cylinder had grown
deeper, and trembled side to side with the gusts of the flame,
the reflection had started to move over the wall like a liquid,
washing in and drawing back like waves on the sand, or the
tide.

"What's doing that?"

"It's Sam's light," he said.

23

*W*HEN DANNY WOKE UP, the light that leaked in around the windowshades was that yellow-turquoise he'd seen from the Promenade on his way home, and Sam's candle had shrunk back to just the small, simple flame in its pool, as if the whole show in the night had only been Danny's imagination. He went to the windows and pulled up all three shades on the side of the room that faced west, toward the city, filled with a restlessness he could remember feeling as a boy, before the swimming had given his energy a direction.

By the time the family started stirring, Danny had eaten breakfast and dressed; as soon as he could get into his room, he loaded all his things into his gym bag, wedging the fraternity paddle in lengthwise. His mother stood over the dripping filter pot and just nodded as he told her his plans; she didn't try to convince him to stay. He could come back when he was ready to go through Sam's belongings, to see what he wanted; she thought it was only fair that he get first pick. She insisted he take home a bag of leftovers. "I'm packing up all the candy and cookies for you—your sister and I will each gain twenty pounds if it stays here." Then she went back upstairs to get dressed so she could give him a ride to the train station.

When Danny and Joan were ready to head out the door, everyone assembled in the front hallway. It reminded him of the ceremonial farewell he'd gotten when he'd gone off to college, only now he was going off to his *life*. Dave shook his hand, slapped him on his bad shoulder and said, "You really ought to get into Manhattan to see us more often," and though Danny was tempted to make some crack like "The bridge runs both ways," he just smiled and said thanks, that he would. His sister still looked a little tight-lipped about the nose business but hugged him anyway. Ida took his hands into her trembling but still-iron grip. "We're both in Brooklyn now, you know. You ever ride the D train? It wouldn't kill you to come see your grandmother." Cindy made him write down his Sackett Street address and phone number. Esther shook her head and pulled him to her. "You're really a doozie, kid." Then Joan said they'd better hurry, Danny might miss his train, and with a quick glance at Sam's clock he was out of there, driving under the arching limbs of bare trees that closed overhead like a tunnel in summer, among the morning commuters.

His mother was crying when she pulled into the train station. He told her not to worry: he'd call her that night, and he'd come home again soon. And no, he wouldn't do anything crazy—anything else, that is.

The Long Island Rail Road was crowded at rush hour. By the time the train pulled up and Danny lumbered to an open door with his gym bag and food bag banging into his knees, there were no seats; it only got tighter as the train slid from one bedroom town to the next toward the city. On the long run under the river, the lights blinked out; from all sides, he was jostled by strange, invisible bodies. From Penn Station, the A train was also packed. But when he changed at Washington Square, he practically had his pick of seats on the F train to Brooklyn.

Danny wedged his bags tight between his feet and closed his eyes over visions of his apartment, of running into the woman he'd met in the laundromat. He let himself drift to the rhythm of Broadway-Lafayette, Second Avenue,

Delancey, East Broadway, and then the rocking, rattling stretch between stops that meant you were speeding between the two boroughs. When he felt the burst of sunlight through his closed eyelids, he jumped up, but it was too late: he'd already missed the Carroll Street stop; the train was speeding out of the tunnel. Forgetting his bags, he lurched across to the opposite window to watch as the car climbed above ground, rising into the world of frozen backyard gardens, empty clotheslines, flat roofs; rising high enough to see—through the flashing gaps of the avenues, looming above the invisible harbor—the Statue of Liberty.

He held the view of the Statue as long as he could before the tracks curved and the train slowed for the Smith Street station. He could have grabbed his bags and gotten off there, climbed down the stairs and crossed under the tracks, and waited on the Manhattan-bound platform for the next train back to Carroll Street. But instead he just sank back down on the seat. He had an idea. It was something he'd never done, though he'd thought about it a couple of times since he'd moved in to Sackett Street.

The train went back underground just past the next stop, and Danny dozed off and on for the rest of the ride, waking to the conductor's voice breaking over the loudspeaker with names he remembered from some buried chapters of the Wingers' Brooklyn history: Church Avenue, Avenue I, Bay Parkway, Kings Highway; waking to the light rushing in as the train rose back above ground just before Ditmas Avenue; opening his eyes again and again to what looked like practically the same view: the bare trees, the squat brick buildings, the monotonous row houses with their plastic awnings in garish shades of orange and green, the vast, yawning mediocrity that was the Brooklyn his father had wanted out of; and once, as though in a dream, opening his eyes to a cemetery stretching on either side of the tracks, an ancient-looking harbor of stones with Hebrew inscriptions rising out

238

of a sea of ivy gone wild, the old Jewish graves packed in as tightly as Brooklyn.

He was awake by the time the train was slowing toward the Aquarium stop, and from the elevated tracks he could see the glinting ocean, the Cyclone and Wonder Wheel, the rusted tower of the old Parachute. At the last minute, he grabbed his bags and stumbled out of the car; there was still one more stop before the end of the line, but this got him close enough. The platform was shielded on either side by corrugated sheet metal, painted light blue and splashed with graffiti, but when he walked down the stairs the water and rides came back into view, and he was hit in the face with a blast of northerly wind, off the ocean. He dug out his hat and gloves from his gym bag and climbed on down to Surf Avenue.

Inland, the tracks loomed above a motley row of store-fronts snaking up to the battered hulk of the Shore Hotel; what Danny remembered as colorful junk stalls manned by hawking, heavily accented vendors were shut up behind green metal security gates, their dilapidated awnings flapping like Small Craft Warning flags. On the ocean side, the chain link fence around the Cyclone was padlocked, and topped with ribbons of barbed wire; the boardwalk was deserted, and the only thing stirring among the closed-up trailers and dismantled rides in Astroland Park was the odd drink cup or ticket stub. Of course all the rides and arcades and refreshment stands were shut down for the winter. He should have expected that, told himself that he had, but he knew that in his half sleep on the train he'd been imagining Coney Island in summer, with the smell of hot dogs and cotton candy, the tinny music and blinking lights, the screaming that twisted and plunged with the loops and dips of the Cyclone track, and in the middle of all of it, a dark-haired boy clutching his father's hand, afraid in that crowd he would lose him.

He stopped and leaned into the fence alongside the Cyclone, and saw his father's face as he pushed Danny in through the gate to take his first ride, where Danny didn't laugh or even scream, but just shut his eyes and gripped the safety rail for all he was worth, calculating the chances that he really would die, that the car wouldn't hold to the track, not understanding why his father was making him do this. Now he noticed the sign on the ticket booth at the corner, CLOSED FOR REPAIRS UNTIL FURTHER NOTICE, NEW YORK CITY DEPARTMENT OF PUBLIC HEALTH, and remembered reading it in the paper, the Cyclone getting shut down, though he couldn't remember the details—whether there had been an accident, or the safety inspector just thought one was imminent: all those cars running over those rickety wooden tracks so fast for so many years, something had to give sometime. But that wasn't the point. The point was what it had been like when it was new, and a nickel, all the rides that boys like his father had taken, before there was anything like rockets or satellites to make the roller coaster seem small, and all the dreams they'd had at the top of the highest loop, looking away from the sprawl of Brooklyn out over the ocean.

Danny pushed himself on up the block. He was sure at least Nathan's had to be open; he could get something warm there. He walked with his head down, his eyes were tearing now from the wind, but he looked up when he heard the strains of some music drifting across from the track side of Surf Avenue. He peered up the block and spotted the big white sign with red letters, B & B CAROUSEL. He blinked and looked back again to make sure: it was open; in the row of locked-down storefronts, a square of color and carnival light.

He crossed the avenue on a broad diagonal (the street was as abandoned as the amusement park) and even when he stood in front of it he couldn't believe he was seeing right. The place seemed vaguely familiar. Had he been here with his father, or was he inventing that? It was just the size of a regular storefront, but the carousel fit inside of it perfectly. The music was playing, the lights were blinking, but the merry-go-round was still, and Danny stood just inside the building gaping at the gilt scrollwork, the fancy horses, the chariot. Maybe his father had taken him here after he got so scared on the Cyclone. Danny was trying to remember when the voice sounded out of the back, "Can I help you, son?" and the balding proprietor waddled out from around the side of the carousel.

Danny was startled, but the man looked kindly enough, someone's grandfather. "Just looking, thanks. You keep this thing running all winter?"

"Sure," the man said. "Have for twenty years anyway. Usually somebody coming out the Aquarium wants to treat their kids to a ride."

Danny let his eyes travel along the carousel's elaborate canopy. "You got the gold ring and everything?"

The man nodded, all business. "Ring's around back. You get it, the second ride's free, but it isn't easy."

The man disappeared again to change Danny's five. Danny took his time stepping around the outer circle, choosing his horse; the carousel lurched into motion just as he spotted the blue one, with the silver-white saddle and mane. It moved up and down on its silver pole but slowly, slowly. Danny had plenty of time on the first revolution to get a good look at the ring, to gauge how far he'd have to reach up from the horse's back to take hold of it. Then the carousel began to turn faster, and for a couple of spins he didn't go for the ring; he was watching the circle of mirrors that spun in the carousel's center, counter to the direction the horses were turning, so when his reflection was caught in a mirror it raced across with a tremendous illusion of speed, until he could barely make out his own face, his horse was just a blue streak, and he imagined in one flash around that he saw his father sitting on the same horse behind him, holding fast to his waist, lifting him up and up as the glinting tease of the ring hurried by them. And then Danny stood himself and started to reach, though he saw what the man had meant, the ring was pitched way too high. But still he kept reaching, the horse running by it faster and faster still, the lights blending into a circle, the music distorting, and underneath everything his father's voice in his ear, *Higher, higher!* and it wasn't any time to talk back.

His body was stretched taut like a band of elastic, a racing dive. He was coming up to the ring, and though the carousel was still racing, it was as if in slow motion, the way he could see the space between his hand and the rim of gold shimmering, growing narrower. *Now! You can get it!*: he couldn't tell if it was his father's voice, or his own, that had spoken. But he did know, as he reached, that this wasn't the end; it was only the start of the ride they were taking together.